### "I want to apologize for last night. I was rude and ungrateful. I'm sorry."

Her words came out in a staccato rhythm, sounding more rote than sincere.

"You haven't apologized much, have you?"

Tara frowned. "Why do you say that?"

"You're not very good at it."

She opened her mouth, then closed it again.

"You have most of the words right," Matt explained, "but the delivery's wrong. You see, you're supposed to sound like you mean it, not like you're saying whatever's necessary to get me to do what you want."

She raised her eyebrows. "Well, guess what? At this point I would say whatever it took to get you to do what I want." Her voice was low. "I was afraid—"

"Yeah." She'd been afraid he wouldn't come back. Probably because he'd told her he wouldn't. "Sorry about that."

"It's okay." Her expression grew serious. "As long as it doesn't happen again."

Dear Reader,

Building and rebuilding—isn't that what life is all about? I've lived in many old houses, and therefore I've worked on many old houses. I am a renovator and builder at heart and it seemed natural to incorporate these aspects of my life into my debut book.

When I first got the idea for this story, I envisioned an independent woman who does things on her own because she's always had to. She's never depended on anyone, except for a few close childhood friends, until she's forced to by situation. My hero, on the other hand, is in the process of rebuilding. His career has been shattered by a devastating revelation and he is determined to make things right again, regardless of personal cost. He, too, is learning to reach out and accept help. While they work on their lives, they're also renovating the kind of house I've always wanted to live in. And they do it well.

I hope you enjoy my book as much as I enjoyed writing it. I would love to hear from you. Please contact me at jeanniewrites@gmail.com.

Happy reading,

*Jeannie Watt*

# A DIFFICULT WOMAN
*Jeannie Watt*

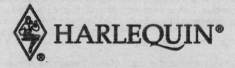

**HARLEQUIN®**

TORONTO • NEW YORK • LONDON
AMSTERDAM • PARIS • SYDNEY • HAMBURG
STOCKHOLM • ATHENS • TOKYO • MILAN • MADRID
PRAGUE • WARSAW • BUDAPEST • AUCKLAND

ISBN-13: 978-0-373-78124-9
ISBN-10:  0-373-78124-5

A DIFFICULT WOMAN

www.eHarlequin.com

Printed in U.S.A.

To my parents, for their love and support over the years, and for teaching me the meaning of tenacity.

To Gary, for believing in me and for cooking when I was busy writing.

To Jamie Dallas and Jake, who grew up with their mother writing—and rewriting—and encouraged her to venture beyond Chapter Three.

To Mike Allen and Charlie Hauntz, who always asked, "How's the book?"

To Roxanne, Tim and Echo— the best proofreading team ever.

To Victoria Curran and Kathleen Scheibling, without whose direction and help this book would not have been possible.

My heartfelt thanks.

# CHAPTER ONE

TARA SULLIVAN, as a rule, did not watch men, but this one was proving to be an exception. She leaned her shoulder against the kitchen doorframe and, for the umpteenth time that morning, paused to watch her carpenter nail the front porch back together. It had been a while since she'd had someone capable working around the place, and somehow she felt compelled to keep an eye on him.

*Probably because I half expect him to disappear.*

Tara smiled grimly, as she pushed off from the doorframe and crossed the worn linoleum to the pantry, where she still had half a dozen shelves to wash before she could paint.

If he quit, he quit. There wasn't much she could do about it. Luke had said his friend would stay for at least two weeks or until Luke's shoulder healed, whichever came first. Tara sincerely hoped that was true because it was the only way she was going to get this place done in time for the reunion.

She sloshed her sponge into the soapy water and started to scrub. At least this man was from out of town, so Martin Somers had no influence over him.

When she was done with the shelves, she carried the wash water to the big kitchen sink, awkwardly dumping the basin before turning it over to dry. She glanced at the clock as she wiped her hands on a towel and realized she didn't have much time before her appointment. It was a routine matter, just a few signatures to finalize things, but routine or not, Tara was in no hurry to get to the bank. Too many bad memories.

She went through the door to the mudroom, hung the apron she'd been wearing on a hook and then carefully made her way out onto the side porch, where the sun tea was brewing. The boards creaked under her feet, but she knew the safe spots and managed to retrieve the jug without crashing through the old flooring. The carpenter continued to work, keeping his head down, concentrating on the boards he was hammering into place. Muscles flexed beneath his thin white T-shirt with each blow.

"Hey," Tara called. The dark head came up. Sunlight reflected off his wire-rimmed glasses.

"Want some?" She hefted the jar a little as she

spoke. It was getting hot outside and she didn't want the man passing out from heatstroke.

He hesitated, then nodded, getting to his feet.

"I'll bring it to you," Tara said. She nudged the side door open with her toe and disappeared into the mudroom. Her reluctance to have him in the house drinking tea with her had nothing to do with fear or caution, and everything to do with boundaries. Because Tara had boundaries. And she let very few people cross them. It seemed that whenever she did, pain and disappointment ultimately followed.

MATT CONNORS hadn't been certain what to expect the first day on this job, but he had not expected his new boss to be beautiful. Even dressed in baggy jeans and a loose tank top that read Night Sky Night Hawks across the chest, and with a smear of pale blue paint across her forehead, there was no denying her beauty. Her long, very dark hair was pulled back into a thick braid, accentuating the shape of her face, the slightly aquiline line of her nose, the high cheekbones. Her eyes were startlingly blue and more businesslike than friendly, so he had been surprised by the offer of tea. She'd given him a cool nod as she delivered the icy beverage, complete with lemon wedge and sprig of mint, and Matt accepted the tall glass with an equally impassive expression. He'd made a perfunctory stab at conversation when he first arrived that morning, more to try to regain a sense of normality in his daily life than for social reasons, but the boss had quickly made it evident that she wasn't looking for pleasantries. She wanted her porch rebuilt and that was just fine with him.

Matt studied her striking profile for another moment as she inspected his work, and then he took a long, grateful drink of tea. It was hot for the end of May and it had been a while since he'd put in so many hours under the Nevada sun. Ten years, in fact, since he'd worked his way through college on his stepfather's construction crew before attending the police academy.

"How's it going?"

"Pretty good. I reinforced the two bad joists, but I have some work ahead of me here." He gestured to the boards he was replacing.

"Another day on this porch?" Tara asked.

"Probably more like two."

Disappointment crossed her face.

"All right," she agreed, as if she had a choice in the matter. She pushed the long braid over her shoulder. "I have to go to the bank. Do you mind being here on your own?"

"No." To him the bigger question would have been, did she feel comfortable leaving him alone at her house? She must've guessed the direction of his thoughts.

"Luke trusts you." The simply stated fact seemed to be enough for her. "Did you bring any water?"

"In the truck."

"Good."

Her very blue eyes held his for a moment and then she turned and went back inside, the old wooden screen door banging shut behind her.

Matt took another swallow of tea, his eyes still on the door. Tara Sullivan was a woman of few words. He set down the glass and picked up his hammer. It didn't really matter to him—if anything it made things easier. He was not there to make friends with her. He was there as a favor to his uncle, his former construction boss, a man who thought he was saving Matt's life.

TARA ALWAYS HAD the feeling when she crossed the threshold of the bank that every eye in the place was on her. The problem was that it wasn't entirely her imagination.

The manager of the Night Sky branch of U.S. Trust and Savings had been one of the tellers on duty at the Reno branch when her father had made his brazen attempt at easy money fifteen years ago. He never let her, or anyone else in Night Sky, forget it.

Damn but she wished that when her aunt Laura had finally realized the house was falling down around her she'd applied for the renovation loan with an out-of-town bank. But no. She'd conducted her business locally and Tara had inherited both the house and the debt to a bank she never wanted to set foot in. And it was a huge debt. Tara'd been astounded by the amount, wondering at first how her aunt had managed to secure it at her age on such a dilapidated house. But then she'd realized just how much property values had gone up over the past decade, and decided that maybe it was the land and not the house the bank had counted on for security. The only blessing was that the interest rate had been low enough to make the payments manageable, and after today Tara hoped to continue with her low-interest payments for a very long time.

"Miss Sullivan. Have a seat." The manager pulled his gold pen a little closer as he spoke.

"You are here regarding the balloon payment on your loan, due October first." The manager raised his eyes from the paper to meet hers. Tara did her best to look friendly. He did not.

"I met with the assistant manager last week. We talked about refinancing the last payment. I submitted my request in writing."

"Yes. I have it here." The corner of the man's mouth twitched, giving Tara the feeling that this was not going to be the slam dunk the assistant manager had indicated it would be.

"He said that it was very common to refinance a balloon payment. Practically expected." His exact words had been "just a technicality."

"That is *if* circumstances are the same as when the loan was secured."

"The circumstances can hardly be the same, since my aunt is now deceased," Tara pointed out.

"Exactly," the man said. "And according to the information here, you are not currently employed."

His information was correct, thanks to the statewide cut in the education budget. The Elko community college now had one less English instructor on its payroll. But that didn't mean she was without income.

"I'm freelancing. Technical writing. I have two projects scheduled to begin next month. I've brought you copies of the budget. I'm certain I'll have more work after that."

The manager barely glanced at the papers she set on his desk.

"Freelancing." From his tone, she may as well have said she was panhandling.

"Yes. And as soon as the funding situation at the college is rectified, mine will be the first position hired back. It's written into my contract, which I have right here." She pulled a paper out of the stack on her lap.

"And when might that be?"

Tara sucked in a breath. "The HR director expects it to be within the year."

"I see. And, when you get your job back, is there any guarantee that it would not again be downsized in the next round of state budget cuts?"

"No, but I will be getting another job as soon as my house is refurbished and the reunion is over."

"Here in Night Sky?"

"I hope."

"Then you have nothing lined up."

Tara pressed her lips together and shook her head. Her sense of foreboding intensified.

The manager smiled with mock regret, paused a beat, and then pushed Tara's papers back toward her with an air of finality.

"I don't want to appear harsh, Miss Sullivan, but I do not believe it would be in the best interest of the bank to extend this loan under such tenuous circumstances."

Suddenly numb from head to toe, Tara forced herself to speak.

"You'd get your money back, plus more interest—"

"Your aunt got a lower interest rate by agreeing to the balloon. That was the arrangement she made, the contract she signed. When one enters into a balloon mortgage, it is with the understanding that refinancing is not guaranteed and that the entire loan balance is due on a particular date."

"Look—" Tara pulled in another breath, tamping down cold panic "—can't you give me a break here? I mean, this bank loans money." She gestured at the plastic banner stretched over the tellers' windows, advertising second mortgage rates, just in case the little worm in front of her had forgotten. "I'm current on my payments. I've proven I'm trustworthy, in spite of being laid off.... I'll pay higher interest if you'll refinance the balloon. I don't care. I just need to make payments." She paused before adding with the utmost sincerity, "It will be very difficult to make the payment and keep my brother in college." *More like impossible, but he didn't need to know that.* "I can do it if you extend the mortgage."

The bank manager merely blinked at her, obviously unmoved.

Tara swallowed hard. "I would really appreciate it if you'd help me with this."

It killed her to beg, but she'd crawl on the floor if that was what it took.

"It might be good for your brother to go to work for a while and then continue his studies."

"No," Tara replied firmly, making a supreme effort to keep her temper in check. "It might be good for him to continue his studies right now. He's completed his sophomore year at UNLV and has just been accepted into a prestigious engineering internship program in California. It's a private college and highly competitive. He needs to go right after summer school or he'll lose his slot. He has financial aid, but it won't be enough to cover both schooling and living expenses. If we could refinance this for even a few years…" Tara lifted her chin. "I want Nicky to have a decent shot at life."

The manager shook his head, making no attempt this time to feign regret. "I'm sorry, Miss Sullivan," he said in a "business is business" tone. "Payment is due October first."

"So I have to chose between my brother's education and the balloon payment."

"If that is your situation, then, yes."

"And if I can't make payment at that time?"

"I believe you will eventually lose your collateral."

There was no mistaking his meaning.

The bank would take her house—the house her great-grandfather, one of Night Sky's founders, had built for his growing family over a hundred years ago. The house that had been the one source of constancy in her turbulent life.

Tara hitched her chin up a notch.

"Not if I go to another bank and take out a loan to pay off your loan."

The man fiddled with the gold pen for a moment before he said, "You may find it difficult to get a loan in your current situation, unemployed and with your only collateral already tied up as a lien on another loan." He raised his beady worm eyes to meet hers. "Practically impossible, I would guess."

This guy was playing hardball.

"*If* it looks like you will not be able to make this payment—" the worm's voice broke into Tara's thoughts "—for the sake of your credit rating, you might want to sell the house first and use the money to settle this loan."

*Sell the house....*

The words echoed in her head as she slowly raised her gaze to meet that of the man across the desk from her.

Her jaw tightened as she suddenly understood exactly what was happening. This man had been well aware of the fact that she was going to have to choose between Nicky's education and making the payment, and he was going to take advantage of it—most probably for one of his best customers. The Somerses would like nothing better than to get their hands on her house, for both punitive and economic reasons. Tara's property abutted the rear of theirs and provided the perfect opportunity for them to expand their empire of vacation retreats for the rich and semifamous.

The manager met her gaze blandly, with just the barest hint of smug satisfaction.

Tara narrowed her eyes slightly as the comforting calm of battle settled over her, a calm that, from the man's subtle shift of expression, was being misread as acceptance.

"Sell my house...." Tara spoke the words thoughtfully as she gathered her purse and papers. She rose to her feet.

"Sell my house," she repeated matter-of-factly. She didn't speak loudly, but she did speak clearly, and the manager's eyes darted around the room, as though trying to ascertain whether she was attracting attention. She was. He cleared his throat.

"Just a suggestion for your own financial—"

"I will sell my house when hell freezes over." Tara raised her eyebrows as she politely inquired, "Does that time frame work for you?"

"Miss Sullivan..." the manager protested as two customers, whose fathers had presumably *not* tried to abscond with federally insured funds years before, sent curious looks their way.

"I can promise you two things," she continued. "First, your bank will get its money. Second, Martin Somers will *not* get his slimy hands on my house because the bank is *not* going to foreclose." Tara allowed herself a grim smile. "And you can tell him that."

"Miss Sullivan, I have no such intention—" But Tara simply raised her fingers to her lips.

The man hushed, probably because he didn't want to risk having her stay a second longer than necessary. She held his beady gaze for a moment, then turned and stalked out of the bank.

It wasn't until the door swung shut behind her that she indulged in several deep shaky breaths. Her heart was pounding. *What? What on earth was she going to do now?*

Tara strode to the Camry, yanked the unlocked door open and dropped behind the wheel, slamming the door shut behind her.

Nicky needed more money than she'd ever made in a year, including salary and freelance work....

Tara leaned her head back and closed her eyes, fighting tears of frustration. She should have known it wouldn't be easy. Nothing ever was. She opened her eyes, determined.

No financial institution was getting her family's house. It wasn't going to happen. Nicky was taking his internship and she was going to make the balloon payment. On time.

Now, all she had to do was to figure out how.

TARA HAD BOTH a throbbing headache and a sketchy idea of what to do by early evening. She stood for a moment at her bedroom window, watching as Matt got into his old, but meticulously cared for, Ford pickup—almost a twin to her own old truck—and drove away, leaving a rooster tail of dust in the red light of the setting sun. The dust slowly settled and Tara turned to lean against the windowsill.

Her finances hadn't seemed that bad prior to her visit to the bank that morning. She wasn't rolling in dough, but she'd had enough money to meet her monthly bills, including the mortgage she'd inherited, and she had Aunt Laura's life insurance to pay for Nicky's college expenses. But now, even if she cashed out her meager 401K and added it to Aunt Laura's life insurance, she still didn't have enough.

Damned bank manager.

She'd sunk too much money into the house; most of the remaining supplies and furniture were either already purchased or contracted for, and sitting in storage, or were awaiting pickup. Even if she returned what hadn't been used, it was only a drop in the bucket. No, she had only one direction to go. Forward. She'd put this house together and do her best to get a loan or grant or private money before October 1.

She let out a sigh and then realized she'd been sighing way too much for one day. It smacked of defeatism. She'd had to be tough for herself and Nicky while they were growing up. She wouldn't let herself break down now.

She crossed the room to the staircase, running a hand over the stripped banister as she descended. She'd been trying to decide between dark oak or walnut stain. It looked as if she'd better decide soon.

The clock chimed six as she went to the kitchen to get her paintbrushes. She'd be able to get in at least five more hours and still be in bed before midnight, which was about the time Nicky would be getting home. He planned to stay for ten days and do what he could to help with the house before heading back to Vegas to finish his last classes during the summer session. She hadn't told him about the balloon payment and she wasn't going to, because she knew he'd postpone school in a heartbeat if he thought she were going to lose her house.

But she wasn't going to lose the house.

Not without a fight, anyway, because if there was one thing Tara knew how to do, it was how to fight.

*How do you say no to a man who'd been more of a father to you than your father or your stepfather had been?*

*You don't,* Matt thought as he strode up the walk to his temporary home. *At least not right off the bat...especially when the guy was trying to help.*

The Anderson house, as it was known to the locals, was more of a cottage than a house, built after World War II as housing for a tungsten mine and then moved in to town when the mine closed down in the early 1960s. A living room, two bedrooms, a kitchen and a bath—more than enough room for a man trying to put his life back together. It was one of Luke's rentals and Matt had it to himself, since the old man had figured he'd want privacy. He'd been correct.

Matt did not want to wake up thrashing from some nightmare with Luke in the house. Some things were private.

The backyard of the house opened onto an alley. On the other side of it across a gravel parking lot, was the back door into the Owl Club, Night Sky's only casino. It boasted twenty-four-hour fun and sometimes it lived up to its reputation, despite the fact that Night Sky's population hovered around the 1,200 mark, which included the outlying county.

Matt took a quick shower, changed into jeans and a T-shirt and headed across the alley to meet Luke for dinner. A fat cat waddled out from under the back porch and threw himself lovingly against Matt's legs. Matt gently eased the animal aside and kept walking. The cat seemed to have come with the house and he drove Matt crazy, staring at him through the window with its huge yellow eyes.

When Matt came in, he saw Luke seated in one of the red vinyl booths, cupping a tall glass of iced tea in both hands and passing time with a buxom waitress. The waitress smiled at Matt and shook back her blond curls. Matt gave her a nod as he slid into the booth.

"How'd it go?" Luke asked.

"I think the work's going to take longer than she wants it to."

"But you'll be able to get it done."

"No problem," Matt said as he reached for a glass of ice water.

Luke glanced up at the waitress, who was watching Matt with unabashed interest. "Becky, this is Matt. He took my place at Tara's today. I was supposed to work on that porch of hers, but my shoulder's acting up so bad I couldn't hammer."

Becky squinted her eyes. "You're working for Tara?"

He nodded.

"I'll bet you're earning *that* pay," she said with a snort before turning to Luke. "Now, what can I get you guys? The special's good tonight."

Matt gave his order after Luke, following the waitress with his eyes as she sauntered back to the kitchen, her hips swinging under the short pink skirt. When he glanced back, he saw that the old man was smiling.

"Not what you're thinking," Matt said dryly. "'I'll bet you're earning that pay'?"

"Yeah. Well, Tara tends to say what she thinks and do what she wants."

"She pisses people off," Matt translated with a half smile.

"That she does," Luke agreed before taking a swallow of tea. He grimaced.

"I can see it," Matt replied, as Luke regarded the tall glass in front of him with disgust.

"What I wouldn't give for a beer," Luke muttered. He took another swallow of tea, and grimaced again. "Reacts with my medication, you know. And even if I wanted to live dangerously, Becky there—" he nodded at the waitress as she emerged from the kitchen with their prefab salads "—knows I'm taking it and won't serve me."

"Rough life," Matt said. "Having somebody look out for you…whether you want them to or not."

"Isn't it?" Luke asked with equal irony. His expression became more serious. "This isn't a bad town to hang out in for a while, Matt. Think things through."

"The small-town cure for what ails you," Matt said, a corner of his mouth twitching. "I'm not sure it'll work on a big-city boy. Besides, I thought I was here to help you."

Luke's eyebrows went up. "You are," he said innocently.

Yeah, he was. The old guy could barely move his arms. But he knew there was more to the situation than that. They both knew it. Since the incident—well, both incidents, the emotional one and the physical one—Matt's life hadn't been the same. If he'd owned a dog, it probably would have run away.

"I'm doing okay, Luke," Matt said softly, intently, trying to mean it.

Luke's gray eyes held an expression of deep understanding. "Yeah. I know, kid."

Matt wondered if he did, and then felt ashamed of himself. Luke had spent thirty years in construction before retiring to Night Sky, his hometown, and he'd seen two tours of duty in Vietnam. He was also a good man—the kind of man Matt always thought his late father had been up until a few months ago when the staggering truth had come to light.

After dropping the salads on the table, Becky leaned over Matt, brushing cozily against him as she pulled the condiments closer. She smiled as she straightened and ran her hands down the sides of her skirt. The invitation was obvious. Matt smiled back noncommittally and picked up his fork.

"Not a lot of fresh blood in this town," Luke murmured after she had reluctantly left.

"Tell me about Tara Sullivan."

"What about her?" Luke asked.

"She just seems like an unusual person. Easy on the eyes, but all business."

"She is all business. And sometimes her bite is as bad as her bark." Luke speared a giant chunk of iceberg lettuce, then picked up the steak knife and sawed it into edible pieces.

"Why do you work for her?"

"I like her."

Matt glanced up. He'd sensed from the moment that Luke had sent him out to the place that this woman was important to him. He just didn't know why. Luke continued to tackle his salad. "I know she can put people off, but she's honest and… well…let's just say she hasn't had an easy time of it around here."

"Not an easy time?"

"Nope." The word was flat and final. "I worked for her aunt after I retired. Laura was too busy with too many things to maintain that old house, but she loved the outdoors. She designed the gardens, the pathways and such around the place, and I made them happen. After that, it seemed natural enough for me to maintain things. I've been doing it ever since."

"You do a nice job." The old house was surrounded by almost two acres of groomed landscaping. Near the house, the design fit in with the Victorian theme—an old gazebo, wooden archways, shade trees, grass and winding paths. Farther away, near the barn and shop, the landscaping melded into the surrounding meadows, which acted as pasture for the two donkeys Tara apparently kept as pets.

"Gives me something to do, and Tara needs a guy around now that Nicky, her brother, is away at college."

Matt had a feeling that Tara could handle things quite well without a man around, but he kept his thoughts to himself. With no immediate family of his own, Luke had a tendency to adopt people. Like Matt. And apparently like this Sullivan woman, too.

The meals arrived and after Becky was done delivering the hot plates, Matt let the subject drop. He wasn't that interested in Tara Sullivan. If Luke's shoulder kept him out of commission, and it looked like it was going to from the stiff way the old man was moving, Matt'd have a few more weeks at the house, tops. Right up until the end of his leave.

How much did he need to know to hammer a few boards back into place?

Not much. In fact, he had a strong feeling that the less he knew, the less involved he got with anyone in this town, the better.

## CHAPTER TWO

THE BOSS LADY was hot about something. Matt could see her pacing the porch as he turned his truck into her long gravel driveway. As soon as she heard his engine, she tossed her braid over her shoulder and stalked into the house. He could practically hear the door slam.

This should be fun, he thought as he pulled to a stop. He hadn't slept much the night before and he wasn't sure he was ready to face Tara in a snit. She reappeared almost immediately with a cell phone, scanning the horizon as she held it to her ear. The boss lady had cleaned up, and rather nicely, too. Instead of baggy jeans, she wore tan denims that did justice to her long legs and a scoop-necked blue shirt that hugged her breasts and flat abdomen. A chain with some kind of a pendant nestled in an interesting hint of cleavage. She looked...different.

She watched him get out of the truck, still

holding the phone to her ear. It was fortunate, Matt thought, taking in her killer expression, that he had expertise dealing with people in all kinds of moods.

"What's wrong?" he asked quietly as he came to the bottom step.

"Brothers." She let out an aggravated breath as she lowered the phone, but Matt saw anxiety as well as irritation in her eyes.

"Anything I can do?"

She opened her mouth to answer, and then her expression changed. Matt followed her gaze and saw a plume of dust in the distance. When the vehicle came close enough to identify, Matt shifted his attention to Tara, watching as her face first softened with relief, then tightened again. This did not bode well for the troublesome brother.

Tara stalked down the steps and brushed past Matt as an older silver Dodge pickup pulled in between his truck and a Toyota Camry. A fair-haired kid in his late teens or very early twenties was at the wheel and Matt could tell that he knew he was in trouble.

"You *said* you'd be home last night," Tara hissed at her brother, who tried a sheepish grin, then gave up. "I had assumed that meant before the sun came up!"

The brother got out of the truck. "I'm sorry, T. Josh and I got stuck up behind Bounty Peak." He gestured at the muddy undercarriage of the Dodge. "My cell wouldn't get service there."

Tara sucked in a breath and let it out again. "Listen to me. In the future, you *call*. I don't care if you have to hike to the top of Bounty Peak to get service, you call." She pushed a piece of paper into her brother's hand. "And I'm sure I don't want to know *why* you were behind Bounty Peak in the first place. Here's the list we talked about. Do what you can. I've gotta go."

Matt had seen the same look on his mother's face more than once during his own turbulent teens—fully justified fear, followed by relief, and then anger at being made to worry unnecessarily. He felt a little sorry for both Tara and the kid.

"I'm late for an appointment," Tara explained abruptly. "I'll be back in a couple of hours. You're pretty well lined out, aren't you?"

Matt nodded and Tara gave her brother one more smoldering look before walking swiftly to the Toyota, muttering under her breath. Matt and the brother stood side by side as the car peeled out of the driveway and turned onto the county road.

"She yells at me when I do that." The blond kid turned to Matt. "I'm Nicky Sullivan."

"Matt Connors. You worried her," Matt said as he shook the kid's hand.

"Yeah. I guess I should have called when we got out of that mud hole," he admitted, "but I figured I'd be home in an hour." He tilted his head, his blue eyes narrowing. "And I think I'm old enough to stay out all night if I want to."

"Probably not to her."

"I guess," the kid agreed. "Hey, you want some breakfast before you get started?"

Matt shook his head. "I had the special at the Owl."

Nicky grimaced. "Sorry, man."

Matt smiled in spite of himself. Dinners weren't bad at the casino, but breakfast had proven to be an adventure. Eggs came in one form. Bouncy. Bacon bordered on scorched. The toast was usually okay, though, and that was what he'd ended up eating that morning after trying all the various components of the special.

"Come on, at least have some coffee. Tara makes great coffee."

A thermal carafe sat on the counter of the obviously recently renovated kitchen and Nicky shook it. It sloshed reassuringly and he reached for two mugs.

"If I had been any later, she'd have dumped it out," Nicky reflected as he poured.

"Important appointment?"

"It is for her." Nicky settled on one of the antique chairs and stretched out his legs. He took a drink of coffee, closed his eyes, took another. "Long night," he muttered. "Anyway, the local school is celebrating its centennial this year and there's going to be a big reunion of all graduates. Tara wants a piece of the action."

"How so?" The coffee smelled great. Matt took a seat on the opposite side of the table and sipped. *Starbucks, move over.*

"She wants to use the reunion to help her kick off her bed-and-breakfast business. She's trying to host a function here."

"Bed-and-breakfast?" Matt almost dropped his cup. *Tara Sullivan was going to deal with the general public?* Nicky smiled at him.

"She's good with paying customers," the kid said, accurately interpreting Matt's expression. "We lived in the basement apartment of a bed-and-breakfast for five years while she was going to college. She ended up running the place from time to time for the owners, so she knows what she's doing. Of course, getting the house ready in time is kind of a challenge."

"The kitchen's not bad," Matt said tactfully. Only the worn linoleum needed replacing. Everything else, from the fancy retro range to the huge fridge, looked new.

"You should see the rest of the place—and I'm only here for ten days. I'll do what I can, but frankly, I have no idea what I'm doing." Nicky rolled his shoulders, working the kinks out. "Believe it or not, I'm an engineering student. But I'm a lot better with calculations than I am with a hammer and a saw."

Matt enjoyed the kid's candor. "Why doesn't she just hire a contractor? Money?"

Nicky grew serious. "She has to watch the budget, but the problem is all the local contractors are 'booked.'" He said the word in a way that caught Matt's attention.

"What do you mean 'booked'?"

Nicky's mouth tightened into a semblance of his sister's smirk, but it wasn't nearly as deadly. "She'd kill me for talking about this, but it's nothing you won't hear in town. There's this family that runs an inn nearby. Real successful."

"Somers Country Inn?"

"That's the one. They're ticked off that Tara is opening a competing business."

Matt frowned. He'd seen the Somers Country Inn when he'd been driving around a few days before, trying to fill the empty hours, trying not to think. It was a few miles away from the Sullivan place—a huge two-story cedar ranch-style building surrounded by picturesque cabins, outbuildings, split-rail fences and giant cottonwood trees. It smacked of luxurious hospitality with a pseudorustic flavor. The kind of exclusive out-of-the-way place where the rich would go to rough it. There was no way that Tara's little Victorian, even if it were fixed and decorated, could compete with that place.

"Rumor has it, and it's only a rumor," Nicky added in a way that made it clear it was anything but a rumor, "old man Somers has fixed it so that nobody wants to work with Tara. I mean, we had no trouble getting help with the roof, the foundation and the kitchen. It wasn't until the plumbing…"

"What happened with the plumbing?"

"When we changed it over from iron to PVC, she had the guys plumb in a bunch of bathrooms—one for each bedroom, you know. That's when the community found out she was planning to open a bed-and-breakfast, and suddenly no one was available."

Matt gave the kid a long look before draining his cup. Nicky filled it again without asking.

"She finally got an electrician to come from Elko, but he was twice as expensive as the local guy. Now all that's left are the floors, walls and stuff that needs to be fixed like the doors and the porch. Luke tries to do what he can around here, but he gets those arthritis attacks." Nicky nodded at Matt over his coffee cup. "It's decent of you to help him out."

"No problem," he replied, looking at his watch. "Any idea what time your sister will be back?"

Nicky shook his head. "Unfortunately, no." He pulled the paper Tara had given him out of his pocket and smoothed it on the table. "But since this list is twice as long as it was the last time I saw it, I think I'd better get busy."

TARA PUSHED OPEN one of the double doors of the convention room at the community center. She was late for her first meeting of the Night Sky Business Association and she would have to make an entrance instead of slipping in as she'd originally planned.

Almost every chair in the room was filled and all heads turned her way as she started down the aisle between the rows, looking for an empty seat. A few people seemed surprised to see her, but most just stared unsmiling or nodded. She wondered, as she always did, if anyone was sincere in offering the simple greeting. She was, after all, a

Sullivan. Daughter of a convicted felon and the latest in a long line of troublemakers.

Her mother's family had been upstanding citizens, but no one seemed to remember that, and she couldn't really blame them. Almost everyone here had had some sort of unpleasant run-in with a member of her late father's family.

Martin Somers was in the front row, dressed in his expensive faux cowboy clothes, his thick gray hair perfectly combed. He, too, nodded as she advanced down the aisle, but it was only for show. He was just like his son—charming and personable until you scratched the surface. Too bad more people didn't figure that out. Too bad she had to figure it out the hard way.

She scanned the room until she finally connected with one honest-to-goodness friendly face, an ally. Jack Hamish gestured to the empty chair next to him.

"Hey, Tara."

"Hi, Jack." Tara nodded at the giant of a man she'd known since he'd been the biggest kid in their kindergarten class. "Thanks for the seat," she murmured as she sat. "Are these meetings always this crowded?"

"Could I please have your attention?" The microphone whistled before Jack could answer and

Tara glanced up to see perfect Stacia Logan adjust the stand, a glittery bracelet sliding up her tanned forearm with the movement.

"I'd like to welcome you to this combined meeting of the Night Sky High School Centennial committee and the Night Sky Business Association.

"A little background for those of you who were unable to attend our first meeting last week. My company, Night Sky Development, has been contracted by the chamber of commerce to ensure the smooth operation of the hundredth reunion of the high school. The chamber and I, in association with various Night Sky high class officers, have been hard at work for almost six months planning this event. We've made a lot of headway, but there's still a lot to do and that's where *you* come in." She paused for emphasis before continuing.

"We have several hundred people coming. I'm certain that a lot of them will be staying with family, but those who aren't will need rooms. For that reason we'll be making and sending out brochures listing accommodations along with the schedule of events within the next few days. What we need today is an idea of how many rooms you will have available, price, etcetera, as well as input into where to hold the various functions. We'd also like to hear ideas for activities and promotions we might not have thought of…."

Stacia continued her spiel and, as Tara listened, she calculated what she had to do to have the house completed by June 24.

"Stacia?" Martin's voice jarred Tara back to the present. "I have a comment. I think that we should have stipulations regarding the accommodations brochure."

"Stipulations?" Stacia asked with eloquently raised eyebrows, giving Tara the distinct impression that she was delivering a rehearsed line.

"Yes. I think we should require that only accommodations up and running on the day we mail the brochure be included, just in case," he emphasized the words, "the promised rooms are not available."

There was only one establishment that he could have been referring to, only one establishment that wasn't currently operational, and everyone knew it. Tara's blood pressure jacked up, but she made an effort to control herself as she said in a calm, clear voice, "Are you talking about my place, Martin? Because if you are, I can assure you my accommodations will be done on time."

Martin scowled at her. "How can you guarantee that?"

"The same way you can guarantee that your establishment will have all of its rooms available. Can you be absolutely certain there won't be a fire or flood—or some other disaster—at your place before the reunion?"

Tara raised her eyebrows, but before Martin could reply, a snide whisper came from the back of the room. "Gee, *who* would set fire to Martin's place?"

A muffled chuckle followed and Tara stifled a groan. Everyone knew Tara's uncle had once attempted a career in arson insurance fraud. He might have been successful, too, if he hadn't locked himself into the first old building he'd tried to torch, leading to his subsequent rescue, arrest and prosecution. Surprisingly though, other than her father, he was the only Sullivan who'd spent any significant time in jail. Most of the rest of the family managed to get away with time served.

The laughter grew, but somehow Tara kept from shifting in her chair to face the person who had made the comment. Jack didn't. He turned and glared.

"Martin has a point," an elderly woman announced with prim conviction, bringing attention back to the front.

"So does Tara," came another unidentified voice from across the room.

This time Tara did turn, but she couldn't identify her surprise defender.

"Look," she said, wanting to put a stop to the debate, "my rooms will be ready. I wouldn't put myself on the accommodations list otherwise." She paused, and then added in a low voice, "So, I'll tell you what, Martin. You worry about *your* establishment and I'll worry about *mine*. I wouldn't think my five rooms would be that much of a threat to you."

Martin's face reddened slightly as a few low chuckles bounced around the room. Stacia tapped the microphone for quiet and Martin turned abruptly toward the front of the room. Tara suspected she hadn't heard the last from him.

"So, are you really going to have that monstrosity up and running by the reunion?" Jack asked an hour later as he held the door open for Tara.

"I'll have at least two floors done," Tara said as they stepped out into the unseasonable heat. "Maybe three if my carpenter hangs around."

"I'd help you if I weren't so damned busy at the casino. Losing the assistant manager really cramped me up hourwise."

"I'm doing okay," Tara said in a tone she almost

believed. "You know, I didn't expect to be accepted at these meetings with open arms, but I didn't expect Martin to launch a public attack, either."

She stopped at her car and unlocked the door. "I guess I should have been nicer to his son."

"Or vice versa," Jack replied evenly.

She smiled, but didn't reply. She was just glad Ryan Somers hadn't been at the meeting. Night Sky was small and she had to run into him every now and then, but that didn't mean she had to like it.

"Well," Jack said, settling a big hand on her shoulder, "congratulations on surviving your first business association meeting."

"No thanks to Martin…or Stacia," Tara added. "I wonder what's up with her?"

She and Stacia had never been friends, but they'd never been enemies, either. They'd simply traveled in different social circles having little to do with each other.

Jack rolled his eyes. "Honey, if you spent less time in that big old house, you'd know that Stacia and Ryan Somers are a couple."

"Stacia and Ryan?"

"They're engaged."

Tara's eyes widened. "No." Jack was right. She had to get out more.

"For over a week, I think."

"How perfect," Tara murmured, turning the idea over in her mind. Ryan liked money. Stacia had money. "Perhaps Ryan has spoken of me in an unflattering way."

"Yes," Jack agreed in a like tone, "and rumor has it you also spoke poorly of Martin Somers in the bank yesterday. Mrs. Randall told the girls all about it at lunch."

"Guilty," Tara admitted without a trace of remorse.

"Stacia mustn't like having her future father-in-law disrespected," Jack surmised. "You have to remember, Tara, that it does not pay to cross the prom queen."

"*I* was the prom queen," Tara reminded him in a dark tone. It still made her cringe when she thought about it.

"Yes, but in my heart," Jack replied solemnly, "Stacia will always be queen."

"Yours and hers." Tara grinned before she opened the car door. "I gotta go, Jack."

"I'll save you a seat next week."

"I'm counting on you."

NICKY WORKED DILIGENTLY around the house, checking tasks off his list and stopping every now and then to talk. He was an earnest, likeable kid and Matt didn't have the heart to shut him down when he'd asked about Matt's background. It was the last thing Matt wanted to discuss. He'd made a vague reply and steered the discussion back to Nicky and his college plans.

Nicky accepted Matt's redirection of the conversation and Matt liked him all the better because of it. Neither of them mentioned Tara, who'd returned home around noon looking tired and not very happy. She'd fixed lunch for the two men before disappearing upstairs without a word. Matt didn't see her for the rest of the day, but every now and then he wondered what had made her unhappy.

It was nearly six o'clock when Matt finally got into his truck and drove back to town. But he didn't go home. Instead, he went to the grocery store, bought a sandwich and a Coke, got into his truck and started driving again, following a gravel road out of town.

He didn't have it in him to go to the Owl for dinner. As much as he appreciated what Luke was trying to do for him, he didn't feel like talking and he didn't have the energy to dodge Becky's come-ons. He didn't want to spill his guts and he didn't want to pretend to be normal.

He just wanted to have a little time to himself, alone, and try to think about…nothing.

"HEY, BABE, I HATE to ask, but can you fill in at the bar this evening? Maggie and Becky both called in sick with that damned flu, which leaves me a staff of exactly none."

Jack's gravelly voice actually sounded desperate, causing Tara to frown as she balanced the phone on one shoulder and attempted, unsuccessfully, to pound the lid back onto a can of walnut stain. She gave up, put the hammer down and took the phone in one hand as she brushed strands of hair back from her face with the other.

"What time?"

She did not want to fill in at the bar. She had so much to do, and it was Friday. The regulars would be out in rowdy force, but there was no way she could leave Jack in a lurch.

"Six would be okay."

"I'll be there."

"I'll make it up to you. I promise. Oh, and babe?"

"Yeah?"

"Check in the mirror for paint smudges before you come."

Tara smiled as she punched the end button and surveyed the room. So much for getting the trim primed tonight.

FOR A PERSON who avoided crowds, she was spending way too much time surrounded by people, Tara mused as she pushed her way through the mob in the Owl Club, balancing a tray of drinks. Usually when she filled in for Jack, she manned the bar while the other waitresses hauled the orders, but tonight she shared the bar with Jack and delivered drinks whenever a restaurant order came in. In the bar area, people got their own drinks—*thank goodness,* Tara thought as she squeezed sideways between two large men.

She nearly dropped her tray as some fool, who was either new to town or too drunk to recognize her, firmly pinched her butt. Tara didn't stop to see who it was—she didn't have time to deal with the jerk. It was payday at not one, but two of the nearby gold mines, and too many people wanted to celebrate getting their check by spending their check. Tara had never understood that particular philosophy, but she was more than willing to help them achieve their goal.

She delivered the drinks to the table of revelers with a polite smile that faded as soon as she turned and faced the throng of people spilling out of the bar.

"Hey, sweet cheeks, get me another. Okay?" A very drunk Eddie Johnson waggled his glass at her, and she barely restrained herself from shoving it into his leering face. Instead she took the glass without a word and headed for the bar.

Eddie would figure out soon enough that she wasn't coming back. Jack wouldn't serve him in the condition he was in and she needed the glass, which would certainly have to be washed and reused before the night was over.

And it was going to be a long, long night.

THE LAST THING Matt expected when he went to the Owl Club for dinner was that he'd have to wait for a table. Or so he thought until he finally took his seat and saw Tara Sullivan push through the crowd carrying a tray of drinks. She was wearing Levi's that weren't exactly tight, but somehow molded to her in a way that made every male in the room take notice. She also wore a red satin shirt unbuttoned into an enticing *V* and again the pendant dangled on the chain between her breasts. Matt was suddenly very curious about that pendant. He was also curious why she was playing barmaid after a full day of painting the interior of that monstrous house.

*None of your business.*

But, man, she did draw the eye.

Even the women watched her. Her dark hair wasn't braided tonight, but was instead twisted up onto the back of her head and held in place with a big silver clip. Little strands escaped, curling around her temples, giving testimony to both the heat of too many bodies and the number of trips she must've made through that crowd. It looked as if everybody there was having hard stuff with dinner. Not him. He didn't want to be responsible for Tara having to push her way through that mob again.

"*If* you touch me or call me sweet cheeks again, Eddie, you will be sporting your *cojones* somewhere in your abdominal cavity."

Matt's head whipped up at the tight, angry words, clearly audible over the buzz of the crowd even though Tara was in the bar area, almost out of view. Almost, but not quite. He automatically started to rise at the sight of her facing off with some drunken jerk whose surprise was rapidly becoming belligerence as his friends laughed. The guy opened his mouth to say something that would have probably gotten him into a whole lot more trouble when Jack Hamish, the manager of the Owl and resident giant, suddenly appeared by Tara's side. Matt forced himself to sink back into his chair and let Jack take care of his employee, which he did by escorting the offending patron outside.

When the door closed behind Mr. Sweet Cheeks, Matt pulled his eyes back to the menu on the table in front of him, but adrenaline still charged through his body and his muscles were taut, ready to react.

He let out a slow breath and closed the menu.

Maybe he'd have that drink after all.

But he'd go to the bar and order it from Jack.

MATT CONNORS was at the bar and Tara wondered why, with a zillion people filling the small space, her eyes zeroed in on him. He ordered Scotch straight up and after Jack finished pouring, Matt raised his gaze and unerringly met hers. Her chin went up as she felt a surprising connection between them. He seemed different here, somehow, and he had caught her staring. Tara's mouth tightened and she got busy filling the rest of her order. She left the bar without looking up again. But she felt him watching her, dammit. And it made her feel ridiculously self-conscious.

The rest of the evening passed in a long blur of shouted orders, sloshed drinks and loud music. Eddie had sneaked back in and Jack threw him out again. He'd had some time to sober up and had not taken his second ejection well.

And Matt had stayed. He stood for a long time, leaning against the wall under Edgar, the stuffed horned owl, watching the crowd, and occasionally her, unnervingly alert behind those wire-rimmed glasses, before finally moving to a vacated stool at the far end of the bar. He didn't socialize, although a few of the town belles had given him their best shot, and he had switched to club soda after the one Scotch. Tara hadn't the slightest idea why she noticed these things on such a busy evening.

"You saved my life tonight, babe." Jack's voice rumbled from behind her.

"No problem." Tara gave the bar a wipe as she spoke. It was close to one o'clock and the crowd was finally thinning…but Matt was still there. Maybe this was what he did at night. Maybe he worked for her during the day and spent his evenings at the bar. Watching. She wondered vaguely why he was in Night Sky in the first place. Maybe waiting to get on at a mine. That's why most single men came to the small town and hung around. Yeah. That was probably it.

Ginny, the graveyard waitress, had breezed in a few minutes before and came out of the back room tying on her apron. She glanced at the swollen tip jar, raising an eyebrow.

"Maggie and Becky are going to be sorry they got that flu."

"I hear it's a rough one."

"Trust me, you don't want it. Knocked me

off my feet for two whole days, then I staggered for two more."

"Then I won't get it," Tara said. "I've too many things to do."

"How's that house coming?" Ginny asked. "I'm dying to see it."

"It'll be done for the reunion," Tara replied. Ginny was fairly new in town and she had always been friendly. Tara appreciated that, knowing that the woman must have heard all the talk about the Sullivan family, but had still chosen to make her own judgments.

"Invite me for a tour."

"All right." Tara gave Ginny a speculative look. "You know, I was wondering if you might have some time when I hire temporary day help."

Ginny grinned. "Just call."

"Right now it would only be during the reunion. I can't pay all that much, but after I'm more established…"

Ginny's smile didn't waver. "Call," she repeated.

Tara nodded. "You have no idea how happy I am to hear you say that."

MATT WATCHED as Tara Sullivan neatly folded her apron and headed into the back room, reappearing seconds later with a small purse dangling from one shoulder.

"Wait a minute," Jack said in gruff voice. He grabbed the purse, unzipped it and stuffed as much of the contents of the tip jar into it as would fit.

"I would have come back tomorrow," Tara protested.

"No. You'll get busy on that barn you call a house and forget. This way I know you have at least some of the money."

Tara gave Jack a tolerant smile. "Thanks. But don't call me again unless it's an emergency."

"I have subs lined up for the next few days."

Tara nodded gratefully. "Good." She surprised Matt then by glancing over at him, as if checking to see if he were still there, before turning and walking out the door.

Mr. Sweet Cheeks' friends were bellied up to a table near the door and they had watched her exit with enough interest to catch Matt's attention. He decided to make certain that she got to her vehicle safely.

*Old habits,* he thought as he pushed the door open and the warm night air hit his face.

He eased sideways into the shadows after the door swung shut behind him, leaning against the building and keeping his eyes on Tara as she crossed the big gravel lot. Someone needed to tell her to park closer to the door. She had her keys out and was nearly to Nicky's Dodge when she stopped in her tracks.

*Mr. Sweet Cheeks.*

Matt wasn't exactly surprised, and as he moved swiftly across the lot, he could see Tara wasn't surprised, either. After her first startled movement, she took a defiant stance.

"Don't even think about it, Eddie," Tara said to the guy who'd sauntered out of the shadow of a pickup. "Just leave me alone."

"Or…?" he asked in a wicked voice.

"That *cojones* promise still holds," Tara said tightly.

The guy laughed and took a step toward her.

"I'm warning you—" She heard the crunch of Matt's feet on the gravel and sent a quick startled glance his way. Matt ignored her and headed straight for Mr. Sweet Cheeks. The guy also looked startled, then smug. He hadn't, after all, done anything. Hadn't even touched her. Matt didn't let that slow him down for an instant. He hated guys who preyed on women. The next thing Mr. Sweet Cheeks knew he was backed up against the same pickup truck he'd been hiding behind.

"Do…do you got some…some kind of problem, man?" Mr. Sweet Cheeks stuttered.

"No," Matt answered quietly. "You do."

Even in the dim light Matt could see the man blanch. Then he got stupid and took a wild roundhouse swing followed by an attempted knee to the groin. Matt automatically blocked both movements, then sent his fist deep into the man's midsection. The guy doubled over and fell sideways onto the gravel.

Matt watched the man gasp for breath, then glanced over at Tara. The gratitude he expected to see wasn't there. Instead she looked stunned and irritated.

"What?" he asked.

Tara just shook her head and watched Mr. Sweet Cheeks struggle up to his hands and knees. She grimaced as the guy retched.

"Is he going to be okay?" she asked.

"His private parts are not in his abdominal cavity, so I would say, yes, he's going to be fine."

"I guess I should say thanks."

"I guess you should," Matt agreed.

Tara's blue eyes looked silver in the glow of the streetlight. Silver and ungrateful. "Thanks." The word was clipped, sarcastic.

"I'm overwhelmed," Matt muttered. Mr. Sweet Cheeks staggered to his feet and away to his waiting friends. He stumbled a few times before he made it to the door.

"I said thanks," Tara repeated, reading the obvious annoyance in his face.

"And you truly meant it," he said sarcastically.

Tara didn't reply, but Matt could see she thought he'd overreacted. Maybe he had, but that didn't change the fact that he'd helped her out of a dicey situation.

He shook his head and reached to take the keys from her hand. She hadn't expected it, so he was able to do it. He unlocked the truck door, opened it and stepped back, holding out the keys. Tara took them, her chin up.

"I can understand why you felt the need to... intercede."

"But...?"

"But that was Eddie Johnson. It's not the first time I've faced him down."

"And...?" Matt prompted, sensing there was more.

"And I fight my own battles, my own way. I don't need help," she stated with an air of finality.

Matt looked down at her from his superior height, wondering why this was the straw that broke the camel's back. He didn't need this. Not on top of everything else.

"Well, you know what, Miss Sullivan? You can fight your own battles and you can fix your own porch. Good night."

Matt had the satisfaction of seeing her beautiful mouth pop open before he turned and started back across the lot to the alley that led to his house. But even as he stalked away he listened to hear the reassuring sound of her door finally slamming shut and the engine of her brother's truck roaring to life.

*Old habits...*

# CHAPTER THREE

HER CARPENTER HAD fired her.

Tara clenched her teeth as she drove, still having a hard time adjusting to the fact. Half a porch to go, plus several other very necessary jobs, and he had fired her. What was she going to do now? Luke couldn't help, even though she knew he'd try.

She'd just have to get along without any help. This wouldn't be the first time she and the *Time-Life Home Improvement* series had gotten a tough job done together.

*Yeah, right. She could do this alone. Who was she kidding?*

*If only Nicky weren't leaving next week.*

But he was. He needed the summer school credits and, frankly, she needed hands a little more skilled than Nicky's.

Damn that Matt Connors. And Eddie Johnson. And Martin Somers. And… The list was just too long.

Nicky was sprawled on the sofa, wearing old

sweats and watching a hideous Vincent Price movie when she got home.

"Don't you ever sleep?" she muttered.

He gave her a lazy smile. "You got an e-mail," he said, lowering the volume of the bloodcurdling screams emanating from the bleached blonde on the television screen. *House on Haunted Hill*. Nicky's favorite bad movie. "I printed it out."

"Where?"

"On the table," he said.

Tara wearily brushed the loose hair off her forehead as she crossed the room. It had better be good news. This had been one long, rough day. She read the printout, then crumpled it in her fist.

"I cannot believe this," she said, rolling her eyes to the ceiling.

Nicky frowned at her. "You sent out all those party brochures. I thought you wanted to book a reunion function here."

"I did." Tara uncrumpled the paper and read it again. The Night Sky High School graduating class of 1965 wanted to hold an afternoon cocktail party here before the reunion dance. And they wanted to pay her well for the privilege. A Mr. Nathan Bidart, former class president, had requested the booking, and he also wanted three rooms. Three rooms. Just like that. Almost the entire second floor. And she hadn't even advertised rooms; Bidart must have simply assumed. And he was in business, which was the market she was targeting. Her stomach hurt.

"Did?"

"I don't have a carpenter anymore."

He put the movie on mute. "What did you do?"

Tara shrugged, then rubbed her neck. "I was ungrateful."

Nicky gave a snort. "So what do you do now? You can't hold an outdoor party with half a porch. You have to call Bidart and tell him you can't host it, or find a new carpenter."

"Tell me something I don't know," Tara said, yawning. She released the clip that held her hair, then groaned as the barrette popped into two pieces. She stared down at the sterling silver conchos in her right hand, the French clip in her left.

The perfect end to a perfect evening. Disgusted, she tossed the pieces into the fruit bowl where Nicky kept his keys and headed for the hall.

"I'm going to bed."

She caught sight of Nicky shaking his head before he picked up the remote and settled back into *House on Haunted Hill*, and felt extremely glad he didn't know about the balloon payment. One Sullivan worried sick about finances was more than enough.

STUPID BIRD.

Tara usually loved waking up to the sounds of the birds in the ancient cottonwood trees outside her window. Usually. But after a long night of calculating in her sleep, and trying to figure out how in the world she could get everything done, Tara was in no mood for cheerful birds.

Matt had done the decent thing and tried to help her and she had done the knee-jerk thing and refused that help. She'd fought her own battles since she was eight years old and some kid had taunted her about having a daddy who stayed too long at the beer joint. That kid had ran home crying a few seconds later with a bloody nose and Tara had discovered she did indeed have the power to fight back. She didn't have to listen to all the talk about her father, whom she loved and was fiercely protective of, especially since she didn't have a mother.

Of course, that had been before her dad had committed armed robbery and reinforced the general opinion that there was no such thing as an honest Sullivan.

She and Nicky had moved into the big Victorian house with Aunt Laura shortly after her father's arrest. It hadn't been a happy time. The kids in school remembered how fiercely she'd defended her father and wouldn't let her forget it. The adults in town hadn't treated "that Sullivan girl" much better.

As soon as she graduated high school, she moved to Reno, taking Nicky with her, never dreaming that someday she'd be back, trying to make a place for herself in the community.

She pushed the covers aside and sat up, glancing briefly at the photo of her father she kept on the bureau and feeling the usual mixed emotions. The picture had been taken when he was about the same age as Nicky and the resemblance was strong. Dark blond hair, an easy grin. Tara looked nothing like him. She took after her dark-haired mother, who was smiling in the matching silver frame. Her mother had died when Nicky was three and her father had died in prison of pneumonia when Tara was eighteen—just a few months before he was due to be paroled. Sometimes, even though she hated herself for it, she wondered if maybe that had been for the best.

*No sense dwelling on it.* It never did her any

good. And right now she had a porch to rebuild and a few new doors to hang.

Nicky groaned when he traipsed into the kitchen an hour later and saw the stack of home improvement books sitting on the table where his plate should have been. He walked to the coffeepot, giving the table a wide berth. He filled his cup, took a revitalizing drink, then leaned against the cabinets. His expression clearly said that he knew from experience how dangerous how-to books could be.

"It's not that bad," Tara said without raising her eyes from the pages of one.

"Yes," he said bluntly, "it is."

Tara looked up.

"Remember what happened the last time you moved beyond your abilities?"

"Wiring can get confusing. All those junctions..."

"Look, T. You're good. I'll give you that. And you learn fast, but you don't have that much time."

"Your point?" she asked sourly.

"Tell me what happened last night."

He brought the coffeepot, filled both of their cups, then took a seat across the table from her.

Nicky shook his head when she finished telling the story. "One punch to the gut, huh?" He was obviously impressed. Eddie was a big guy.

"Neatly done, too." Although she had thought there might be more to Matt Connors than met the eye, Tara hadn't expected him to know how to fight like that. His moves had been quick and automatic. Well-practiced.

Silence hung between them for a few seconds and then Tara closed the book in front of her.

"I guess I should go and see if I can talk him into coming back."

Nicky nodded, his eyes fixed on the kitchen window. "You shouldn't have any trouble finding him."

Tara's eyes widened in surprise. "You're kidding." She jumped to her feet and crossed to the window. Sure enough, Matt Connors's pickup was turning into the drive.

"Let's hope he's not here for his tools," Nicky commented as he watched the truck roll up the drive.

"Let's hope," Tara echoed.

"Or his last paycheck."

Tara scowled at her brother over her shoulder as she headed for the front door. "You're a real ray of sunshine, you know that?"

"Just don't blow this, okay?"

"I won't blow it," she replied flatly.

*I can't blow it.* She took a moment to collect herself, and then stepped out onto the porch.

MATT EASED HIS PICKUP to a stop next to Nicky's Dodge. He turned off the ignition, but he didn't get out of the truck right away.

Damn, but he was tired.

He'd had some alleged coffee at the Owl that morning, knowing he probably wasn't going to get any from Tara, but now the casino brew was burning a hole in his gut. It wasn't in his nature to leave someone in lurch though and, no matter what had happened last night, the Sullivans were apparently in one.

Numb from lack of sleep, he stared at the porch. Tara stood on the top step, keeping the advantage of higher ground. Matt let out a breath and pushed the truck door open.

Squaring time.

He made his way up the walk as far as the bottom porch step, and for a moment he and Tara simply stared at one another. She was dressed for work, but her feet were bare, and her hair hung to her waist in a loose ponytail. She looked tired and yet she also looked good. Must be the hair he thought, wondering what it would feel like to hold handfuls of it.

*And what would it feel like spilling over his chest?*

The thought came out of nowhere. *What would it feel like if he got a grip?*

"I'm glad you're here," Tara said, breaking the silence. "I want to apologize for last night. I was rude and ungrateful. I'm sorry."

The words came out in a staccato rhythm, sounding more rote than sincere.

"You haven't apologized much, have you?"

Tara frowned. "Why do you say that?"

"Because you're not very good at it."

She opened her mouth, then closed it again.

"You have most of the words right," he explained, "but it's the delivery that's all wrong. You see, you're supposed to sound like you mean it, not like you're saying whatever you have to."

Her eyebrows rose. "Yeah? Well, guess what? At this point I *would* say whatever I have to to get you to do what I want."

Not what he expected. He almost smiled, but Tara didn't notice. She was staring at something in the distance as she worked out what to say next. When she looked back at him, her expression was grudgingly sincere.

"When you hit Eddie last night, I was shocked and…unnerved, I guess. I hadn't expected any intervention and then, out of the blue, there you were." She held his gaze for a few seconds. "I'm sorry for not being more appreciative. I know you were trying to help. It was just kind of—" she pressed her lips together momentarily "—scary help."

Okay. That was a revelation. It hadn't occurred to him that of the two of them, she might have considered him more of an unknown than the big guy she'd been staring down. "I guess I can understand that."

Tara studied him matter-of-factly, almost fatalistically. "Are you here to pick up your check?"

"Nope."

"So—" she tilted her head "—are you coming back to work?"

He gave a nod.

There was a cautious silence, then, for the first time since he'd met her, Tara smiled. At him. A slow, totally fascinating curve of her lips that changed her beauty into something warmer, more approachable, a hundred times sexier. He felt as if his breath had caught in his throat, which was ridiculous. It was only a smile.

"That's great." Her voice was low. "I was afraid—"

"Yeah. Sorry about that."

"It's okay." Her expression grew serious. "As long as it doesn't happen again."

"It shouldn't…as long as you pick on someone your own size."

Her smile was more wry than sensual this time, but once again, Matt felt a response he wasn't ready for.

"Do I still get lunch?"

"Twelve sharp." She raised a eyebrow. "I have some breakfast on, too, if you're interested. It should be ready in about ten minutes. Nicky'll probably have more coffee brewing by now."

*Breakfast that didn't include bouncy eggs and burned toast? Coffee that didn't bottom out on the pH scale? What a concept.*

"Consider me interested."

THE SUN WAS SETTING by the time Matt finished for the day. He left Tara inspecting the porch, which was practically done, and although she hadn't said much, she'd worn a satisfied smile that somehow made the hours worth it.

He pulled up in front of his house a few minutes before he was due to meet Luke. He figured he had just enough time to wash the sawdust off before he made his way across the alley for another fun-filled night at the Owl. He'd just turned on the shower when he heard a sharp rap at the door.

He cranked the water off, pulled on his jeans and his glasses, and then walked barefoot over the old hardwood floor to the front entry. The rapping continued, rattling the small curtained window in the door. He pulled the door open and found himself facing a uniformed deputy.

"What happened?" he demanded, hoping the guy wasn't there to tell him Luke'd had a heart attack or something.

"Nothing's happened." The deputy's tone was professional, his dark eyes carefully appraising. Catzilla peeked in from behind his legs. "I'd just like to talk to you for a minute, Officer Connors."

*Officer Connors.* Not only did the guy know who he was, he was pretty damned formal about it.

"Is this official?" Matt asked. He didn't know how it could be…unless it had something to do with the parking lot incident last night. *Assault, maybe? Oh, that would go over well with the lieutenant. He was just itching to get something on Matt.*

"I'm not on duty right now."

Matt stepped back to allow the man in. The deputy expertly blocked the cat's entry before he closed the door behind him. He gave Matt another quick appraisal before introducing himself. "I'm Rafe Sanchez. A friend of Tara's."

"Tara? She had you check me out?"

"No. I heard what happened with Eddie Johnson last night."

There was a beat of silence while Matt put two and two together. Sanchez wasn't on duty and Johnson didn't seem like the type to press charges. "So you decided to check me out."

"Yep."

Matt wasn't insulted. He understood looking out for your own.

"What'd you find out?"

"You're with the Reno PD. You're a friend of Luke's. You're on vacation."

Matt nodded. "Yeah."

"How long will you be in town?"

"A few weeks."

"And then you'll be going back to work?"

Something in Sanchez's voice caught Matt's attention and he realized Sanchez had facts. At the very least, he knew about what happened, maybe about Matt's father, too. Matt let out a soft breath.

"I guess you're here to make sure I'm not a basket case, ready to go off the deep end around Tara."

"Something like that."

Matt appreciated the fact that the guy didn't try to hedge. Matt wanted to assure Sanchez that he was only a little burned out, not some crazy on the brink of exploding, but his training had taught him the less said the better.

"What do you think? Am I safe?"

"You'd better be." Sanchez studied him intensely before adding, "I just thought you should know that."

The message was crystal clear. Where Rafe Sanchez and Tara were involved? It was a definite possibility, one that he didn't particularly like. He didn't need someone checking up on him, making certain he was treating the girlfriend all right.

"Don't worry. I'm probably in more danger from her than she is from me," Matt muttered darkly. To his surprise, the deputy actually cracked a smile.

"Maybe so." He gave Matt another long look, but it wasn't so intense now. "You know, if you have any problems—"

"Yeah." Matt didn't let him finish. He didn't need anyone else in his business. "I'll let you know."

Another faint smile. "Thanks for your time."

"Thanks for the warning," Matt replied with quiet irony.

The deputy let himself out of the house. Matt waited until he heard the front gate bang shut, then headed back to the shower.

"YOU'RE LATE," Luke said as Matt sat across the table from him fifteen minutes later.

"You look well entertained," Matt responded,

nodding at Becky, who sauntered away. He reached for the beer Luke had ordered for him. He'd told Luke the night before that he didn't like having a beer with dinner when Luke couldn't, but the older man had insisted, saying he wanted to live vicariously. "Deputy Sanchez stopped by to check me out."

"He probably heard that you and Tara had trouble last night."

Matt's eyebrows went up. "Yeah."

"What happened?"

"We—" Matt's mouth twitched "—had a misunderstanding."

"Involving Eddie Johnson."

Matt tipped the top of his beer toward Luke in silent agreement. The old man probably knew as much or more about the encounter than Matt did. "We made up. I spent the afternoon at her place working on the porch. It's practically done."

"Good. I'm hoping to be able to come out tomorrow and take a look, see if there's anything I can do."

Matt gently set his bottle down as he tried to come up with a way to say this without getting Luke's dander up. Finally he just said it. "Maybe you should take it easy a while longer. You know…let the medication take effect?" He didn't want his friend to hurt himself, but he didn't want to insult him, either. Thin line there.

"Maybe," Luke replied after a lengthy silence. He pulled the tea bag out of his cup and squeezed the last bit of moisture out of it. "How're you sleeping?"

Matt raised his eyes to meet Luke's. He hadn't told Luke about his insomnia, but he supposed that his exhaustion had to show.

"I know stress," Luke said as he put the tea bag aside. "I saw action similar to yours while I was in the service. I was only twenty." Luke shook his head. "You gotta experience it to understand it."

That was an understatement.

"How'd you get past it?" Matt shifted back in his chair, not certain he wanted to explore this.

"Time. Change of scenery. More time."

Luke let the comment sit for a bit as he stirred sugar into his tea. "When I heard from my brother how things had been going for you—your dad…the standoff—I had a feeling. Thought maybe you should get away for a while, and since I needed help…" His mouth quirked up at the corner. "But you've figured that out. Time and a new place. It helps. Some."

After an uncomfortable silence, Matt said, "I appreciate it." He didn't necessarily think the change of scenery would provide a wonder cure, but it couldn't hurt. And the time away would recharge him, help him get ready for the next stage of battle. He gave Luke a half smile and a gentle warning. "I don't know I'll be as talkative as the last time you helped me out."

Luke nodded his understanding.

The last time, Matt had been an unhappy kid, working for his stepdad, Luke's brother, building apartments while on vacation from college. Torn. His mom had been pushing him to study engineering, education, law—anything but criminal justice. She hadn't wanted him to become a cop like his biological father.

Matt, however, had been fascinated by law enforcement. And hungry for approval from the man he'd only seen a week or so every summer after his parents' divorce.

Luke had been his crew's boss, and he'd also been the only person who simply listened to Matt without offering an opinion, the only guy who just let him talk.

"Mom thinks it's 'lovely' that I'm spending my vacation with you." A corner of Matt's mouth lifted. "I'd kind of appreciate it if she kept thinking that."

He hadn't given her any facts, except what was

printed in the newspaper, and in the paper he'd come off looking pretty good. She didn't know about the insomnia, the dreams, the lieutenant's vendetta. Matt was thankful she lived almost seven hundred miles away.

"I wouldn't dream of telling her otherwise," Luke replied. "My brother would kill me if I upset your mom."

"Thanks." Matt didn't want his mother upset. Again. She'd suffered enough trying to keep him out of law enforcement and, ironically, after all of the turmoil Matt never did develop the relationship he'd hoped for with his father, even after landing a job in the same PD. Their relationship had never felt like that of a father and son. It was more like that of two guys who worked together, two guys who didn't have a lot in common. Later, after his dad had been killed, Matt and the rest of the department discovered his father had a good reason for not letting anyone into his life.

He wiped condensation off the bottle with one finger. "What's Sanchez's relationship with Tara?"

"I don't know the particulars," Luke replied, apparently amused by the abrupt change of topic. "But I think if you upset Tara, you'll be dealing with Rafe."

"I'll keep that in mind," Matt said dryly.

"It'd be easier if you just didn't upset Tara."

Matt shrugged. "Too late for that."

Luke's eyebrows drew together for a split second and then he burst out laughing. He was still smiling when he gestured Becky over and ordered up another round of Budweiser beer and Lipton tea—hold the sugar.

MATT CONNORS was MIA.

The table was set and his breakfast—or what was left of it—was shriveling up in the warming oven. They'd made a deal the day before and she'd agreed to give him meals in lieu of some pay. He'd seemed to like the idea, so she didn't understand why he'd skip out on the first day.

She finally gave up waiting and started painting another bedroom, but every now and then she paced to the window, scanned the county road. *Where was he?*

It had been over two hours since she had fed Nicky and sent him to Reno with a shopping list almost as long as he was tall and instructions not to come back for at least two days. Nicky had spent six years of junior high and high school in Reno while Tara went to college, earning first her bachelor's degree, then her master's in English, and she knew he had friends to see and stuff to do before he headed south again. He'd already spent most of his short vacation scraping, sanding and painting. Enough was enough. Nicky was still a kid.

A sudden ominous thought struck her and she tucked a loose wisp of hair behind her ear as she laid down her brush and headed for the phone. Tara dialed the number to the Anderson house and tapped her foot as the phone rang. And rang.

Tara's nerves started to hum. If Eddie and his numbskull buddies had hurt her carpenter in some kind of misguided attempt at revenge, she was going to—

"Yeah…?"

The voice on the phone was thick with sleep.

"Matt?" Tara said cautiously.

"Tara." His voice was instantly alert. "What time…?" She heard fumbling and then he muttered an expletive. "Sorry…I overslept. Give me twenty. I'll be right over."

He hung up before she could reply. Fifteen minutes later he was at her door, his hair still damp from a shower. He hadn't shaved and the dark stubble gave him an entirely different look. An incredibly sexy look.

Tara suddenly realized she was staring and stepped back, letting him in.

"So what'd you do last night?" she asked as she led the way to the kitchen. "Tie one on?"

"I was up late."

He didn't look so much hungover as exhausted, so she let the subject drop and tackled the matter at hand. "I'd like to get the porch finished and the gazebo fixed and painted, but…" She paused, studying him with a slight frown. "I need you to adjust the height of the new doors before you do that, so that I can stain them."

She had bought several solid wood doors to replace damaged and missing ones in the house, only to find that while the doorframes were consistent in width, they were not consistent in height. In fact, some of the frames weren't even true and it was going to take finagling to get the doors to hang and swing correctly. It wasn't something she wanted to leave until the last minute.

"Show me what you got," he said. She watched as he crossed the room to the porch door, thinking, in spite of herself, that he wore those worn-out Levi's very well and wondering why she hadn't noticed it before.

Until he'd taken on Eddie, she hadn't realized his long lean body was almost solid muscle. That awareness was having a definite effect on the way she was looking at him now, so she was glad he didn't have the ability to read minds when he glanced over his shoulder and caught her staring.

"Do you want your breakfast?" she inquired innocently.

"What kind of shape is it in?"

Tara grimaced.

"I think I'll hold off until lunch."

Tara was impressed that he didn't expect her to cook another meal for him. She led the way to the prefab metal shop where the doors had been stacked. The shop had a woodstove and a cement floor and was, all in all, a comfortable place to work. Her aunt Laura had been an artisan who specialized in pottery and soap-making, but she had done a little of everything and had collected quite an assortment of woodworking tools.

Matt went immediately to the table saw, inspected it, then moved on to the tools hanging on the pegboards lining the wall.

"Find what you'll need?"

"Yeah." He shoved his hands in his back pockets. Tara's eyes automatically followed.

She had to stop doing that.

"The doors each have a sticky tab on them, telling where they'll be hung and the measurements of the frame," she said briskly. "I'll be wallpapering the parlor. Lunch is at noon."

Matt Connors nodded. He reached for a saw and Tara headed for the door, glad to have made an escape before he caught her gawking at his butt again.

## CHAPTER FOUR

IT WAS FUNNY HOW wallpapering always seemed like such a good idea until she was actually doing it—and hanging paper in an old house that had spent almost a century settling only added to the fun. At least she knew enough now, after that first horrendous experience in her own bathroom, to avoid stripes.

Tara soaked and folded the first strip of vintage rose paper into a book, then hung the plumb bob and drew her reference line. Classic rock played on the radio and she hummed under her breath as she positioned her stepladder and tackled the first strip, applying it to the wall, then smoothing it from the top down to the newly stained and varnished wainscoting.

"One down," she murmured as she stood back to view the colors.

"How many to go?"

Tara jumped at the unexpected voice.

"How long have you been there?" she demanded. She shouldn't have left the front door propped open, but she'd never had trouble with vermin before.

"You really do need to work on your manners, Tara."

"Speaking of which, you should knock before you slither into someone's house."

Ryan tilted his blond head back, looking down his nose at her, his perfect lips curved into a perfect smile. Perfectly nasty, that is. Tara gave him her best smirk in return. It made her shudder to think how she'd once been taken in by this guy. Used and discarded. And the kicker was that most of the populace of Night Sky still bought into Ryan's charismatic golden boy facade. They assumed that any trouble between her and Ryan had to be her fault. She was a Sullivan, he was a Somers.

But Tara wouldn't let him upset her, because that was exactly what he wanted to do.

"Filed any restraining orders lately, Ryan?"

That hit the mark. His eyes narrowed, but his voice was smooth as he said, "Again, that manners thing, Tara."

"Why are you here?"

"Why do you think?"

"To harass me?" Tara suggested, her eyebrows going up.

Ryan regarded her for a long moment. "Now why," he finally asked in a much too quiet voice, "would I want to harass you? What possible reason could I have?"

He moved another step closer, so that he was only inches away—so close that Tara could feel the warmth from his body, smell his expensive aftershave. And suddenly it was all she could do to hold her ground. Memories, sharp and painful, flooded her.

She hadn't expected the reaction and it threw her, but she fought to pull herself back together. Ryan had no idea how traumatic their physical encounter had been to her. He was so egotistical that he'd actually thought that she'd want to do it again.

Through sheer willpower, Tara forced herself to look Ryan in the eye. And then she noted with some satisfaction that she had left a pretty good bump on his once classic nose.

"Oh, yeah. That's right," Ryan said sarcastically. "I remember now. Your lies. My job."

"I had nothing to do with you losing your job," she said bluntly. And it was true. She'd had nothing to do with his being fired from his cushy job with the accounting firm in Elko, where he'd hoped to become a partner. Jack had. But Ryan didn't know that and she wasn't going to tell him.

"You're a liar, Tara."

Tara simply shifted her weight as she waited to see what was coming next. She didn't have to wait long.

"Actually I'm here because of the crass attempts you've been making to embarrass my father in public."

"What are you talking about?"

"Oh, I think you remember raving in the bank about my father trying to steal your house."

She didn't remember using the word *steal*, but in Night Sky, embellishment was the rule rather than the exception.

"Ryan, surely you have better things to do than chase rumors."

"Tara," he murmured, "if you keep doing things like that—if you embarrass my father or falsely accuse him, especially at this reunion—you'll be very sorry."

Tara studied Ryan as if he were a nasty insect. "I can't wait to see what you try to do to me that you haven't already done."

"I haven't taken your house."

"And you won't," Tara responded with a grimly confident smile.

"I will if you don't come up with a hell of a lot

of cash, and it won't be stealing. I'll take it just to torch the place, if nothing else."

"Will you be using Daddy's money?" Tara asked. "Or Stacia's?" She smirked. "Congratulations, by the way. Helluva catch."

Ryan acknowledged her touché with a slight sneer, which turned into a rather nasty smile as he raised his hand to her face.

"Touch me even once and you will be a sorry man."

His perfect lips curved even as his hand stopped in midair.

"You know Tara, you really…challenge a man."

It was both a threat and a reference to their past.

"I'm sure Stacia would love to know I still *challenge* you," Tara replied with mock sweetness. "Now, kindly get out of my house and off my property."

She spoke the words matter-of-factly, hoping against hope that Ryan wasn't aware his presence unnerved her, that her heart was beating harder than it should be.

"And while you're at it, tell your father to mind his own business. He isn't getting my house and he isn't going to stop me from opening my business."

Ryan merely shook his head and moved even closer, his smile fading. It was the first indication

Tara had that he might honestly be a threat. Her body tensed, instinctively preparing for defense, when the side porch door scraped open and they heard booted footsteps in the kitchen.

Ryan's head swung around and, from his startled expression, Tara knew he'd been aware her brother wasn't here. He hadn't expected anyone—had probably thought Matt's old truck was her own.

And that frightened her.

"Do you need something, Connors?" Tara called as the footsteps continued down the hall toward the parlor. Matt appeared in the doorway a second later, frowning when he saw that Tara was not alone.

Ryan was already several feet away from her. He smiled as Matt entered the room, wearing his charm like an exoskeleton. Tara blinked at the change. Incredible. Who'd believe her side of things when confronted with…this? Ryan extended a hand.

"Hi. Ryan Somers."

Matt dusted his own hand on his jeans and accepted the handshake with a nod, his expression unreadable. "Matt Connors."

Ryan waited, but when no further information came, he glanced at Tara with a this-isn't-over look in his eye. "I won't keep you any longer," he said congenially. "Stacia will be in touch."

"Yeah," Tara replied softly. "I can't wait."

"Nice to meet you," Ryan said as he walked past Matt.

Matt followed Ryan with his eyes until the man was through the front door.

"What happened?"

"What do you mean?"

He gave her an impatient look. "I'm not stupid, Tara. Something happened."

Tara shrugged. She picked up her wallpaper brush and idly ran her thumb over the bristles. "Did you need something?"

"No. I just came in to remeasure a frame." His mouth tightened as he studied her carefully composed expression.

Tara dropped her gaze. She wished he'd go back to work so she could have her breakdown alone. It was the first time she'd been alone with Ryan since...she couldn't think about it now.

"Is there anyone in this town you don't have some kind of a problem with?" Matt muttered as he turned to leave.

"No." She'd snapped the word. Tara drew in a sharp breath and made an effort to bring her voice back to a more even tone, "Now, would you do me a favor and let me get back to work?"

To her relief, he gave her one last look and then

walked out of the room and down the hall, the sound of his footsteps fading as he passed through the kitchen and back out onto the side porch.

She walked to the window and watched Ryan's BMW roll down the driveway and turn onto the main road. She hugged her arms across her middle and found that she was shaking. And, worse than that, she was close to tears.

Tara swallowed, disgusted with herself for being so weak, for letting Ryan intimidate her. She needed to get hold of herself. Ryan couldn't hurt her again as long as she stayed out of his way. She just needed to think logically, not let fear get the better of her.

She was still facing the window, arguing with herself, when she heard Matt come back into the room. She didn't turn around.

"Tara?"

"Matt. Go. Please." She spoke in a fairly normal voice, if a little husky. She just didn't know for how much longer she'd be able to hold on.

"Tara," Matt replied in a tight voice, "I'm not going away."

"Why?" she asked, abruptly swinging around. "Do you want to see me cry? Is that why you're back? Do you want to see me cry, too?"

"What do you mean, 'too'?" he asked quietly.

Tara stilled at his very logical question. "Oh,

man." The words came out as a whisper. She dropped her chin, but he reached out to tip it back up with his thumb and forefinger.

"What do you mean, 'too'?" he repeated. "Did that guy want to make you cry?" he asked.

"He wants to see me crawl."

"Why?"

She shook her head, afraid that if she spoke, her voice might break.

"Not ready to discuss it?"

She shook her head again, pressing her lips together, hoping he didn't notice that her eyes were shiny.

Matt looked down at her and Tara stubbornly held her tears at bay until, with the air of a man acting against his better judgment, he reached out and gently put his arms around her and pulled her against the warmth of his solid chest. And, for reasons she didn't quite understand, Tara let him do it. It had been a very long time since anyone had tried to comfort her and, dammit, it felt better than she imagined it would.

"It's okay," Matt whispered. She exhaled and leaned into the warmth of this man she barely knew. She let him hold her until Nicky drove into the yard few seconds later, unknowingly breaking the spell she had fallen under.

She frowned as she stepped back out of Matt's loose embrace and he gave her a quizzical look.

"I don't do this."

"What don't you do?" he asked softly.

"I don't act like this," she answered. "I never act like this."

"You don't let people comfort you?"

She shook her head.

To her surprise he smiled. "Hold still, Tara."

"What?"

"Hold still." He moved a step closer and once again he tipped her chin up. But this time he slowly and, oh so gently, kissed her and Tara felt her knees go weak.

"Hey, T." Nicky burst into the house and Tara took a stumbling step backward just before her brother strode into the room.

"Looks like you're making some headway," Nicky said to his sister, oblivious to the stunned expression on her face. "Hey, Matt." He went on into the kitchen, talking the entire way. He reappeared with a pitcher of orange juice and a glass. He filled the glass, drank it, filled it again.

"What a time," he said shaking his head. "Remember Tiff? The blonde I dated my freshman year? She works for the Hilton now. I got the Hollywood suite for the single-room rate. We had to pretend I was twenty-one, but nobody figured it out. It was great." He paused and looked at his sister. "You all right, T?"

"Fine," she mumbled, pulling her attention away from Matt and the feeling he had managed to evoke in her traitorous body. The jerk. First Ryan and now this. Kissing wasn't part of the deal. Tara might have allowed herself to ogle Matt when he wasn't looking, to appreciate what he'd been blessed with, but he was not supposed to kiss her. That was how complications started. Complications she knew from bitter experience could lead to pain. Mental...physical...

She muttered a short expletive. "So everything went okay?" she said to her brother, pointedly ignoring Matt.

"I got everything on the list. It should only take about an hour to unload it all."

"Do you need help?" Tara asked.

"Got it covered."

As soon as Nicky left, Tara turned on Matt. "Don't ever do that again."

"Okay," he agreed. But he looked unrepentant as he stared down at her. Unrepentant, unfazed and sexy. Men wearing glasses weren't supposed to look sexy. He followed Nicky out of the room, leaving Tara seething.

She was tired of men. She just wanted to get away from them for a while. She whacked off a piece of wallpaper, slid it through the wetting tray and folded it on itself with two decisive thuds. *Whomp. Whomp. Men.*

MATT DEBATED ABOUT even showing up for lunch. He was kind of afraid of what she might feed him; besides, he had some things he needed to mull over.

What had he been thinking, kissing Tara Sullivan?

He hadn't been thinking. He'd been reacting. He'd done what seemed natural at the time. And it had felt good, holding her, kissing her, even if it had only been a shadow of the kiss he'd wanted to lay on her.

Matt focused on cutting the bottom edge of the door. If he let his mind wander too much he'd be minus a digit or two. He passed the blade over the door, inspected the cut and measured the finished length.

She'd definitely been startled when he'd kissed her, and she was royally pissed right now, but she had kissed him back. She'd liked the kiss—at the time.

Well, she didn't like it now, for whatever reason, and Matt had to respect her feelings. He smiled humorlessly. That he was still on the property attested to the fact that she needed him. She needed him to help her accomplish something, and now he knew it was something more than just getting a house ready for a cocktail party.

TARA THREW TOGETHER a chicken salad. She was still upset. Between Ryan and Matt…she needed to talk to someone. But who? She had no one except for Jack, Rafe and Luke. Men. Not likely to understand, even if she cared to explain. She could just imagine how they'd react to *Hi. Ryan came to visit today and, I hate to admit it, but he frightens me. Why? Oh yeah, I didn't tell you everything that happened between us, did I? Well, let me fill you in…my first sexual experience was kind of brutal…and then he came back for more….*

Tara brushed under her eyes with the back of the hand holding the knife, telling herself it was the onions making her tear up.

She could never see herself explaining what Ryan had done. She didn't even know if she could find words to convey how deeply she'd been affected by it. The act had been consensual—in the beginning—and that made the selfish way he'd used her body, with no consideration for her or the fact that it was her first time, hurt even more. She'd trusted him.

Tara put down the knife before she hurt herself. The chicken salad was as done as it was going to get. She put plastic wrap over the bowl and shoved it in the fridge. The guys could make their own sandwiches. She had work to do.

It took most of the afternoon and four walls of rose paper, but Tara finally came to the weary conclusion that it was pointless to obsess over Ryan or Matt or anything else. She had made it clear to Matt that what had occurred between them was never going to happen again, and she didn't think he was the kind of guy who pushed things—not the way Ryan had pushed them. Anyway, she hoped he wasn't, because she needed him. A working relationship. He worked, she compensated him monetarily and there were no gray areas.

Tara hated gray areas.

And as far as Ryan was concerned…today had been an eye-opener. She didn't doubt for a moment that he'd stopped by for the exact reason he had given—because she'd made a few unflattering public statements concerning his father. She knew better than most that with the Somerses, image was everything.

But for the first time, Tara was beginning to see the depth of anger Ryan carried within him; anger that wasn't caused solely by losing his job or having his nose broken. No. She suspected that anger was part of his personality, simmering just below the surface, and that it was a part of himself he hid extremely well. He had to. He was a Somers with an image to uphold.

Thinking back, though, she could see that she'd had glimpses of the anger during their relationship, culminating on the night they'd finally slept together, when he'd lost both patience and control. But at the time she'd thought it was the situation. Now she suspected it went beyond that. He seemed more volatile than before, possibly because he blamed her for his being back in a hick town like Night Sky, essentially on his father's payroll.

She was going to have to be more careful around the man. That didn't mean she was going to let him push her around.

TARA WAS GOING to work his butt off.

In the three days since he'd kissed her, Matt had cut and hung the doors, finished and painted the side porch and started replacing parts of the gazebo, all in virtual silence. Tara wasn't talking to him, except when giving orders, but she did feed him well. The woman had a knack for cooking, which worked well, since he had a knack for eating. He was wishing he had a knack for conversation, because, surprisingly, he found himself wanting to coax Tara out of her silence. He wanted to find out more about her, more about what had happened with that guy who had wanted to make her cry.

As if she would tell him.

Tara kept her secrets. If anything, she was as guarded as he was.

And he wondered why.

That night Matt had the dreams, and they were the worst ever. He jerked awake in a cold sweat, his heart hammering. Adrenaline continued to pump through his body as he sat up in bed, making his breath come in rasping gasps.

He was never a hero in his dreams…he never saved anyone's life. Someone always died, and most of the time it was Matt. His father was usually the one who pulled the trigger. To see his own father raise the gun, to watch the bullet enter his flesh in slow motion, to see the small, deadly hole in his chest, the blood and bits of tissue fly in full Technicolor. To lie on cold pavement, feeling life trickling away, wondering why…

Matt knew he had to move, had to do something until he calmed down.

He swung his legs out of bed, sat on the edge, pushing his hair back from his forehead. The clock read 3:30 a.m. He wouldn't be going back to sleep before he drove to the Sullivan house at 6:15 a.m.

He walked into the bathroom and turned on the shower. Twenty minutes later he let himself out his back door and crossed the alley to where the twenty-four-hour fun of the Owl Club beckoned. The fat cat followed him as far as the gate, then sat, apparently winded by the long walk from the porch.

It was a Monday morning—a very early Monday morning—and business was pretty slow. Matt sat in one of the booths near the bar, thinking that he might try that notorious breakfast special— available twenty-four hours a day—again.

There were two small groups of people at the bar and he could see a few miners eating breakfast in the restaurant, either before or after their shift. Deputy Sanchez was also eating breakfast. Matt knew he could probably join him, talk shop, but right now he just wanted to concentrate on...nothing.

"Hey, sweetie." Pink trousers appeared in his line of vision. Matt raised his tired eyes.

"Hi, Ginny." He knew all the waitresses by name now. There weren't that many of them. Jack kept a skeleton crew.

"A little early for you, isn't it?"

"Trouble sleeping," Matt said truthfully.

"Want anything?"

Matt thought. "Tea," he finally said.

Ginny's eyebrows went up. "Tea?" she asked dubiously. "Okay. Want a shot in it or something?"

"No. Just the tea." He stared down at his blunt-tipped fingers with their woodworking scars after Ginny left. He liked carpentry, but he was committed to police work. Only one of those two occupations gave him nightmares, though. Maybe he needed to think about that.

He blew out a breath. Nothing to think about. He was a cop and he wasn't going to quit.

A cup clinked onto the table, followed by a glass. Next came the Pyrex teapot. He glanced up to see not Ginny, but Becky. And she obviously intended to join him. Matt gestured to the opposite side of the booth. Becky smiled and sat, pushing her curls over her shoulder.

"You on duty?" he asked. She shook her head. She had a lot of hair. Not hair like Tara's, but bigger, blond hair. But she did smell good.

He smiled. "Then I guess I don't have to tip you."

"Guess not," she said as she squeezed his knee under the table. She left her hand there as she stirred her drink with the other. "You never really struck me as a tea drinker."

Matt smiled politely at her comment, then put the bag in the cup and poured the water over it.

"You haven't been eating here as often."

"I'm working," he said. "Meals come with the job."

"She's a good cook."

"Yeah, she is," Matt agreed, halfway amused at how "she" suddenly came into the conversation without being identified. He figured in a town this size everyone knew everyone's business.

He let the tea brew for a minute, then pulled the bag out. He usually only had tea when he visited his mom and stepdad down in Las Vegas, and the smell of the orange pekoe brought back comforting memories—or would have if Becky's hand had not been inching higher as she leaned forward.

He put his hand over hers, stopping her progress up his thigh. But he didn't move her hand away. He just pushed it down closer to his knee and held it there. She raised her eyebrows in a silent question. He shook his head. She pulled her hand away and brought it up to hold her straw as she sipped, then gave him an "oh well" smile. There were obviously no hard feelings.

"Girlfriend?" she asked.

He decided it would be better for her ego if he said yes. So he did, neglecting to mention that she was now long gone, driven away by the effects of stress. His stress.

"Things happen," she said. "And if they do…"

Matt smiled broadly. He couldn't help but appreciate Becky's honesty. He decided to take advantage of it. "Do you know who drives a white Beemer? Blond guy."

"Oh, that would be Ryan Somers." A look of dawning realization crossed her face. "Did he go to see Tara?" Becky leaned forward as she asked the question, giving him one heck of a view of her assets. "Oh, man," she whispered even though Matt hadn't answered. "That would be something to see those two together again."

"They were together?"

Becky wrinkled her nose. "They were, but…"

Matt waited. Becky stirred her drink and her heavily mascaraed eyes narrowed. "They *were* together for a while about a year and a half ago…maybe a little less…and everyone was kind of surprised because the Somerses are rich and influential, you know, and the Sullivans…well, Tara's dad did die in prison. Not exactly the people the Somerses hang with. And Ryan is the *nicest* guy. Everybody likes him, but Tara—" Becky's mouth formed a commiserating little smile "—you work for her. You know how she is."

Matt kept his face carefully expressionless, hoping for more information. He got his wish.

"Anyway," Becky continued as she fiddled with her straw, "Tara *is* very, very pretty and Ryan always was a sucker for a pretty face. And they were both from Night Sky, living and working in Elko. It was probably natural that they hooked up for a while, but then—" Becky leaned closer again, but thankfully kept her hands off his thighs "—according to Ryan, Tara started getting real possessive. Following him, things like that and he had to end it." Becky shook her head. "Possessiveness... Not his thing. And then rumor has it he applied for a restraining order against her because she hit him or something during one of their fights."

Becky let out a sigh, as though wondering how anyone could raise a hand to Ryan Somers.

"He moved back here right after they broke up and opened an accounting business. Some people say it was to get away from her. He's been back over a year now."

"How long has Tara been back?"

"Two months?" Becky guessed. "She lived in Elko while she was teaching, but spent her weekends here working on the house. After she lost her job, though, she moved back for real. Nowhere else to go, I guess. I heard that Ryan was unhappy when she moved back, so that's why I'm surprised he went over there."

Becky sipped the last of her drink through the straw, then pushed the glass away with a sigh. "You know, the sad thing is that nobody really knows what happened, except for Ryan and Tara, and neither is talking. He's too much of a gentleman and she keeps to herself. And you know what that means, don't you?"

Matt shook his head and Becky grinned.

"It means that the rest of us have to speculate, and speculating is something we do very well here in Night Sky."

"I'll remember that," Matt replied dryly.

Becky gave him a sassy smile. "You'd better." She leaned forward again, suggestively. "So tell me…this girlfriend…is it serious?"

## CHAPTER FIVE

ICE. COLD AS.

Matt rammed his ball cap backward on his head in frustration as he watched Tara march away. Orders for the day given, orders received.

Nicky had left for Vegas early that morning, but while that might account for some pensiveness on her part, it did not explain her curt behavior. Matt wondered if Ryan Somers had been in contact with her again, and whether he should do something about it if he had.

About an hour after he started working on the gazebo, Tara's old Ford truck, which was the same year and color as his own, showing that the woman had remarkable good taste in classic vehicles, pulled out of the drive. She hadn't told him where she was going, but he'd seen another huge shopping list on the table and figured she was probably going to Elko. That meant he was going to be rooting through the fridge for his lunch. Fine with him. He just didn't want to cross her in the mood she was in.

Things did not go much better once she got home, almost eight hours later. The truck was stacked with food, building supplies, paint, wallpaper, bags of cat food and grain. It was no wonder she looked as if she were about to drop. Matt stopped hammering and went to help her carry things into the house.

"I can handle this," she snapped.

*Dismissed.*

Matt swallowed his anger and went back to work, finishing up the gazebo and hammering in the last nail with a single blow, before going to sit on the bench inside and watch as Tara lugged bags and boxes in. Trip after trip. Finally he'd had it. He strode over to the truck and took the bag of grain she was attempting to heft. She rewarded him with a glare.

"I hear you have a girlfriend."

Matt stepped back in surprise. So she'd had a chat with Becky, or someone Becky had talked to. He shrugged noncommittally, wondering what his pretend girlfriend had to do with anything.

"Then why in the hell did you kiss me? Do I look like some kind of plaything to you?" She practically spit the words at him. "Someone to amuse you for a while?"

He started putting the pieces together.

"Well?" she demanded, hands on hips. He also noticed then that she was flushed and it wasn't entirely with anger. She wasn't looking well and he needed to put an end to this.

"Shut up, Tara."

Clearly startled, she stared at him. Good, he had her attention. "I don't have a girlfriend. I told Becky that to make her back off." He settled the fifty-pound bag on his shoulder. "Where do you want this?"

Silently, Tara pointed to the barn. Matt delivered the grain and came back for more. Tara was just returning from the house. They met at the tailgate.

"Do you really think I would use you?" he asked as he dragged the next bag of grain to the edge of the truck bed.

"I don't know you."

He cocked his head to one side, his eyes narrowing behind his glasses. "Take a wild guess."

"That is what I'm saying," Tara replied in a tight voice. "*I don't know.* I'm not good at judging those kinds of things—even with people I thought I *did* know." She grabbed an armful of wallpaper and stalked to the porch.

Another piece of the puzzle fell into place, a piece with Ryan Somers's name written on it.

Matt lifted the grain and took it to the barn.

When he came back, Tara was still in the house. He hauled the other two bags of grain, took two twenty-pound bags of cat food to the barn, thinking that his cat could probably eat both of them in one sitting, and then went into the house carrying two buckets of paint.

Tara was stirring the contents of a Crock-Pot. She didn't bother to look up when he came in the door and put the paint next to the stack of wallpaper. Matt's stomach rumbled as he inhaled the savory aroma of the stew. But there was a very real possibility he wouldn't be eating stew anytime soon.

"When did you hear about my 'girlfriend'?" he asked.

Her eyes drilled into him. "This morning."

"Before I got here?"

She nodded, sipped the broth she'd spooned up.

"Rafe stopped by. He said you'd been at the Owl late last night—"

"Early this morning," Matt corrected her, wondering once again about Rafe's relationship with Tara.

"Early, then."

"I couldn't sleep." The words came out before he thought about them.

"Why?"

He hunched his shoulders. Her eyes narrowed,

but she accepted his nonanswer. Neither of them was being straight with the other, and they both knew it. Neither of them was trusting by nature. And neither was going to willingly share the details.

Matt decided he could accept that, as long as it was mutual. But he had to set her straight on one important point.

"I wasn't using you, Tara."

"Thank the Lord for small favors," she muttered before stalking to the cupboard and taking out one…no, two bowls. "Come and get it," she said in a clipped voice.

Matt dished up, but hesitated before sitting at the table, wondering if she really wanted him there. It was the first time they'd eaten together, the first time she hadn't given him his food and disappeared with her own.

He got his answer a split second later in the form of an impatient nod. He sat and began eating. Tara swallowed about three spoonfuls of stew, then pushed the bowl away. She was pale except for the flushed red spots on both cheeks and she looked cranky enough to hunt bears with a switch. She pulled an envelope out of her back pocket and put it on the table. Matt glanced at the letter and then at her.

"Official confirmation from Mr. Bidart of Bidart

Industries," she explained. "For the reunion. Three rooms and the party. Plus a deposit."

"That's good."

Tara nodded wearily. "Yeah. It is."

"But...?"

Tara hesitated and Matt knew it was hard for her to say what was on her mind, that confiding did not come easily to Tara. So he was surprised when she abruptly said, "I'm afraid I won't have the house done on time."

She leaned back in her chair. "I need this booking. And I'm working against time here."

She lapsed into silence, her pensive gaze settling on her stew until Matt said, "Look at me, Tara."

She did.

"I promise we will get this house done."

"You sound confident."

"You need your house done, we'll get it done."

She reached for the envelope, studied it briefly, then tapped the edge on the table. Her brows drew together. "How come you're being so nice, when I haven't exactly been pleasant?"

Matt shrugged. "I need the work."

"No, really."

"Really." He did need the work, just not for monetary reasons.

"All right. Whatever." She took her bowl to the

sink. "Eat as much as you like," she said, gesturing to the Crock-Pot before she started for the door.

"Where are you going?"

She gave him a none-of-your-business look that Matt weathered for several seconds before she decided to reply. "Upstairs to work."

*Of course.*

MIND OVER MATTER.

Tara gritted her teeth as she prepared to paint the trim in one of the bedrooms. If she could get the trim done tonight, then she could roll paint tomorrow. Then it would be her first finished bedroom. She stood up after stirring the paint, causing her head to swim, but she refused to give in.

*I will not get sick. I will not get—*

Tara raced for the bathroom.

*No fair.* First her application for a loan from a small, privately owned bank in Elko had been regretfully denied and now this. Talk about adding insult to—

She clutched the bowl as her stomach heaved. Again. And again. Tara weakly leaned back against the old-fashioned claw-footed tub once her midsection stopped convulsing. Her eyes were damp and she felt as if she were going to cry—partly from frustration and partly because she felt so very, very rotten. She leaned her head back, closed her eyes, giving mind over matter once last shot.

It didn't work. Her head started to throb and she let out an unconscious groan. She turned her face so that the cool painted iron of the tub was against her cheek.

"Tara…"

Matt. She hadn't heard him come into the bathroom. She wondered if she'd even been conscious when he did. She had no idea how long she'd been on the bathroom floor, propped against the tub.

"Go away," she said weakly as her stomach started to roil again.

She moved to the toilet, but nothing came. A few seconds later she felt Matt crouch down behind her. His hands stroked her hair away from her face, and then he held her head until the heaves were over. When they stopped, she collapsed back against him, no longer caring about her stupid pride. She just wanted this to end. His arms came around her, holding her against his chest. Her head flopped back onto his shoulder.

"Matt…I…" She tried to wet her dry lips.

"I know." His hand smoothed soothingly over her hot forehead as he spoke. "You want me to leave."

Painfully, she shook her head, rolling it against

his chest. "No," she whispered. "I want to go downstairs."

"No problem," he said. He gently helped her to her feet. She felt herself sway and swallowed dryly, fighting another wave of nausea as she waited for her head to stop spinning.

"Can you walk?"

"Yeah." She took a couple small steps forward. Matt kept hold of her elbow, steadying her. They made it as far as the stairs and then Matt gave up steering and lifted her. "Where's your room?"

"Off the kitchen." The trip down the stairs jostled her sore body. She turned her head into the comfort of his chest. She needed him to take her to her bed, to put her down, stop jostling her, but when he did, she suddenly felt cold.

"Can you get undressed?'

"Yeah," Tara assured him weakly as she collapsed sideways and drew her knees up to protect her sore stomach. *Undressed. In just a minute…* She was surprised to feel him taking her shoes off, untying the laces, prying them off her feet. Socks followed. Then…nothing. She let out another painful sigh, pulled her knees tighter against her chest. And fell into a deep, fitful sleep.

MATT STOOD and stared down at Tara. She wouldn't know or care if he helped her undress and made her more comfortable—until later. Then she'd care. She'd gone bonkers over one kiss once she had heard he supposedly had a girlfriend, and not because she had any serious feelings for him. It was because she was afraid of being someone's plaything. It was obvious that she'd dropped her defenses before, let someone get close and then that someone had used her.

And Matt was pretty certain he knew who that someone was. And what he drove.

There were two sides to every story, he reminded himself, before promptly disregarding the notion. Ryan Somers was a bully. Matt knew it instinctively, even if Becky seemed to think Ryan was a great guy. Matt had seen Ryan come to torment Tara when her brother was gone and she was alone. Great guys, even ones with nice smiles and firm handshakes, did not do things like that.

Well, Matt thought as he unfolded a heavy afghan and settled it over Tara's body, Ryan had him to contend with now, whether Tara liked it or not.

Matt didn't go home that night. He sat in Tara's room while she slept, reading a spy novel he'd found in the living room bookcase. He'd helped Tara to the bathroom twice, holding her head while her stomach attacked, and she had leaned heavily on him on the trip back to her bed, something he knew she wouldn't normally allow herself to do, physically or emotionally. Her stomach had not acted up in over an hour and she slept less fitfully now. But she still had the fever and as soon as she woke up again he was going to get some aspirin into her.

Tara's room had been a surprise. He had expected a room that fit in with the Victorian theme of the rest of the house, but this room was wild with color—the gypsy colors Tara looked so good wearing. There were bright comforters and afghans, satin pillows, Persian rugs on the hardwood floor. Self-contained Tara had a bit of a wild side. The only sedate touch in the room was the chair in which he sat—a rather beat-up dark leather recliner he could imagine Tara escaping to when she needed to get away.

Tara murmured in her sleep, pulling the afghan up to her chin, huddling into herself, shivering. Matt closed the book, put it on the writing desk. She opened her eyes when he knelt by the bed and he felt the impact of connection as their gazes met. She tried to smirk. Couldn't do it. Matt smiled. Her eyes drifted shut.

Matt spread a blanket over her, but she still

shivered. He looked for yet another blanket, but they were all beneath her, covering the bed. A huge shudder racked her body and then Matt, who'd honestly had every intention of sleeping in the chair, took off his glasses and eased his long body onto the bed, feeling it give with his weight as he pulled Tara, blanket, afghan and all, against him. She sighed and immediately snuggled against him, making his heart lurch at the unexpected action. Her body was still quaking. His arms tightened and he settled his cheek against her silky hair and closed his eyes.

Tara's shivering finally stopped, but Matt continued to hold her, hesitant to leave. The unsettling thought struck him that maybe he needed her warmth.

It was almost midnight when the phone rang. Matt jerked awake, surprised to find Tara still in his arms, surprised at how natural it felt to have her there. He carefully eased himself away from her. She didn't even stir. He grabbed his glasses and strode out into the kitchen, answering the phone with a clipped, "Hello." The phone clicked dead.

Matt shook his head and went back into the bedroom. He stopped in the doorway, looked at the woman sleeping in the bed and wondered what on earth he had been thinking when he'd stretched out and pulled her against him. He hadn't been thinking. He'd simply been reacting. Again.

Matt shoved a hand through his hair, suddenly irritated that he had given in to temptation. He was just settling himself into the leather chair when the phone rang again. This time he picked it up on the second ring. "Hello."

Silence.

"Hello," he said again. If this was Somers…

"Who is this?"

Matt instantly recognized the voice and gave an inward groan. "Hi, Nick. It's Matt."

*What the hell are you doing there?* Matt could practically hear the kid's very reasonable yet unspoken question, so he filled in the blanks. "Tara's got the flu. I'm sleeping in the chair—" *liar* "—in case she needs anything."

"She's sick? How bad?"

"She's sleeping. She'll feel better tomorrow."

Nicky was silent for a moment then said, "Tell her I'll call her tomorrow. And don't let her kill herself working on that house until she's better."

Matt smiled in spite of himself. "I'll try," he said dryly.

He heard Nicky's voice relax a little as the kid said, "Do your best."

"By the way," Matt asked, "did you call a few minutes ago?"

"Yeah, I figured it was a wrong number when you answered."

"Why are you calling so late?" Matt asked, curious.

"Oh, I usually call at this time," Nicky said matter-of-factly. "That way I can tell T to stop working and go to bed."

THERE SEEMED TO BE cats everywhere when Matt started to slide the big barn door open early the next morning, so he stopped pushing for a moment and watched the animals scramble away. Had his own adopted fat cat ever been that speedy? Somehow he didn't think so.

The animals raced to a low-sided black rubber tub and looked at him expectantly, and Matt saw then that there were actually only two adult cats and a litter of half-grown kittens. Somehow it seemed as if there were more. He went over to the bags of food he'd hauled in the day before and he grinned as he saw several holes in them. He hefted one of the leaking bags as best he could and filled the black tub.

The donkeys were waiting outside the barn, both obviously hungry and impatient to be fed.

Matt knew enough about the equine species to know that he needed to feed them hay. He had no idea how much, so he filled the manger and figured that they could regulate their own intake. From the greedy way they both dived into the dried grass, tossing it in the air as they looked for the good stuff, Matt decided that self-regulation was out. He hoped he hadn't overfed them and they wouldn't get sick or something.

There seemed to be no one else to feed, except for himself and Tara, so Matt went back into the kitchen and began to familiarize himself. Tara had everything a cook could possibly need, including some gadgets he couldn't even identify, and from what he'd tasted, she knew how to use the stuff.

He wasn't a bad cook by any means, but he was definitely not in her league. The things he used were simple. Bowls, spoons, measuring cups, knives, things like that. He left the food processors and espresso makers to the professionals. He started opening drawers and cupboards, looking for rudimentary items to make breakfast for a sick person.

He had just finished making oatmeal when he heard scuffing footsteps.

Matt looked up, surprised to see Tara on her feet and standing in the doorway. She was wearing a

T-shirt emblazoned with the logo for the UNLV Running Rebels and a pair of baggy, overly long gray sweatpants that had to belong to Nicky. She'd unbraided her hair and it fell down her back in long waves. "Do me a favor," she said in her husky, sore-throat voice. She handed him a hair elastic and turned around.

"I'm not much of a braider," Matt said roughly. She'd keel over before he got the job done. Besides, it would be best, after last night, if he didn't touch her, especially because he wanted to touch her.

"Just make a ponytail. It hurts to lift my arms." She glanced over her shoulder, her expression surprisingly unguarded. "It hurts to do anything."

She obviously had no recollection of him being in her bed the night before, which was probably a good thing, he decided as he tentatively gathered the long hair.

Now he knew what Tara's hair felt like. It felt great. Silky and sensual as it slid through his fingers. And it was hard to control. He bit the corner of his lip and concentrated on pulling the strands through an elastic that didn't seem up to the job.

He brushed his fingers over the smooth skin at the back of her neck when he was finished, fighting an urge to follow with his lips.

"Thanks," Tara murmured. She moved to the nearest kitchen chair and sank down, her elbow on the table propping her head in her hand. She was pale and her forehead was furrowed with pain.

"I fed your animals…I think," Matt said. "They have food in front of them anyway."

"Again, thanks," Tara said in a low voice. "And thanks for last night."

"Uh, no problem."

"I should call Nicky."

"He already called. He said he'd call back this afternoon."

"Good." Tara closed her eyes.

Matt wondered why she was even out of bed. Surely she didn't plan to work…. "You look awful," he said bluntly. "Go back to bed. I'll do the work today."

Tara opened her eyes and gave him a dark look. Matt ignored it. "Do you want to eat first?"

The horrified expression on her face almost made him smile.

"I made oatmeal."

"Don't." Tara held up a hand. "I'll go back to bed for a while if you promise not to threaten me with food. *Especially* oatmeal."

"Deal."

She got to her feet, swaying a little before she

started toward the door to the back of the house. Matt could hear her muttering something under her breath.

"Tara?"

She stopped in the doorway.

"I'll work for both of us today, okay? That way you can concentrate on getting well instead of worrying about what you're not getting done."

Her expression shifted and she actually smiled. "Maybe you could do enough work for Nicky, too," she suggested in her husky voice.

He smiled back. "That should be easy. Nicky doesn't know how to do much."

She held his gaze, her voice low and matter-of-fact as she said, "I've been kind of rotten to you lately. I'm sorry."

"Tara…"

"Yes?"

"Go to bed."

MATT CLIMBED the stairs to the third floor, figuring he'd start at the top and work down, inventorying the work ahead of him. The top was not good. In fact, it was pretty bad, and Matt could see why Tara only planned on finishing the first and second floors in the short amount of time they had left. There were two baths plumbed and framed in, but no wallboard, no doors. There had probably been four rooms on that floor at one time, but the walls had been torn down, leaving only one plaster-and-lath load-bearing wall in the center of the scarred floor. It needed a lot of work to make this area habitable, but Matt could see the potential. The view alone was fantastic.

He went to lean on a rough windowsill and peered out across the valley—pastures, green irrigated fields and vast expanses of government grass and sagebrush. Night Sky to the east and the Sandoval Mountains to the west.

It was peaceful.

Serene.

A place where he didn't really belong. His place was the city. Vegas or Reno. Crowded, loud, impersonal. Sometimes ugly, always active.

So why did he feel this unexpected attraction to a place unlike anywhere he'd ever lived before?

*Because he was flipping crazy from lack of sleep, that's why.*

He abruptly pushed off from the sill and went back down the stairs.

The second floor was in a lot better shape. The walls in all of the bedrooms had been patched and primed, some had been painted. The floors had been stripped and refinished. There wasn't a stick of furniture anywhere. Matt wondered if Tara had it stored somewhere or if she planned on a shopping spree. The rooms needed the molding replaced and none of them had overhead light fixtures—just capped-off wires protruding from the ceilings. Matt found a trouble-light in a bedroom, clamped to the closet door, that answered his own question as to how Tara worked after dark.

The hall had a working light fixture, but it was a simple ceramic base with a bare bulb. He switched the light on, illuminating the scuffed-up walls, which had yet to be primed, or even washed. One woman could only do so much.

He turned the light back off and was heading for the stairs when he caught a flash of white out one of the bedroom windows. He stepped inside the room in time to see a white BMW cruise by on the county road. Matt's pickup was parked prominently in front of the house and was apparently all the incentive Ryan needed to keep moving—unless, of course, the guy had an innocent reason for driving by Tara's isolated house at approximately twenty miles per hour. Always a possibility…but somehow Matt didn't believe anything Ryan did was innocent. The Inn was a couple of miles in the opposite direction. There wasn't much in the direction Ryan was heading.

Matt watched the vehicle until it was out of sight. He waited and then, about ten minutes later, it reappeared, traveling faster on the return trip, but still not at a normal speed for the road.

As soon as the BMW rounded the bend heading toward town, Matt went downstairs and let himself out the kitchen door, crossing the grass to the gazebo. He had another couple of hours of work left on the old structure, then he figured he'd see what he could do inside. Of course, Tara would be up and around and trying to do things before she was recovered, but there wasn't much he could do about that.

Tara surprised him, though, by staying in bed most of the day. She was asleep when Luke dropped by to see Matt's work and to fertilize the roses.

"Looks good," Luke said as he inspected the gazebo. "Heard you had a late night last night."

"Yeah." Nothing happened in this town without everyone knowing about it. "I couldn't sleep, so I went over to kill some time."

"I hear you have a girlfriend."

Matt gave Luke a dark look and the old man laughed. "So, where's Tara?"

"Sleeping. She's got that flu that's going around. How long you going to be here?"

"A half an hour or so."

"I have to run to town. I hate to leave her alone."
*Especially with Ryan cruising around.*

"I'll stay within shouting distance in case she needs something."

"Thanks."

When Matt returned an hour later, Luke was gone and Tara was sitting at the kitchen table, sipping a glass of water.

"Where's Luke?"

"Appointment at the clinic. They called with a cancellation. He wasn't going to go, but I told him I was fine." She smiled. "He left about twenty minutes ago, all excited because the doctor is going to try a new medication. If it works out, he can drink beer."

"That should do him some good," Matt said with a grin. He liked it when Tara smiled. "How're you feeling?"

"Good enough to work tomorrow."

"No doubt."

Tara took another sip of water. "You know, Connors, it occurred to me today that you spent the night in my house and I know nothing about you."

That was true. And he could see where that would be cause for concern for a single woman living alone.

"Luke trusts me," he pointed out.

"Yeah. Now I want to know why. How do you know Luke?"

"His brother is married to my mother. He's my stepuncle I guess. He was also my boss once."

"And what do you do for a living? Carpentry? Contracting?"

"I'm a police officer for the city of Reno."

Tara's eyebrows went up. "You're in law enforcement?"

"Is that so surprising?" Wasn't it normal to have a cop refurbishing your house?

"No…it just clears a few things up for me." Tara didn't explain. "And you're here because…"

"I came to help Luke until he feels better. It seemed a decent way to spend my vacation." It was his turn for a question before she delved too deeply into the matter of his vacation—like why he had about twice as many days as he should have. "How long have you known Luke?"

Tara thought for a moment. "He knew my aunt from school. When he moved back here, he started doing the gardens for her, but I was already in college. I guess you could say that I really got to know him after my aunt died. He kind of stayed with the place."

"So only a year or two?" It was Matt's turn to

be surprised. From the way Luke talked about Tara, Matt had assumed he'd known her since she was a child.

"Yeah. But he has been very good to me. He was someone that…I don't know…I guess I trusted from day one."

"That doesn't happen often for you?"

"Like never?"

"Imagine that?" The words came out low and teasing. Tara smirked at him and ping-ponged the subject back to him.

"Where are you from originally?"

He leaned back against the counter, folding his arms over his chest. "Las Vegas. My mom and stepdad live there."

"Your real dad?"

"He's dead."

"So's mine," Tara said, running a finger over the ridges on the side of her glass.

"Is it just you and Nicky, then? Or do you have more family somewhere else?" Matt purposely shifted the direction of conversation again and wondered if Tara was going to let him get away with it.

"You've been in Night Sky for more than a week. Are you telling me you don't know my entire history?"

Matt didn't try to hedge. "I know your dad went to prison." He didn't feel like telling her that his dad probably should have gone to prison, too. Would have, if he hadn't have been killed in the line of duty.

"He did. Bank robbery. I was twelve when he was sentenced and eighteen when he died. Pneumonia."

"Your mom?"

"Died when I was ten."

"Who raised you and Nicky?"

"I did, in a way. We lived here with my great-aunt Laura, after my father was arrested." Tara smiled reminiscently. "She was a bit of a free spirit. She took care of us, but wasn't exactly... traditional, shall we say?"

"Your aunt was eccentric?"

"I prefer to think of it as having unique tastes and skills. See that penguin on top of the refrigerator? She carved it for Nicky when he was little."

Matt reached for the brightly painted bird. "I've never seen a purple penguin."

"It reminds me of her. She was always creating something. Sometimes she would literally forget to go to bed if she was in the middle of a project. She never married, but she had lots of—"

"Cats," Matt guessed, still holding the sculpture.

"Burros and goats. She made cheese and soap

from the goat milk and adopted the burros from the Bureau of Land Management whenever she could."

That explained the long-eared residents.

"Buddy and Billie are the only burros left. I sold the goats…. The cats are *mine*," she said darkly. "The place was overrun with mice before I got them."

"I didn't say anything."

"Yeah, but I know the cliché."

"House cats. Not barn cats." His eyes crinkled at the corners. "And I wouldn't exactly call you older.

"Good save." Tara held out a hand and Matt passed her the penguin. "Well, I've really enjoyed this conversation about *you*."

Matt acknowledged her point with a half smile. "Is there anyone who could come and stay with you tonight?"

Tara frowned. "Not really. I'm feeling a lot better anyhow. I'm sure I can make it through the night on my own."

"I saw Somers drive by here today. Slowly."

Tara stilled for a moment and then shrugged before carefully placing the penguin on the table in front of her.

"You don't have very good locks on your doors and none to speak of on your windows."

"Never really needed them."

"You may need them now." He was silent for a moment. "I want to stay one more night, Tara. I'll install new locks tomorrow."

"I don't need to be protected Matt. I'll be fine on my own."

"Tara—"

Her expression grew stubborn. "I appreciate all you've done, but no more rescues. Okay?"

"Rescues?" Matt felt a stab of irritation, more from her tone than what she said.

Tara pressed her fingers to her forehead. "I knew I'd blow this," she muttered. "Look, no offense, Connors. I want you to keep working here and, frankly, I kind of enjoy your company, but you've been my personal white knight lately."

"Last night I had to stay."

"Okay, forget last night. But I've taken care of myself since I was twelve. When I do need help, I like to ask for it, and get it on my terms. I don't want a self-appointed bodyguard."

Matt wanted to argue, but realized she was right. He had been shoving his way into her life.

"I understand where you're coming from," Tara continued, "especially now that I know you're a cop, but honestly, Matt, I don't need a hero...I need a carpenter."

## CHAPTER SIX

THERE WAS A THIN LINE between being ungrateful and stating facts, but watching Matt's reaction, Tara didn't think she'd crossed it. Yet.

"I hadn't intended to be your hero," he replied in a low voice. His expression was frank, borderline troubled. "But I still think I should stay one more night."

Tara stared at him, which seemed better than throwing something at him. "And if I don't agree," she asked stonily, "are you going to do something stupid like sleep in your truck in the yard?"

He shook his head. "I'll go back to town."

"Honestly."

"Yeah." He paused. "I think."

Tara let out a breath. It wasn't so much that she minded him staying at the place. It was a big house, after all. A guesthouse. No, it was the feeling that she was becoming dependent on this man in ways she hadn't anticipated that bothered her. But, on the other hand, if Ryan did come back, she wouldn't mind watching Matt knock the snot out of him. She knew he'd do it so much better than she could.

A corner of her mouth tightened. "One night, and that's it."

There was a flash of relief in Matt's hazel gaze, there and then gone.

"One night," he agreed.

MATT BEAT TARA to the kitchen the next morning. He was standing at the stove with his back to her when she entered, stirring what she hoped was not oatmeal. Oatmeal was the only hot breakfast Aunt Laura had ever made and Tara had had enough to last a lifetime.

He turned, smiling as he took in her bedraggled appearance. Old sweatpants and one of Nicky's big T-shirts. Very alluring, no doubt. She'd tried to smooth her hair, but the wisps that had escaped the elastic stubbornly refused to be tamed and she'd given up.

She took comfort, though, from the fact that Matt looked just as disheveled as she did. His hair was tousled and he was barefooted. The dark stubble was back on his face. He wore a shirt, but it was fastened by only one button at midchest, as though he'd thrown it on at the last minute and otherwise she would have found him standing at the stove, wearing only his Levi's and his glasses. The thought pulled at her and suddenly the scenario seemed just a little too intimate.

"Something wrong?" he asked.

She shook her head. "No." Other than the fact that he looked downright sexy and she was noticing.

He gave her a look that clearly said, *yeah, right,* and Tara pressed her lips together, half-afraid he'd guessed the direction of her thoughts.

"Nothing's wrong," she said as she crossed the room to grind the beans for coffee.

"You're probably just sore because I beat you out of bed."

Tara gave him a face-saving smirk as she measured the grounds, and he grinned. She turned her back on him as she went to the tap, letting it run until the water was icy cold. Whatever he was cooking smelled great and it wasn't oatmeal.

"What's for breakfast?" she finally asked, attempting nonchalance.

"Frittata."

Her inner cook was immediately interested. This she had to see.

Matt glanced down at her as she peered over his arm into the skillet filled with eggs, potatoes and ham. Heaven help her, despite the rich aroma of the sizzling ingredients, she was also aware of his scent—warm, masculine, somehow both comforting and stimulating. *Oh, man.* His eyes crinkled slightly at the corners, and Tara felt her cheeks grow warm.

"If you can cook like this, why have you been eating at the casino?"

"Nothing to cook with at Luke's house, and I didn't feel like investing for only a couple of weeks." He gave the pan a little swirl. "I didn't know if your stomach was ready for something this substantial, but you said no oatmeal."

"No," Tara said, drifting back, putting some space between them, "this is fine. Uh, what's the red stuff?"

He shifted as he used the spatula to loosen the egg at the edge of the pan and Tara took another step back. "Roasted red peppers. I found a jar in the pantry. Hope you don't mind."

Tara shook her head. "No. Not at all. I was afraid they were pimentos."

"Don't like pimentos?"

"Not much." She didn't even own pimentos, for Pete's sake. She turned and went to get the coffee cups, trying to get a grip on herself, and then jumped about a foot in the air when someone knocked on the back door. Both she and Matt whirled around as Rafe pushed the door open and walked in, stopping dead in his tracks when he saw Matt at the stove. His dark eyes immediately shot to Tara.

Matt also cast her a glance, eyebrows raised, but she simply pulled out another cup. No explanations. She didn't owe anyone anything. She saw Matt shrug before he expertly flipped the frittata. Rafe was frowning at Matt, who had obviously just rolled out of bed.

She filled a cup, handed it to Rafe and motioned to a chair.

"Hey, Rafe," she murmured with studied casualness as she took the opposite chair. "Have time for breakfast?"

Rafe started to shake his head, then changed his mind and nodded. "Yeah. I'll stay."

"Good. There's enough for three, isn't there, Connors?"

"Yep."

She was about to get up and set the table, when Matt pulled out another plate and placed it in the oven on top of the other two warming there. Then he took a pitcher of orange juice out of the fridge and set it on the table. He looked like a man who knew his way around her kitchen.

Tara read the unspoken questions in Rafe's eyes, and reconsidered her no-explanation plan.

"Matt gets meals as part of the job," she said, keeping her voice low enough that she didn't think Matt could hear.

Rafe's expression was impassive. "So why is he cooking?"

Tara let out a soft sigh. "I've been sick. He spent the night," she replied, giving up. Rafe would find out anyway. "This is none of your business, Rafe. I don't need another brother."

"Tough."

"It was no big deal."

Rafe raised one eyebrow. Clearly *he* thought it was a big deal that she'd let a man she barely knew spend the night. Tara stared at her coffee cup.

"So how are you feeling today?" Rafe asked with a slight edge to his voice.

"Fine." Matt set the frittata on the table along with a bottle of hot sauce.

Breakfast was a rather stilted affair, long on tension, short on conversation. Rafe and Matt engaged in a bit of civilized verbal sparring of the male variety, while Tara ate her meal in silence. She walked Rafe out to his SUV after they finished, for once glad to see him on his way.

He leaned back against the vehicle and studied

her through his sunglasses. She'd known Rafe forever. He had been part of her misfit band while growing up, the poor kid from an immigrant Mexican family who wanted to be a cop. They'd even dated briefly in high school, the *only* time she'd dated in high school, before deciding they were meant to be friends. But that didn't mean he had any say in her life.

"Don't," she said warned him.

"Tara, what do you know about this guy?"

"I know he's a cop," she replied, hoping the fact that Matt was one of the brethren would slow Rafe down. But he was obviously already aware of it.

"Tara…" He let out a frustrated breath. "There's more to this guy's history than you know."

"Like…"

"Like, he was involved in a critical incident a while ago."

"What kind of critical incident?"

"It was a shooting followed by a standoff. Connors pulled a John Wayne."

Tara frowned.

"He took matters into his own hands. It's a wonder he survived."

Tara felt a chill. "Maybe he had a reason for pulling this… 'John Wayne.'"

"He probably did. But Tara, what I'm saying is that usually when guys do things like that…well, it might be for reasons other than the obvious. They have something they need to prove, or something they need to live down."

He paused and let the words sink in. "And sometimes, after situations like that, there are post-traumatic reactions."

"You're not saying he's dangerous?" Tara asked incredulously.

Rafe shook his head. "No. I'm just saying he has a history and he might have some issues. You should be aware of it. I'd feel better if he wasn't spending the night."

Tara chewed her lip as she digested the information. Rafe looped an arm around her, pulling her to his side. She leaned her head against him.

"Jealous?" Tara asked in a weak attempt to lighten the mood.

Rafe dropped a brotherly kiss on her forehead. "You bet." His expression grew serious, though, as she stepped away from him. "Call if you have any trouble."

"I'll call," Tara agreed wearily.

Rafe gave her one last long look. "I think this guy is all right, but damn, Tara, you never know."

MATT GLANCED THROUGH the window at Rafe and Tara as he finished washing the dishes. He had no doubt that Tara now knew whatever Rafe Sanchez had dug up on him. He wondered if that included his father's history. He wasn't going to ask.

He still wasn't certain what Tara and Rafe's relationship was, either. During breakfast, she'd treated him with the easy camaraderie and congenial disrespect that comes from growing up together, but then they had embraced before Sanchez got into his rig and drove away. He'd kissed her, but not on the lips. There was something there….

His mouth tightened as he turned on the tap water. Tara had made it very clear the night before that he had no business butting into her life. And he had to admit she was right.

TARA RUBBED HER FOREHEAD with the back of her hand, trying to ease the tension that had been building there since breakfast.

*A John Wayne.*

*What kind of John Wayne?*

Luke knew Matt, so he must know Matt's past. He wouldn't have had Matt working for her unless he trusted him. Therefore, Matt must be trustworthy.

Or so she hoped. She needed Matt to finish the house. But more than that, she was attracted to him.

He was the first man since her awful experience with Ryan who had sparked any kind of reaction in her. And, to her astonishment, she liked having a reaction. It felt good in a secretive sort of way, and it took her mind off mortgages and balloon payments and Nicky's education. She'd probably never do anything with Matt, but at least she was *interested.*

It gave her hope that someday she might feel whole again.

MATT DROVE AWAY from Tara's house at dusk. She'd firmly eased him out the door after feeding him dinner, and he had gone quietly—because he'd promised to, and because he knew that her perception of him had probably changed drastically since talking to Rafe that morning.

It was for the best, he told himself, unnerved that he was thinking about her differently lately. He'd gotten a glimpse of the hurts and scars Tara was hiding under her tough veneer. And, regardless of her assertion that she didn't need a white knight, he felt a strong desire to protect her from new wounds. Maybe even to help soothe the old scars.

But he wasn't the man to do it.

Lisa, his ex-girlfriend, had driven home the point that stress, retribution and relationships do not mix. As things were now, he could walk away, with no one the wiser that Tara was starting to get to him. He had issues he needed to settle in Reno and he didn't want any distractions in his life when he did.

He felt better about leaving her alone now that all of her doors had new locks—if she actually locked them. The side door had had no lock at all until today. Tara, for being so protective of herself emotionally, was not very security conscious. But he hadn't seen the white BMW all day, and maybe it had just been a fluke that Ryan had been in the vicinity the other day. All he could do was hope, since it was obvious Tara wasn't going to let him hang around after hours.

JACK WASN'T AT the meeting.

Tara sucked a breath through her teeth as she searched the crowded convention room. Jack was a hard man to miss. On the plus side, though, she didn't see Martin Somers, either.

Ryan was obviously taking his place. Drat.

Well, Ryan wouldn't attack in public. He had an image to uphold—that of poorly used ex-lover and all-around good guy. He would mind his manners.

Tara sat in the first empty aisle seat she came to, next to Lydie Manzo, owner of the Hair

Affaire. Nodding a hello, she received a hesitant nod in return. Lydie looked as if she wanted to say something, but Stacia started the meeting before she could speak.

The secretary was reading the minutes when Dottie Gibson bustled in, uncharacteristically late. She had obviously planned to sit next to Lydie, who shrugged helplessly, as though Tara had strong-armed her way into Dottie's chair. Dottie gave an indignant huff as she realized there was no seat near her friend, reversed course and finally settled two rows behind Lydie.

The meeting continued with an update on correspondence, but Tara could still hear Dottie rustling. The committee reports came next. Various people stood and gave updates. Tara jotted notes.

The last committee report was for the Welcome Back luncheon. Dottie and Lydie were co-chairs, but Dottie rose to speak. The menu the caterer provided had been approved and was adaptable to adding new guests at the last minute. The high school swing choir would sing and, Dottie announced with a girlish laugh, having obviously recovered from the seating incident, they had come up with an interesting luncheon entertainment. A prom-dress parade.

"What exactly is that?" Stacia asked, and Dottie Gibson, queen of the 1966 prom, happily filled in the blanks.

"We have located several vintage prom dresses, including one from the 1930s. We're having these dresses cleaned and mended and they'll be modeled during the luncheon by high school girls."

There was a murmur of approval and Dottie beamed before outlining her plan.

"Weren't you a prom queen?" Lydie whispered.

Tara kept her expression pleasant as she nodded at the woman beside her. She needed to make an effort to be part of the community, she reminded herself, and she *had* taken Dottie's seat. This wasn't the time to make a scathing comment about the "honor" of being both queen and the butt of the joke.

"Do you still have your dress?"

Tara forced a smile and nodded again.

If they wanted her dress, they could have it. Aunt Laura had preserved it. Practically embalmed it, in fact, but Tara didn't blame her. Her aunt had made the dress herself, sewing zillions of pearls into intricate designs over the pale gray satin. It was a masterpiece. Tara never told her aunt about the embarrassment she'd suffered that night, and she truly hoped Laura never knew. Of course in Night Sky, that was highly unlikely.

"All right," Stacia said, interrupting Tara's thoughts, "the last item is the donation jars for the new gym floor. The boosters are really hoping that donations from the reunion will send them over the top and construction can begin in August. If you haven't already volunteered to have a jar at your business, please raise your hand so Ernest can get your name."

Several hands went up, including Tara's.

"Uh, okay…" Ernest Stewart, the booster club president, looked a little overwhelmed at the number of hands. "Uh, keep your hands up until I say your name."

He wrote names, saying them aloud, and the hands went down one by one. When Tara lowered hers she heard Dottie whisper, "We'd better watch *that* jar, if you know what I mean…."

Dottie's voice was low and she may not have meant for everybody to hear, but they did. Tara clenched her teeth, and she was more than aware of quick glances her way, but she kept her eyes straight ahead, pretending she hadn't heard. Several sharp retorts came to mind, but she was going to take the high road, ignoring the fact that Dottie had not once but twice publicly accused her of shoplifting in her convenience store when Tara was a teen. Both times Tara had been thoroughly searched and both times she'd had nothing on her person. After the second time, she'd never gone into the Gibson store again. But the memory of the humiliation lived on. It was one of the reasons she'd taken Nicky with her when she left for college. She wasn't going to subject her little brother to the same blind prejudices she'd had to live with.

The meeting was adjourned shortly after Dottie's rude comment. Tara had just started toward the rear exit when she heard her name. She turned to see perky Sandra Hernandez hugging a clipboard to her chest.

"Tara, you're not on a committee yet and you need to be on one if you're going to participate in the reunion," Sandra chirped like a happy parakeet.

"Fine," Tara said. "Put me on a committee."

"I already have. You're on the prom-dress parade staging committee. Flowers, decorations, dress rehearsal. Things like that."

"Oh?" Tara replied. "Can I be in charge of the slide show?"

Sandra had the grace to blush, before pursing her lips defiantly. "That was none of my doing."

"It was a long time ago, Sandra. Maybe you can't remember that far back. Anyway, I didn't care then and I don't care now. What do I need to do on this committee?"

"Dottie will call you."

Tara refrained from rolling her eyes. *Great. Dottie.* "Thanks, Sandra," she said dryly. "See you."

In the few short minutes she'd spend talking to Sandra, the room had nearly emptied. Tara started down the long L-shaped hall that led to the rear exit. She rounded the corner and immediately regretted her decision to take the shortcut. Ryan was standing next to the isolated door, a self-satisfied smile on his handsome lips.

Tara fixed a stony expression on her face and tried to brush by him, but he stepped into the center of the hall. Short of knocking him over, which she seriously considered, she couldn't leave this way, so she did an immediate about-face and started back down the hall, only to be pulled up short by a heavy hand on her shoulder. Tara immediately twisted out of his grip and turned, ready to do whatever she had to to protect herself, but her tormentor casually stepped away and leaned against the wall.

"I want to talk to you, Tara. Privately. And since your bodyguard *never* seems to leave your house…"

Tara's spine stiffened at the implication of his words…and that he knew Matt was there most of the time.

"I don't want to talk to you," Tara replied through her teeth, holding the man's gaze so that he couldn't surprise her again. Her shoulder was already starting to ache where he'd grabbed her too hard.

"Not even to work a deal out on your house? Save you the embarrassment of foreclosure? You've had time to think since I last spoke to you."

*Translation—you've had time to get turned down for six different loans.* She jacked her chin up and narrowed her eyes.

"I'll risk the embarrassment, Ryan. The house is not for sale and I want you to stay away from me."

"Yeah, Tara? Just what will you do if I don't?" He hooked his thumb in his pocket. "Seems to me, there's not much you can do."

"You might be surprised at what I can do," she bluffed.

"Oh, yeah?" He stepped forward. "Why don't you show me?"

The smug challenge was too much for her. Tara took a deep breath…and screamed.

The startled expression on Ryan's face was well worth the strain on her vocal cords and her pride. She would have much rather popped him in the nose again, but he'd obviously been expecting that. This seemed a better option under the circumstances.

He muttered, "You bitch," and then he was gone, the door swinging shut after him as several people came charging down the hall.

"T-Tara?" Ernest Stewart stuttered, obviously thinking that if something had frightened Tara Sullivan, it had to be bad. "What happened?"

Tara pressed a hand to her heart. "I saw a rat."

"A rat!" Sandra looked faint, but Eva Martini's eyes widened and then narrowed.

"Don't be silly. We have never had a rat in the convention center."

"Yes, Mrs. Martini, you have."

A few minutes later Ernest was arranging traps under the direction of Eva and Sandra. Tara felt bad about her ruse, but she had to prove to Ryan he couldn't push her around, or he would certainly continue.

*Make an offer on her house*...she'd rather torch it than see the Somerses own it.

She shivered as she stepped out into the startlingly bright sunlight and felt the heat wash over her. She wanted nothing more than to go home and sleep for about ten hours, but she still had to drive to Elko to pick up the three antique dressers she'd bought over the phone a few days before.

Aunt Laura had packed the house with antique furniture, most of which was now stored in the barn, but she had favored the unusual over the practical and there weren't enough usable dressers for all of the bedrooms. Tara'd been lucky enough to hook up with Mrs. Felton, an elderly lady from Elko who pronounced herself an antique broker, even though she was actually more of a yard-sale broker, and through her had managed to pick up enough pieces at a fairly reasonable cost to finish furnishing the bedrooms. These pieces would be her last—if they were indeed in as good a shape as Mrs. Felton insisted they were when she had named her price.

*It didn't matter,* Tara thought as she pulled onto the highway that led to the interstate. With the reunion only weeks away, she'd take whatever she could get.

It was close to ten o'clock and the moon was well above the horizon by the time Tara, exhausted, turned back off the interstate onto the state highway leading to Night Sky. The dressers, which had thankfully turned out to be well worth the asking price, were riding nicely under their protective tarp and the thunderstorm that the weatherman had predicted hadn't materialized. All in all, a very rotten day had turned into a pretty good evening.

As she rounded a sharp corner, a red safety

flare all but blinded her. She yanked the steering wheel to the left to keep from hitting the rear bumper of a sedan parked half-on half-off the side of the highway.

Tara cursed as her dressers hit the side of the truck—hard—then bounced to the other side, and finally to the cab as she braked. Once she was at a stop, completely *off* the road, unlike the other car, Tara looked over her shoulder. Was this an actual driver in distress or a ploy to stop an unsuspecting motorist? They were in the middle of nowhere on a little-traveled road....

The sedan, which looked very familiar in the red glow of the flare, had a white distress hanky fluttering from the antenna. Tara opened her door and got out, no longer leery of possible consequences. She only knew one person who drove a classic Cadillac and carried white hankies. Dottie Gibson. And unless she was mistaken, that was indeed Dottie huddled behind the wheel, looking terrified.

Tara grabbed her flashlight and, thinking *first things first,* stalked to the back of her truck to inspect her dressers. She lifted the tarp and was happy to see that none of the wood had splintered. They were probably scratched, but not destroyed. She dropped the tarp and stood for a moment looking at the frightened figure in the dangerously parked sedan.

Tara used the flashlight to illuminate her face as she walked back to the car, hoping she didn't look too ghoulish in her attempt to make herself recognizable to the frightened woman. No sense further terrifying the old…she swallowed as she saw the expression on the woman's face. Fear, chagrin and…relief?

"Flat tire, Mrs. Gibson?" Tara asked as Dottie rolled down the window. Dottie nodded, her eyes round.

"Have you called for help?"

"My cell phone is dead and I forgot my charger." The woman's voice cracked on the last word. "My husband told me…he said…"

"It's okay," Tara soothed. She knew how cranky Mr. Gibson could be. He rivaled his wife. "Have you been here long?"

"Twenty minutes." Tears started welling in the woman's eyes.

Twenty minutes alone, wondering who or what might come by. Tara could understand her anxiety. "You can use my phone if you want to call him while I change this tire."

"Oh, that would be…" Dottie's eyebrows went up. "You can change a tire?"

"I've learned to do a lot of things for myself."

Dottie nodded thoughtfully. "I…I suppose you

have." She rolled her window the rest of the way down. "If you could change this tire, well, I could get home and David wouldn't know I had this flat. He hates it when I go to visit my sister in Elko when it's late, but I had to go. She's tailoring a dress for me...it had to be fitted...." Dottie's words trailed off. "He said something like this would happen and he insists I have the phone. If he knew how careless I'd been—"

"The sooner we get started..." Tara suggested.

"Yes. Yes."

"The first thing we need to do is get your car into a safer position," Tara said. "I'll move my truck and you can park there where it's level, but be sure and get all the way off the road."

"Oh. Can I drive on a flat? Won't it damage something? David said—"

"It won't hurt if you just pull it forward a few yards and it'll be a lot safer."

Dottie looked first dubious and then determined as she cranked the ignition. "Yes. I'll park right where your truck is."

Tara had the tire changed in less than fifteen minutes.

"Tara..."

"That should do it, Mrs. Gibson." Tara wiped her hands on her jeans.

"I have some moist towelettes," Dottie offered and Tara smiled.

"No thanks. Just take it easy into town. You have no spare and the tire I put on is a little low on air. I'll follow you until my road."

"I do need to pay you."

"Thank you, but no," Tara said firmly as she started walking to her truck. "Good night."

"Tara?"

Tara raised her hand in a dismissive wave, got into her truck and waited until Dottie finally glanced at her watch, then got into her own car, started it and pulled onto the road. Tara waved again as the woman drove slowly by, the hankie still fluttering from the antenna.

Pay her, indeed. Tara smiled. She'd been paid in satisfaction and poetic justice and wouldn't have it any other way.

In spite of Ryan, in spite of everything, she felt great.

IT WAS OFFICIAL.

In the back of his mind, Matt had known it was coming. It was the lieutenant's next logical move in his bid to get rid of him without risking a harassment suit.

Matt opened the certified letter and read the

notification that he was required to partake in an FFD—Fitness for Duty—exam before returning to patrol. Failure to comply…

Matt scanned the rest of the letter and then dropped it on the kitchen table.

Rumor had it Lisa had gone out with the lieutenant a couple of times after she'd broken up with Matt. *Gee. What could the lieutenant have wanted?* A little information on Matt's stress level and stability, perhaps? Any signs of domestic violence? Fits of rage?

Matt knew for a fact that Lisa had seen none of the above, and she would have been honest about it, but she had seen obsessive focus, insomnia, lack of appetite. Warning signs. Things to report to the lieutenant.

Matt picked the letter up and shoved it back in the envelope, disgusted.

This was his legacy from his father, a supposed top cop who, along with two other officers, had been stealing recovered money and drugs for years. Ironically, the scheme had come to light shortly after his father had been killed. So in a sense, the old man had gotten away with it, while the other two officers had been arrested and charged.

The department had naturally suspected Matt of being a co-conspirator, but he'd eventually been cleared. On paper anyway. But suspicion lingered and the lieutenant was the most suspicious of all. He firmly believed Matt had to be involved and he subsequently made Matt's life a living hell. If he couldn't indict Matt, then he was at least going to force him to quit his division. But Matt never once considered it, because quitting was the same as admitting guilt. So he'd become "supercop" instead, proving that he was not his old man. Proving the lieutenant was wrong. Proving that he was a good officer.

It had almost killed him.

Well, Matt thought as he put the letter in his suitcase, he wasn't going to let this exam get to him. It was meant to be a slap in the face and it was, but for the past few days he'd been feeling better, sleeping better, and he planned on continuing that way—at least for as long as he was in Night Sky.

Focusing on Tara's problems had helped him shove aside his own, temporarily at least.

Matt's leave was running out, but the house was progressing on schedule and Luke had finally been able to pitch in. His new medication was working better than the old and the inflammation in his joints had diminished to the point that he was able to put in a few hours a day in the gardens. The shift in his attitude had been tremendous and he'd left Tara's early that day to have his reaction to the new medication checked. If it was acceptable, then he'd finally be allowed to give up iced tea in favor of his preferred beverage. Matt was supposed to meet him for dinner that night and either celebrate or commiserate.

When Matt headed out his back door to the Owl, the curtain moved in the kitchen window of the house next door and his neighbor, an elderly lady he'd never met, gave him a little wave and then disappeared. It was a common occurrence, one Matt had found disconcerting at first, but was finally getting used to. Sometimes he even waved back.

As he opened his gate, he saw Luke walking stiffly down the alley toward the casino from his own house.

"You all right?" Matt asked when Luke got closer. The tubby cat had followed Matt across the yard and now he rubbed his head on Matt's jeans. Matt absently leaned down and scratched the animal's ears before he realized what he was doing and straightened back up. The cat rumbled with pleasure.

"Other than going all to hell, I'm fine."

"How's the new miracle drug?" Matt fell in step with Luke.

Luke grinned. "I'm going to try it out tonight. It's called Budweiser."

A few minutes later, Matt opened the door of the casino and let the older man precede him in. A group of men trooped out at the same time, shoving and jostling one another, knocking the door out of Matt's hand and Matt suddenly found himself eye-to-bloodshot-eye with Eddie Johnson.

Eddie paused for only a second, his lip curling, but as he moved on, he bumped Matt with his shoulder, hard enough to make Matt take a step backward. Eddie gave a satisfied snort.

Matt reined in the gut impulse to teach Eddie some manners, knowing there were other things to consider. Like legalities. A pack of nasty-looking friends. The FFD letter tucked away in his suitcase.

He had a temper, but he wasn't stupid.

Matt shook his head and pulled the door open again, entering the dimly lit casino just as Luke was heading back out, a concerned frown on his face.

"It's fine," Matt said as he let the door swing shut behind him. Luke shook his head and expressed his opinion of Eddie and his friends in one succinct plural noun. Matt grinned.

They settled at the bar and Matt watched the action surrounding the pool tables while Luke ordered two Buds with an air of deep satisfaction.

The twenty-to-thirty-something crowd was there, laughing and drinking, doing all of the things that a twenty-to-thirty-something crowd was supposed to be doing. Front and center was Ryan Somers, shooting a pretty good game of pool and flashing a smile that would have made Tom Cruise proud. Just watching him made Matt's blood pressure rise. His mouth tightened as he realized that if this had been the first time he'd seen Ryan, he would have read him wrong. And he was good at reading people. He didn't think Ryan would have fooled him for long, but now he understood how cautious Tara might have fallen for him. The guy was a hell of an actor.

"Well, well," Luke muttered, turning to see who Matt was frowning at, "if it isn't golden boy."

"Don't think much of him?" Matt asked with interest.

"He's two-faced," Luke said as he turned back around in the booth.

Matt raised his beer to his lips and drank. "He seems to have a lot of friends."

"He's good at being two-faced. I arrested him once while I was working weekend auxiliary here for the sheriff's. Nothing too serious, but he was one snotty, petulant kid after he couldn't charm his way out of the situation. Downright ugly when crossed. Daddy rescued him, though, so he never learned a damned thing. You know the story."

*Oh, yeah.* Matt nodded. He knew the story. Knew it well.

"I think he's been bothering Tara lately."

"How?"

"He was at her place a few days ago. Tara wasn't happy about it. Since then I've seen him drive by a time or two."

Luke thought for a moment and then shook his head. "My read on this kid is that he's a petulant bastard, but he's not dangerous. I don't think he has a lot of follow-through."

"You sure?"

"Not one hundred percent, but he spends more than he makes and if he wants Daddy to keep giving him extra cash, he has to keep up the public image. Daddy wouldn't like him to do anything that would hurt the Somers name. Neither would his betrothed."

"He's engaged?"

"Oh, yeah, just recently and to quite a catch. She'll inherit the biggest land company in the valley someday. She's usually here with him. She must be busy with reunion stuff."

Another group, wearing matching fluorescent orange shirts, headed for the tables.

"Is there a pool tournament or something tonight?" Matt asked.

"Yeah, I think so. Jack keeps trying things to get a Monday night crowd in here. I think this is tag-team pool or something. This is one of his saner ideas."

"What else has he tried?" Matt asked as Ginny slid two more beers across the counter, compliments of Jack. The older man picked up his bottle, saluting Jack before he looked Matt in the eye.

"Trust me, son, you're better off not knowing."

# CHAPTER SEVEN

USUALLY WHILE TARA worked, she was figuring strategies to finance Nicky's education and pay off her loan, but today she found herself wondering just what was eating at Matt.

They worked on the second floor for most of the day, Tara painting first the bathrooms and then the long hallway while Matt reinstalled the stripped and refinished molding, and wired the antique-looking light fixtures that had just arrived.

He moved from room to room, brushing past her in the narrow hall, focused as ever on his work, except today he was almost too focused on his work. At one point she had stepped backward, inadvertently treading on his foot as he went by and he'd caught her by the waist in a sturdy grip, sending sparks of awareness through her body before he released her and continued on to the end bedroom to finish the wiring there.

Matt installed all of the fixtures at about the

same time Tara started her second and final coat on the hall. He paused to survey her handiwork.

"Got another roller?" he asked after taking a look at the long stretch of wall ahead of her.

"Yes." She pushed loose strands of hair off her forehead with the back of her hand and then she saw a hint of amusement light Matt's eyes for the first time all day.

"Let me guess," Tara said. "I have paint on my face."

"A little," Matt replied, tilting his head and studying her.

Tara refused to give in to the impulse to check her reflection in one of the bathroom mirrors. "Yes, I have extra rollers. They're down in the mudroom, next to the paint."

Matt was back a few minutes later with a roller and tray and an extra gallon of paint. Tara kept working, oh-so-aware of him as he opened the top of the gallon can and slowly stirred the contents.

He started painting on the wall opposite her, moving down the long passageway, rolling paint at approximately the same speed as she was. They continued to paint, back to back, with rock music playing softly in the background. At times they bumped up against each other in the narrow space, but neither of them broke the silence.

They hit the end of their respective walls at the same time and stood side by side, rollers in hand, facing the last six-foot panel that ended the hall and connected the freshly painted surfaces.

"If you want—" they started at the same time and then Matt looked down at her and smiled. Finally.

"We'll do it together," Tara said, impulsively slopping a line roughly down the center with the end of her roller. "Race you."

And then she dipped her roller and began to paint her side with short, swift strokes. "Loser cooks," she said, dipping the roller again.

Matt frowned at her as if she were a nut, and then took the challenge.

He had the height advantage and was able to roll all the way up to the six-inch swath Tara had painted below the molding before she started rolling. Tara had to jump to reach the top, but she got the job done with only minimal damage to the ceiling. She crouched low then, painting the section closest to the floor and when Matt crouched beside her, she purposely bumped him hard with her shoulder, throwing him off balance.

"Wait a minute…" he protested with a surprised laugh.

She ignored him as she dipped her roller again, about to finish her last section. But Matt reached out and took hold of her wrist, firmly guiding her roller over his side of the line and across his last swatch of wall. Tara pulled her arm free and twisted to face him.

"No fair!"

"You started it," Matt pointed out.

"So?" Tara responded, her eyes locked on his.

"Maybe—" Matt touched the end of his roller on the tip of her nose, leaving a little eggshell-colored dot "—we should call it a draw before one of us gets hurt."

"I wouldn't want to send you home injured," Tara agreed. His expression was still hard, but he was forcing it now. And dear heaven, but he was a handsome man. His face was all planes and angles and hollows, his rounded wire-rimmed glasses the perfect foil to the angles. Dark hair spilled down onto his forehead, as it tended to do when he wasn't wearing a ball cap, and she had the urge to reach out and brush it back.

"That's a danger," he said sardonically.

She grinned then and lifted her roller to put a tiny corresponding dot on the end of his nose. Matt shook his head and let out a breath edged with exasperation before he finished Tara's half of the wall with slow, deliberate strokes.

"Thanks for the help," Tara said as she hammered lids back onto cans.

"No problem. Oh, and by the way…"

She glanced up at him, pushing her braid back over her shoulder.

"I won."

WHAT WAS IT ABOUT a beautiful woman with a smudge of paint on her face?

Matt glanced over at Tara as she dumped the rollers and brushes into the kitchen sink.

Yeah. Smudges of paint in the right places were definitely sexy—sexy enough to pull his mind away from the FFD that he was not going to think about.

Tara dampened a cloth and raised it to his face, holding his gaze as she wiped off the daub of paint.

"Your turn," she said, raising her chin and closing her eyes as she gave him the cloth.

"Hold still," he said unnecessarily as he gently rubbed the paint off her nose and then her forehead. He resisted the impulse to pass the pad of his thumb over the softness of her full lower lip and instead turned toward the sink.

"I'm thinking I'll pass on dinner tonight," he said as he rinsed the cloth and spread it to dry.

"All right." She glanced down at the floor. "Would you like a beer or something before you go?"

He thought it would be best if he got out of there, but he made the mistake of looking at her and changed his mind. It was obvious she wanted him to stay. Maybe she was lonely. Tired of kicking around in this huge old house alone. He understood lonely.

"Maybe one," he said.

"The flooring guys are coming on Monday," Tara said, as she moved to the fridge and opened the door. "I'll need help moving the appliances out of the kitchen."

"No problem," he answered, taking the long-neck she handed him and twisting the cap off. He looked for a place to put it and then noticed the pieces of silver in the ornamental key basket. He picked one up and turned it over in his hand.

"You wore this the night you faced down that guy in the parking lot."

"Eddie."

"Yeah."

Color rose in her cheeks. "I'm surprised you remember."

He smiled. "Oh, I remember a lot about that night." Having a beautiful woman calmly tell you that she didn't need your help with a six-foot-three drunk did tend to stick in one's mind, as did her apology later. He watched with some fascination as she blushed deeper. Very un-Tara-like. He turned the silver conchos over. They were heavy, ornate. "You should have this fixed."

"I will. I just…I've had other things on my mind." A silence followed and then Tara said, "How much longer will you be in Night Sky?"

"Another few weeks."

"And then you go back to work?"

He nodded. What else did she think he'd be doing? Heading off to the asylum maybe? He had no idea what Sanchez told her.

"Are you ready to go back to work?"

Now he understood why she'd wanted him to stay. She wasn't lonely. She was worried about him because of the way he'd been acting today.

He pulled in a breath, formed an explanation for his behavior.

"I know I was a little rugged today, Tara. I apologize. I've got some things I've been thinking about."

"Must be some serious stuff."

"The job. Going back."

"Do you like your job?"

"I did," he answered truthfully.

She had questions. He could see them in her eyes, but she didn't ask.

"So you'll be here for the reunion?" She gave him a break, shifted the subject.

"I'll probably have to leave before that. I'm due back at work around then." Matt took another drink, feeling the tension start to ease. "Where's your beer?" he asked curiously, looking at her empty hands.

"I'm more of the dry red wine type."

"That's funny," Matt said, "I had you pegged as a margarita type."

"Too much work. I prefer to uncork." She glanced sideways at him. "Sometimes I don't even bother with the glass."

Matt grinned at her confession and after a tiny hesitation, Tara smiled that smile that always made his gut do a long, slow somersault. He forced his mind along another path, one he figured would put a halt to this cozy feeling growing between them.

"What did Sanchez tell you about me?"

Tara didn't seem surprised by the sudden question. She frowned thoughtfully before she answered. "He told me you were a police officer, which I already knew. He also told me you were involved in some incident."

"That's all?"

"Is there more?" she asked candidly.

"No. I just wondered if he'd warned you about me." He wanted her to be cautious, to keep her distance from him.

"In what way?"

"Sometimes people aren't exactly themselves after a critical situation."

"Are you yourself?"

"Close," Matt said, but he didn't smile.

Tara remained serious, matter-of-fact. "I don't know what you were like before, but you seem pretty decent now."

Nice opening, but Matt didn't feel up to discussing what he was like before. "Thanks."

Tara took the hint. She fiddled with the barrette for a moment and then redirected the conversation to the house. They talked about that safe subject while Matt finished his beer, and he made an effort to hold up his end. He did pretty good, too, he thought, because when Tara walked him to the door twenty minutes later, she looked as if she were feeling better. Surprisingly, he was feeling better, too. But as he headed to his truck, he wondered how long it would last.

Damned FFD.

TARA SPENT LONGER than she wanted pushing a cart through the nearly empty aisles of the grocery store, trying to remember everything on the list she'd forgotten on the kitchen table that morning.

And to make matters worse, no matter how

hard she tried to focus, she found her thoughts drifting back to Matt.

She wanted to find out what had happened. Find out what was bothering him.

"Good morning, Tara."

Tara nearly dropped a bottle of balsamic vinegar. She turned to see Lydie Manzo strolling toward her.

"Hi, Mrs. Manzo." It was the first time the woman had ever addressed her by name and Tara tried very hard not to look suspicious.

"Lydie," the woman corrected automatically. "Dottie told me about the flat a few nights ago. That was very kind of you."

"No big deal."

Lydie gave her a look. "Yes. It was. Especially after Dottie's past behavior, but that's water under the bridge. It was nice of you."

"Thank you."

"There's one more thing…."

"What's that?"

"Well, Ginny said she'd be working for you on a temporary basis."

"Yes," Tara replied slowly. They had just firmed up the final arrangements the previous afternoon over the phone.

"Do you need any more help for the reunion?"

"Maybe…" Tara hedged, wondering what was coming.

"My granddaughter, Hailey… She just left her husband and, well, between you and me, it's about time. He's a real *bastard*." Lydie leaned close and whispered the last word. "She's working at the shop and trying to put her life back together."

"Sure," Tara said, feeling as if she'd been backed into a corner. She did need help, but she didn't know this granddaughter of Lydie Manzo. "I could use an extra pair of hands."

"She likes old houses and Ginny was raving about yours. If you needed any help *before* the reunion, I'm sure she would be available. And she's real artistic."

"Have her call me."

Lydie reached out and grabbed Tara's hand with both of hers. "Thank you."

Tara left the store in a bit of a daze. Lydie Manzo had asked her for a favor.

It almost made up for her having to face her dress again.

"THIS PLACE IS GREAT!"

Hailey Manzo was a pretty woman. Blond hair, green eyes, vivacious personality, but there was something watchful about her…and the way she held herself sent Matt's sixth sense into gear. A survivor, he thought.

She'd showed up late in the afternoon, driving a small station wagon with a magnetic sign advertising a beauty parlor called the Hair Affaire. Tara hadn't known the girl's full name—had simply introduced her as Hailey after she brought her upstairs to see the work on the almost completed second floor. Hailey had then provided her own last name, stumbling over it, as though she wasn't used to using it. Newly married or newly divorced, probably, and the watchful eyes made Matt think newly divorced. He would have checked for a ring, but she had her hands shoved into her back pants pockets.

Well, whoever she was, and whatever her past, Tara was hiring her to help around the place. It would no longer be just he and Tara working alone in the big old house anymore.

And that, he thought, might just be a good thing.

"I LOVE THIS PLACE," Hailey repeated, her eyes skimming over the kitchen fixtures as she took the glass of iced tea Tara offered. "You're lucky to have it."

"I guess I am," Tara agreed.

"Did Grandma tell you about my—" she quirked a corner of her pretty mouth "—situation?"

"Not much." *Let's see. Newly divorced. Ex-husband is a bastard.*

"Well, in a nutshell, I married too young and the guy I married turned out to be a jerk. I wasted, oh, about five years of my life."

"I see," Tara said slowly.

"I just figured you should know."

"Why?" Tara could not help but ask.

"I work in a *beauty parlor,*" Hailey explained. "Gossip central. I know what this town is like. Frankly, I prefer to tell my own story rather than let someone else do it for me."

"I think we'll do just fine. But as far as working for me goes, I need help with the reunion function, and I'll need help with the housekeeping while the guests are here, but I can't offer anything permanent. It would be on a day-by-day basis."

Hailey nodded. "How about the cooking?"

"I might need some help there."

"I thought maybe we might be able to work out a trade."

*A trade?* "What kind of trade?" Tara asked cautiously.

"Well—" Hailey tilted her head "—this is pretty forward of me, but here it goes. I need a place to do pottery—at least until December."

"Pottery."

The blonde nodded. "I'm a potter and I'm pretty good. You have that shop building and I know from my grandmother that your aunt used to have a kiln in there, so the wiring must be suitable. So, if you have room, well, I thought maybe I could set up my kiln and a wheel and a table. In exchange, I would help you around the place here. It wouldn't be forever. Like I said, I think I'll be able to rent my own place by December. I just hate to think about going that long without throwing a pot. Plus, I make a lot of money at Christmastime and I'd hate to do without that, too."

*Talk about ideas out of the blue. Pottery.*

"I can show you some of my pieces," Hailey added. "In fact, you should probably have some kind of a gift shop here, like they have at the Somerses' place. Local craftspeople."

Tara had toyed with the idea, but decided to put it on hold until she actually got the house finished. "What about the sawdust in the shop?"

"Would there be a lot of woodworking going on in there? I mean, are you a woodworker?"

Tara shook her head. "No."

"If it's intermittent, I can work around it."

Tara circled the idea carefully in her mind. "How about a trial period?"

"Sure."

Hailey seemed utterly confident that things would work out. "And in the meantime, I can paint or clean or cook or whatever you need."

"When will you be available?"

"Any evening, plus Tuesday and Thursday afternoons and Sundays."

"When would you like to set up the pottery stuff?"

Hailey gave her a crooked smile. "I love hearing those words. I have to borrow Grandpa's truck and he's out of town…how about next Thursday afternoon?"

Four days? Tara figured that would be enough time to figure out if she'd made a mistake. "Sounds good."

"YOU HAVE MORE HELP?" Nicky sounded surprised. "Can we afford it?"

"Kind of." As always, his use of the word "we" jarred Tara. She thought of herself as sole keeper of the family coffers, because that made her sole worrier about their financial difficulties. Nicky's job was to educate himself.

Tara carried the phone into the parlor, explaining the deal she'd made with Hailey as she walked. "She'll only be here a few hours a day, but she'll use the shop whenever she wants."

"What's she like?"

"Young, pretty, divorced. Kind of a straight talker."

"What would *that* be like?"

"Okay. Point taken. But…I don't know if she understands boundaries."

"Oh, I think you'll make her understand. And who knows? Maybe you'll become friends."

"Maybe." Tara pressed the palm of her hand to her forehead. She could use a female friend, someone to bounce ideas off without interference from the Y chromosome, but needing a friend and making a friend were two different things.

"Just drop those killer defenses a little, T."

"Excuse me?"

"You heard me. Just imagine the worst that can happen if you take a chance and, oh, let's say, act friendly toward someone. If the consequences do not involve death or bodily harm, well, you might consider going for it."

Great. Now her baby brother was giving her personal advice.

"Thanks for the tip," she said sardonically.

"Anytime. So, how's Matt doing on the house?"

"You won't recognize the place. All the molding on the first two floors has been refinished and put back up. He's replaced the bad pieces. The gazebo is beautiful." She paced past the darkened window as she spoke and then stopped as a shadowy movement caught her eye. She saw it again. Behind one of Luke's hedges. Did the burros get out? They loved to munch on Luke's flowers and she knew there'd be hell to pay if they ate anything now.

"Hey, Nicky, I think Buddy and Billie escaped. I'll call you back tomorrow."

"Sure thing, T. Talk to you then."

Tara collected her catch rope from the mudroom and headed out the back door. She was halfway around the house when she recognized the silhouetted shapes of the animals clearly defined by the bright moonlight in the corner of the meadow. Far away.

A shiver traveled up her spine as she walked back into the house, clicking Matt's new lock shut behind her. It must have been a dog or a coyote. A very big dog or coyote.

Tara walked through the house, checking the locks on doors and windows, shutting off the lights and pulling drapes as she went. She hated having the house shut up on a warm night, but she couldn't handle the thought of someone out there, looking at her.

It was only an animal. A deer, maybe. But if it wasn't…

She moistened her dry lips. She'd never been nervous in this place before. It had always been her safety, her sanctuary, which was one reason she couldn't bear to think of selling the house to settle the debt. And now here she was, pacing and trying to convince herself she'd seen an animal. Ryan had her spooked and she hated it.

Tara didn't own a gun, but she did own golf clubs, inherited from her aunt. She went to the bag, stored in a cabinet in the mudroom, and pulled out an iron, testing the weight. Not as good as pepper spray or a gun, but at least it was something, just in case it wasn't an animal, which it *had* to be. Tara sat in the parlor on the sofa, her golf club next to her, and read until she fell asleep.

The phone rang at three-thirty in the morning. Tara shot up from the sofa, her heart pounding, the golf club in hand, but by the time she got to the phone, the answering machine had picked up and the line clicked dead.

Tara reached out and shut off the ringer before walking back to the sofa. She curled up again, but knew she probably wasn't going to sleep. Her heart was pounding. She didn't know if she were being paranoid, or if someone, like say Ryan, was honesty trying to creep her out. If they were, it was working.

Tara was sitting at the table sipping coffee when Matt showed up the next morning.

"You look bad."

"Thanks," she answered with a smirk. He walked past her to the coffeepot.

"Couldn't sleep?"

"Phone call," she replied, smothering a yawn. "Early in the morning. The machine got it, but they hung up and afterward, I couldn't get back to sleep."

"Nicky, maybe?"

"I already talked to him. It was just a wrong number."

Tara yawned again, and decided not to mention the deer. In the light of day, her paranoia the night before seemed foolish. It had to have been an animal. Her place was too far out of town for someone to walk to easily, and there were no cars around last night. None that she was aware of anyway. Why would Ryan be sneaking around her place anyway?

*Very, very paranoid, Tara.* She was going to have to work on getting over this.

A TALL, LANKY GUY with dark red hair showed up soon after Matt downed his first cup of coffee to help him move appliances and, from the way Tara greeted him, Matt knew he was one of her small group of loyal friends.

"Ben. Matt," said Tara. The two men nodded at each other. Matt could see that he was being sized up, and it wasn't in the now familiar so-this-is-the-guy-who-punched-Eddie-Johnson way, but rather in the Rafe Sanchez you-better-treat-her-right way.

"The floor crew is due in an hour," Tara said, putting a stop to the face-off.

Matt grabbed a hand truck. Ben started taking the porch door off its hinges. Neither man spoke again until the actual lifting began, which rapidly turned into a bonding experience. Tara didn't have ordinary appliances, but rather sturdy, restaurant-quality stainless steel along with some equally sturdy antiques. And they were heavy.

When Tara tried to help, they both insisted that she stand back. She'd shaken her head in disgust while Matt and Ben waltzed and wrestled with big stoves and oversized refrigerators.

One more big mother freezer to go....

Matt stopped with one hand resting on the top of the counter, the other on his thigh, catching his breath. String bean Ben was doing the same. He gestured to the massive appliance.

"Ready for another go, John Law?"

Matt nodded, not one bit surprised Ben knew he was a cop. "Whenever you are, Opie."

TARA WISHED the two guys struggling in her kitchen would knock off the machismo and let her help. There was enough testosterone in the room to float a small boat and she was actually glad Rafe had been called out on an emergency and wasn't there adding to the male hormone-fest.

She really needed to get some female friends. Nicky was right.

"Why didn't you put the floor in before you bought the appliances?" Ben grunted "That is how normal people do it."

"One guess," Tara said darkly.

"Does it start with an *S?*"

"It does." Somers. Good old Martin Somers. He'd let it be known in that underhanded way of his that he was redoing the Inn's floors and anyone who wanted consideration for that contract had better not be doing business with Tara Sullivan.

"Figures. That's why these guys are coming down from Idaho, I take it."

"That's why."

Ben and Matt maneuvered the huge stove through the thankfully large kitchen door and gently eased it down on the porch. "You know,

Tara," Ben said mopping at his forehead with his sleeve, "you might consider how many people really *look* at a kitchen floor."

"When the asphalt backing starts showing through, they look."

Ben took a big gulp of air. "Fine. At least I get a day's breather before we put the stuff back. Maybe Rafe will deign to show by then. This is definitely a three-man job."

"I offered to be the third man," Tara pointed out and was rewarded with two rather withering looks.

"You're both fired," she muttered.

## CHAPTER EIGHT

TARA WALKED BEN to his truck a half hour later, just as the flooring van came into sight. "So that's your protector." He was obviously referring to Matt.

Tara narrowed her eyes. "Why did you call him that?"

"I heard he put locks on all of your doors. Spent a night or two. You know. Stuff like that." He paused. "Rafe's not real pleased."

"Ben, since when is my business your business?" Tara asked sweetly.

"Since big brother Jack shanghaied me into getting a hernia in his place." He gave Tara an unrepentant smile. "Hey," he said as he opened his door, "I hear you hired Hailey Manzo."

*Let's see, I hired her yesterday around 4:00 p.m. It's now 8:30 a.m. and Ben already knows about it.... Yeah, that was about right by Night Sky standards.* "Do you know her?"

"Nice girl. A little wild in high school, but nice. She married a real loser."

"Sounds like my mom. The loser part."

"Lots of women hook up with losers. Fortunately," he added with a crooked smile, "Cherese had more sense."

"Your wife's a lucky woman," Tara agreed, rolling her eyes. "Thanks, Ben."

After he'd pulled out of the drive, Tara went back to the house to check in with Matt.

"Nice guy," Matt commented as she entered the bedroom where he was working. "I haven't seen him before. Is he from around here?"

"Yeah. Ben is Jack's little brother, but he lives in Elko now. He works at the community college where I used to teach."

"Jack and Ben are brothers?"

Tara smiled. Ben was as lanky as Jack was huge. "Hard to believe, I know. Jack volunteered him."

"I'm surprised Rafe wasn't here."

"He had an emergency call." The floor guys were thumping around below them, hauling in rolls of linoleum. Tara leaned her shoulder against the doorjamb and watched Matt as he maneuvered the oak molding. He made a cut, and then checked the fit before tacking it into place. When he glanced up at her, she was still studying him and she didn't bother trying to pretend otherwise.

Their gazes met, and then Matt turned his attention back to the molding as Tara pushed off from the wall and left the room to start her own day's work. But the snap of electricity still hung in the air.

JACK HAMISH'S GOAL in life was to come up with a Monday night promotion that would keep the football crowds coming back during the long months after the Super Bowl and before the first *Monday Night Football* game. He wasn't having a lot of luck. Even the Monday night tag-team pool tourney had bombed after the first night. People preferred to play on the weekends when they could get happily soused without worrying about getting up for work the next day. But, he confided to Matt, who stopped by the bar to meet Luke, he had high hopes for this one—Monday night treasure hunt. Every round of drinks a team bought came with clues that would lead to a trophy Jack had hidden somewhere nearby. The first team to bring the trophy back to the bar got two rounds of free drinks, as long as they were the cheap ones. It was a sure winner.

Matt wasn't so certain.

"It's got to be better than the cricket races,"

Luke assured him when he arrived. "Or the belly art contest."

A pretty good crowd showed up and Matt got to see all of his local favorites before the evening was over. Ryan Somers was there with his fiancée, a small classy-looking blonde with *high maintenance* written all over her. Ryan stood with his hand pressed possessively to the small of her back, the solicitous husband-to-be. Two-faced jerk. Matt had watched him over his beer as he waited for Luke, and even though Somers was subtle, he was aware of every woman in the place. After a few minutes, Matt decided that he couldn't exactly blame him. If his fiancée were any cooler, she'd form frost on her.

Eddie "Sweet Cheeks" Johnson arrived with his band of drugged-out cronies just as Jack finished explaining the rules, so his team was eliminated. No one, including the team, seemed to care. They settled at a table across the room from Matt and Luke, and started drinking.

The waitress sauntered over after the crowd had left on the treasure hunt and Matt ordered a pizza, which Luke agreed to share.

"Thought you were getting meals," she said to Matt, as she waited to get a little dirt.

"New flooring," Matt said. "The stove is out of commission for a day or two."

"Oh." The word had an edge of disappointment. She closed her order pad and headed for the kitchen.

Luke waited until she was out of earshot, and then cocked his head at Matt.

"You know—" he spoke with just enough hesitation to activate Matt's self-protection radar "—they are kind of shorthanded in the sheriff's department here. They're trying for a grant to fund a position."

"No."

"Just thought I'd throw it out as an option."

"I don't belong here, Luke. The small town thing…it works for you because you were born here. I grew up in Vegas. Reno's a small town for me."

"Just an option I was throwing out," Luke repeated.

Matt pulled in a breath. "And I appreciate it. Don't get me wrong."

"Small isn't that bad," Luke grumbled. "Regardless of your profession."

Matt smiled at the older man, who simply gave him a you-dumb-bastard look over the top of his glass. He was, frankly, touched that Luke wanted him to stay in the community, but he couldn't imagine policing in a non-urban area, being totally out of his environment. And more than that, he couldn't imagine leaving unfinished business behind at his present job, especially when it was business that could possibly haunt him for the rest of his career.

Luke left shortly after dessert, but Matt stayed for one more beer, enjoying the spectacle of the triumphant women from the county courthouse celebrating with their free drinks. Eddie went to the bathroom and then, when he came back out, he strolled over to where Matt sat and hooked his thumbs in his pants, rocking on his heels. He'd had so much to drink, Matt hoped he didn't fall over backward.

"You, son," he said in a nasally voice, obviously meant to be threatening, "are lucky I didn't press charges that night you hit me. But—" he smiled nastily "—I like to take care of problems on my own." His tongue had trouble wrapping around the words, but he finally got it all out. "You probably feel safe, since I haven't done anything, but you know what they say…"

Matt waited, curious to find out what they say.

"The best revenge is a *c-o-l-d* revenge." Eddie dragged the single syllable of the adjective out for maximum effect.

"'Revenge is a dish best served cold,' you moron," said Jack directly behind Eddie and, in spite of his slow reflexes, the man jumped. "Now go sit down or get out."

Jack apologized to Matt as Eddie went back to his friends. "He's going to hell in a handbasket. But watch that jerk. He carries a grudge and it only grows."

Matt smiled his thanks. "I'll remember that."

HAVING HAILEY AROUND wasn't bad, Tara decided. She'd stopped by Monday evening to find out what Tara needed help with before the reunion, and also what duties she and Ginny would share while the guests were there. Hailey had to work around her beauty salon schedule, and Ginny had to work around her waitressing, but between the two of them, Tara would have help when she needed it.

And Hailey, it turned out, did respect boundaries and had a few of her own besides. On the surface she was vivacious and easy to talk to, obviously intelligent and matter-of-fact about her train wreck of a marriage, but Tara soon sensed that Hailey, too, had had her share of kicks in the teeth and that she was not all that anxious to talk about them. And as per Nicky's instructions, Tara had made an effort to open up, to be friendly and drop the defenses. Fortunately, Hailey made it easy.

"I know it's a bed-and-breakfast, but I decided I'd offer a cold dinner buffet on Friday and a luncheon buffet on Saturday. Everything is ordered and just needs to be picked up from Elko. The rest of the meals are covered by reunion events."

"And the cocktail party?"

"That's where I want to concentrate my efforts. I mean, cocktail parties are definitely not my forte, but the man who booked it is kind of a bigwig. I'd like to impress him and maybe drum up some return business." Tara opened her notebook. "Here's the menu," she said. "Just light finger food, most of it made ahead of time."

"Who's mixing drinks?"

"A couple of friends," Tara said. Ben and Rafe. She hadn't been certain about Rafe, until he'd stopped by that afternoon to apologize for not being available to help with the appliances and to reassure her he'd tend bar. There'd been tension between them, and she could see he had questions, but he wasn't going to ask them.

"Well, if you need an extra pair of hands, I'm licensed."

"That's good to know because one of my bartenders is a deputy and if he has an emergency, he'll have to leave."

Hailey tilted her head and narrowed her eyes.

"Which deputy?" she asked in a deceptively mild voice.

"Rafe—"

"Sanchez?" Hailey pressed her lips together.

"You know Rafe?"

"We've had a few encounters," she said in a tight voice. "He gave me a speeding ticket a couple of days ago that's going to cost me a week's salary."

"Rafe? Are you sure it wasn't another—"

"I'm sure," Hailey said flatly.

"That's weird. Rafe usually gives warnings…."

An odd expression crossed Hailey's face, but all she said was, "Not this time." She shook her head then and made an effort to lighten the mood. "Don't worry. I can work with him, no problem. I was just surprised at the irony."

*Me, too.* Tara was surprised at more than the irony. She was surprised to hear that softhearted Rafe had handed out an expensive ticket, and to a good-looking blonde, at that. Something more to this story. Definitely something more.

The phone rang shortly after Hailey left. It was an inquiry from a woman who'd just got her reunion packet and was looking for a place to stay. Did Tara have any rooms left? Fortunately, she did. The last one on the second floor. A few minutes later it was booked and then the phone rang again. Another inquiry. Tara was pleasant and told the woman there was a waiting list and she was first on it, but perhaps she'd like to book elsewhere just in case. Tara would get back to her if there were any changes in the near future.

And then Tara jogged up the steps to the third floor to see how many changes she could make before the near future arrived.

She was on the stiflingly hot third floor again the next morning, opening windows, when Matt arrived. She'd spent most of the evening planning, figuring if she had enough linens and furniture, she could make the top of her house not only habitable, but charming—a place people would want to return to. If she couldn't make it an asset, she would have to turn down the bookings, and the thought of doing that killed her.

"Can we turn this into two bedrooms before the reunion?" she asked Matt as soon as he topped the stairs.

"Did we get greedy?" Matt asked, crossing the room to help her with a stubborn sash. Finally he pulled out his knife and dug at the frozen lock until he was able to pry it open.

She gave him a sidelong glance. "I would like

the option of becoming greedy." She wrinkled her forehead. "Can we do it?"

"Possibly." He walked over to the peeling plaster and flicked a hanging chunk to the scarred floor. Tara followed the movement with her eyes.

"I can't afford new flooring up here."

"I think I would leave this floor alone. It'll clean up okay and then maybe with some rugs…"

"Yeah, I was thinking of going with the cottage look, too."

He stared at her uncertainly and it dawned on her that she was speaking Greek to him. "It's a decorating trend. Kind of a beat-up furniture and funky flea-market style with lots of comfy cushions and rugs and color and…" Her voice trailed off as he raised his eyebrows. "Never mind. It's the only look I think I can handle on short notice. My question is, could we have walls on the bathrooms and get the fixtures in before people arrive?"

Matt looked over at the framing in the bathroom area. "I won't have time to build cabinets or anything."

"I have the tub and pedestal sink already. I bought all the fixtures at once to get a discount, so that's not a problem. I have a small armoire that could double as a linen closet. All I really need are walls."

Matt looked around again, and then he glanced down at Tara. "Walls, eh?"

Her mouth turned up at the corners as she saw the answer to her question in his eyes. He didn't have a lot of time, but he would try to do this for her. "Yes. Walls."

"I could do walls," he said in a low voice.

Tara felt the ever-present tingle of awareness grow stronger. "You could, huh?" she answered, her voice a little unsteady, very throaty.

The words hung in the air and something about the way Matt was looking at her made Tara catch her breath.

"Hello…" Hailey's voice rang through the house and the moment, the mood, was shattered.

"Up here."

A few seconds later, Hailey joined them on the third floor. She gave a quick look around. "This floor is a little more challenging than the other, I'd say." She returned her attention to Tara. "Sorry to barge in, but I'm on my way to Elko and Grandma asked me to stop and see if you wanted me to take your dress to the cleaners there. I guess they have some special process that protects older gowns, although I'd say yours probably isn't that old."

"Come on," Tara said, leading the way to the

stairs and stifling an almost overwhelming sense of disappointment. "I'll get it for you."

THE TWO WOMEN went downstairs, leaving Matt to wonder just what would have happened if Hailey had not interrupted them.

No, he knew exactly what would have happened. He just wondered what Tara's reaction would have been. All thoughts of caution and keeping his distance seemed to evaporate whenever he was around the woman. And, dangerously, Tara seemed to be of a like mind. Just what did she want out of this…connection, he guessed he'd call it? A flirtation? Something casual and friendly? Something physical? Heaven forbid… something serious?

Would she pursue it? And if she did, would he?

He was a guy with little willpower where she was concerned, but he couldn't give Tara the time and attention she deserved and he wouldn't risk hurting her.

He headed downstairs to the coffee, planning to make a list of what needed to be done to get the top floor in some kind of shape. He didn't have much time; he might even have to hire day labor, at his own expense if Luke and Tara would allow it, because he wanted to do this for her.

The women were in Tara's room, a room Matt had not seen outside of his fantasies since the night she had been ill. He walked into the kitchen and saw his mug sitting next to the carafe, as it was almost every morning when he arrived.

Man, he would miss this coffee, he thought as he took the first slow sip. Tara had explained during their conversation the other night that she ordered the beans from San Francisco, buying only small quantities and having them shipped express so that they'd always be fresh. It was her one indulgence.

Tara needed more indulgences, Matt thought. As near as he could see, she put all of her energy into her house, her future business, her brother's education, and not a whole lot into Tara.

"I have got to see this in the light," Hailey said as she carried a large box into the kitchen. She set the box on the table and gently lifted the bodice of a dress out of the folds of tissue. It shimmered like mother-of-pearl and Hailey let out a murmur of appreciation.

Matt didn't know much about dresses, but he knew that this one was something special, all pale silvery gray with thousands of tiny pearls on it.

"Did you wear that dress?" he asked, trying to imagine Tara in something besides jeans.

She nodded, looking so instantly defensive that he had to fight to keep from smiling.

"She was a prom queen," Hailey announced as she eased the dress back into the tissue. "She's letting us use the dress for our fashion show."

"You were a prom queen?" He hadn't meant to sound incredulous, but a prom queen? It just didn't jibe with everything else he knew about her.

"Don't rub it in," the prom queen muttered, her gaze lowered as she helped Hailey arrange the folds of tissue over the beaded fabric.

Matt's eyes narrowed suspiciously. "Do you have the tiara to prove this allegation?"

"Shut up, Matt," Tara replied, handing the lid to Hailey, who eased it over the bottom half of the box. When she finally gave him a sideways look, he couldn't keep from grinning. Her jaw first tightened and then it relaxed as she let out a huff of breath.

"My aunt wanted me to go to the prom, so I went. And I came home with a tiara. It was the thrill of a lifetime."

Hailey laughed, missing the irony in Tara's tone. "My prom stunk," she said easily as she hefted the box, holding it in front of her with both hands. "Literally. Somebody threw up on the dance floor and none of the chaperones wanted to deal with it." Hailey's nose wrinkled at the memory and she shook her head. "I'll take good care of this," she said, nodding at the box. "I promise."

"Don't worry about it," Tara replied. "What happens, happens. How many dresses do you have right now?"

"There were almost forty under consideration and from those the ladies chose the fifteen they are going to use, including Dottie's—which is a real scream by the way, but don't you *dare* tell her I said so." Tara held the door open as Hailey maneuvered the box through.

"Your secret's safe with me."

Hailey left with a wave and the bang of the screen door, leaving Tara and Matt alone in the kitchen.

"Prom queen, eh?"

"It was a joke, Matt. I was the butt of a joke."

"What kind of joke?"

She leaned back against the counter, and he could see that she was debating telling him. Finally she relented.

"After my dad went to prison, I was a tad defensive. I didn't play well with others, so others did not play well with me. But—" she shrugged "—being a kid, I didn't see the connection. In fact," she added wryly, "I'm just starting to get a handle on it now. Back then, I had two friends—Jack and Rafe."

Tara shook her head ruefully before she admitted, "I wanted to belong and I wasn't quite sure how to do that. I pretty much had an adversarial relationship with everyone.

She drummed her fingers against the ceramic tile of the counter. "When I was nominated for prom queen, I was at my defensive worst. Kids poked at me. I poked back." She smiled. "And I mean that literally in some cases."

Matt could just imagine.

"I knew the nomination was a joke—it *had* to be —but secretly I was hoping that maybe it wasn't. That maybe it would be a chance to put the past behind me…"

Tara fell silent for a moment, then glanced at Matt. "It didn't work out that way. First of all, my date didn't show. He was one of the jocks. A real catch. I'd been stunned when he'd asked me and then figured it was because of the queen nomination. I finally pretended that he'd called with car trouble so I could borrow Aunt Laura's car and drive myself. I could have just driven out in the country and hid for a while, but my pride wouldn't let me. I hated the idea of those jerks setting me up and laughing at me, so I made an appearance…to show them I was tougher than they thought. Unfortunately, I underestimated my opponents."

She absently twisted her ring. "I was elected queen, and crowned, but since my date hadn't shown, I had to dance the opening waltz with the principal, Mr. Gates. Talk about humiliation." She shuddered. "And then... let's see...during the opening waltz slide-and-light show, a shot of my father in handcuffs came up, but the chaperones took care of that pretty quickly. And then my date finally showed, an hour late, with another girl." Sandra Hernandez to be exact. "He seemed surprised to see me there, but he ambled up and said hello."

"Did they have to call an ambulance for him?"

Tara smiled, shook her head. "I drove myself home after that, and had a rather suspicious flat tire, which I changed in my slip so as not to ruin Aunt Laura's dress. And that was my prom." She tilted her head, an ironic gleam in her eye. "I did learn one lesson from that night."

"What's that?"

"Well, for years I'd felt like I had to defend the Sullivan honor, which is laughable because the Sullivans had no honor. After the prom, I figured it out. But, I still had no idea how to fix what was broken. I'd burned bridges, and Sullivan public sentiment had never been high. I didn't have a lot of, shall we say, social skills, so I simply had to live with the situation. A few months later, I graduated and I left, taking Nicky with me."

"And now you're back. Why?"

He caught her off guard and she said simply, "I love this place, the house, the land. It was my sanctuary when I was younger. My heart feels whole when I'm here." Her words rang with quiet certainty. "Now all I have to do is hang on to the place."

"How so?"

Tara hesitated. She'd already said too much...so why stop now? "Well, that's a story in itself. The house was pretty run-down when Nicky and I were here. Aunt Laura usually had someone come in and put a Band-Aid on urgent problems, only to have them crop up again later. About the time I got hired to teach in Elko, she took out a renovation loan. She was going to put things right once and for all." Tara shook her head. "Little did I realize how right she'd planned on making them."

She paused to gather her thoughts, her emotions. "The loan was huge, although I didn't know that at the time. Aunt Laura had the foundation and the roof fixed first and that ate up a lot of the money, and then she started on the kitchen. After she passed away, I made some amazing discoveries. The size of the loan, the fact that there was a balloon payment…about two thirds of the money was spent."

Tara tilted her head and the braid slid over her shoulder. Matt reached out and wrapped his fingers around the thick plait, holding it for a moment like a lifeline before letting it slide through his grip. Tara let out a small sigh as he released it.

"There was too much invested to stop the renovation, so I continued, with the idea that I'd make the place a bed-and-breakfast and then it could help pay for itself." She shrugged. "And here we are. All I have to do to live happily ever after is get my house up and running, behave myself and overcome old prejudices. *But*—" her eyes widened as she spoke "—not as many prejudices as before. Nicky gave me some pointers. I've made some headway."

"Yeah. I've heard," Matt replied.

She smiled widely, taking no offense. "I'll just bet you have. You haven't been ostracized for helping me, have you?"

"No," Matt replied, "but I get odd looks."

Tara laughed. Matt loved the sound. Light. Melodic. A totally different Tara was appearing before his eyes. And he liked her.

MATT LEFT FOR ELKO right after lunch to pick up the wallboard and a couple dozen other items necessary to begin repairs on the top floor. Tara worked on the second floor while he was gone, painting the closet doors and thinking that the house felt empty without him. She actually felt close to Matt, or as close as she'd allow herself to feel toward another person.

*Experience the man. You can trust him not to hurt you. Let yourself have a decent fling. Get Ryan out of your system once and for all. It looks like he's willing....*

It was starting to make perfect sense, especially after this morning. She didn't want a serious relationship. That led to heartache. But she would like physical intimacy without brutal overtones, to have a lover who could also be a friend and just a friend. Matt seemed like a man who would understand that, help her without hurting her. In fact, he was the perfect man to do that because she trusted him and he'd be leaving soon.

Tara dipped the brush again and started applying paint to the last closet door in the last bedroom, when she heard the crunch of tires on gravel. She moved to the windows facing the road, her heart beating faster as she looked out to see if Matt was back. He wasn't. A white BMW was rolling up the drive and Tara's heart rate quickened even more. Speak of the devil... She did not want to deal with Ryan. She felt as if she should post a sign on the lawn: Attention Vultures—This House Is Not For Sale.

But as the car pulled closer, she saw that Stacia was driving and Sandra Hernandez was beside her. *Great.* Tara put her brush down and started for the stairs. What was this about? An actual visit instead of a phone call. Tara had a bad feeling.

The women walked briskly across the yard, their gazes sharp and analytical as they took in every facet of their surroundings. Tara pushed the screen door open and forced a smile.

"You have a beautiful yard," Sandra commented in her parakeet chirp, as the two women came to a stop near the bottom step.

"Thank you," Tara said. "My aunt was very proud of it."

"I'm sure she was," Stacia interjected coolly before her minion could chirp again.

"Can I help you ladies with something?" Tara asked, hoping that perhaps they were there for some benign reason—the prom-dress parade, a volunteer list, collecting for charity…

"I received a call this morning about your establishment," Stacia replied, giving Tara a look that told her exactly what she thought of Tara's establishment. "There is some question about whether you're actually going to be able to deliver what you've promised in the brochure."

Silence.

"I see," Tara finally replied in a remarkably even voice, considering that a small flame of anger had just ignited inside her. "Who called? Your future father-in-law?"

"It doesn't matter who called," Stacia said in a tone that made Tara believe she'd hit the nail square on the proverbial head. "What matters is that my company is being paid to run this reunion, and I am not going to be embarrassed by someone unable to follow through with commitments."

Tara shook her head. She was too busy to deal with this nonsense. "The rooms will be done."

"I want to see them."

"Excuse me?"

"I want to see your rooms. I want to be sure my company won't be embarrassed."

Tara shook her head. "I'm not giving a tour today." She was not going to be ordered around by Stacia Logan and she was not going to give the woman any ammunition by letting her see half a dozen half-completed bedrooms.

"Tara—"

"The brochure is out, my house is in it and there's nothing you can do about it." Tara paused and then in the name of professionalism, softened the blow. "My rooms will be ready, Stacia. You and your company will not be embarrassed. Now, I really do need to get back to work, so if there's nothing else…"

She waited until it gradually dawned on the two women that they were dismissed.

"No. There's nothing else," Stacia said with icy politeness and turned on her heel. Sandra followed, casting Tara a frown over her shoulder as she went, twisting her neck so far that Tara was surprised she didn't trip and fall. A few seconds later, two German-made doors slammed shut. Tara grimaced at the noise as she turned toward her front door. BMW or not, that couldn't be good for the hinges.

THE NEWS CAME by e-mail, not an hour later. Tara clicked on the icon, hoping for another reservation, and instead received a cyber heart attack. Mr. Nate Bidart of Bidart Industries regretted to inform her that he was withdrawing his reservation. The rest of the words, having to do with deposits and early cancellation, blurred.

She hadn't even seen it coming. Tara had been convinced Stacia had just come out to harass her. She didn't doubt for one moment that she received a call, but as she had said, she'd assumed it had come from Martin Somers, since it was the exact same sentiment he'd expressed during the business association meeting.

Tara reached for the phone and dialed the contact number. She identified herself and to her relief was almost immediately connected to the associate who had sent the e-mail. She forced an upbeat professional voice.

"Hi, this is Tara Sullivan. I'm calling about the cancellation for the Night Sky High School reunion."

"Oh, yes. I am sorry about that, but we had hoped that by cancelling early enough, it would give you time to fill your rooms."

"That's very considerate of you," Tara enunciated. "I was wondering, for my own information, why you cancelled?"

The woman hesitated. "To tell you the truth, I'm not privy to that information. Mr. Bidart is in Night Sky right now, and he called earlier in the day."

It took Tara a moment to find her voice and it took another moment to find words that were not comprised of four letters. This was a low blow.

"He's not staying at the Somers Inn by any chance?"

"I'm sorry, I can't—"

"I understand," Tara said truthfully. "But—" she paused, bit her lip and then went for broke "—if you happen to be in contact with Mr. Bidart, would you ask him to please contact me? I think there has been a miscommunication. I'd like to clear it up—for possible future functions." Plus the one that was stolen right out from under her nose.

"I will do what I can," the associate replied in a no-promises tone.

"I appreciate it very much. Thank you." When Tara finally hung up the phone, she walked straight to the kitchen, straight to the fridge.

She needed a drink. Maybe two. And since she had no wine in the house, she settled for the closest thing she had—Luke's supply of Bud Light.

## CHAPTER NINE

MATT'S FOOTSTEPS echoed as he let himself in the front door of Tara's house. He stopped and listened. No radio playing upstairs. No singing. No humming. Just the sound of a bottle cap bouncing on a hard surface. He followed the noise into the kitchen.

Tara was leaning against the counter, beer in her hand. As Matt came into the room, Tara lifted the bottle in silent greeting, making no effort to put on a game face.

"Bad day?" Matt asked.

A corner of her mouth tightened as she slowly nodded her head.

"Anything major?"

"Pretty much." She gave him a brief description of what had transpired that afternoon, throwing in several colorful adjectives to describe the future Mrs. Ryan Somers and that lady's future father-in-law as well.

"They keep whittling away at me, Matt, and it gets kind of exhausting after a while."

She shook her head, then lifted the bottle to her lips and took a sip. Matt could see by her expression that she wasn't a beer drinker. Well, he was.

"You want me to finish that for you?"

"No. I think I need it." She gestured to the fridge. "Feel free. I'm sure Luke won't mind. I'll just replace it before he starts on the gardens."

Matt pulled another out of the fridge, popped the top and came to lean against the counter next to Tara. Their shoulders touched. He liked the sensation.

"You know," she said, gesturing with the bottle, "sometimes I wonder why I keep plugging away."

"Why do you?" Matt asked conversationally.

She turned her head toward him, her eyebrows raised. "Like I told you. I love this place. Besides, I don't appreciate being pushed around."

He could understand that. She gave him a half smile over the top of her beer bottle and Matt felt an almost instantaneous response as he watched the slow curve of her lips. He was tempted to lean forward and touch her beautiful mouth with his own.

"Ryan wants me to run scared and I won't."

"It takes an awful lot of effort to fight those two," Matt pointed out.

"Sure looks like it, doesn't it?" She lifted her shoulder eloquently and took another drink. This time she didn't grimace.

"Is it worth it?" he asked, having a hard time pulling his eyes away from her mouth. The beer had left a sheen of moisture on her lips and Matt imagined tasting those tiny droplets. One by one. With the tip of his tongue.

"You want to hear the story?" Tara asked. "Decide for yourself?"

"Yeah," Matt said. "I wouldn't mind."

"Then I'll tell you," she said without hesitation, and Matt had a feeling the alcohol was already going to her head. "Ryan's family is originally from California. Martin bought the inn and moved here when Ryan was a junior in high school. He transplanted well. The girls were all nuts about him and it was a pretty sad day for the female populace when he graduated and headed off to college."

"Were you one of the sad ones?"

Tara looked surprised. "No. I pretty much kept to myself back then." The remark hung in the air for a moment, before she said, "I didn't see Ryan again until we were both out of college and working in Elko. He was with an accounting firm and I was teaching at the community college. We met at a Christmas party. He was very, very charming, which I know now is his modus operandi. He told me he remembered me and that he'd heard I didn't date. That wasn't quite true, but..." Tara shrugged. "Anyway, he said he could change all that. I bet him he couldn't...."

The rest of Tara's narrative went almost exactly as Matt had assumed it would. Tara had been the beautiful, but standoffish college teacher and Ryan the guy who decided he was man enough to scale her defenses. Which he did. It was only after he'd dropped his charming facade and scored in a rather self-centered style, as near as Matt could tell by reading between the lines, that Tara realized she'd been a notch on the bedpost, a challenge he couldn't resist and nothing more.

"I know what happened to me is probably not unusual," Tara confessed when she was done, "but it shook my confidence. Broke my trust... hurt my pride."

The last words were so low and bitter, Matt had a hard time hearing them. Tara took one last drink and then set the beer aside. "Such is life."

She moved to the sink and pulled a paint encrusted brush out of the container of water, grimacing as she held it up. She poured dish soap on the bristles and began working it in.

"Why does Somers still have it in for you?"

Tara didn't turn around, but her reply was quick and certain. "Because he got hit in the two places that hurt him most—his pride and his pocketbook. He came to see me a few weeks after our...encounter. He'd had too much to drink and he was ready for another go. I was not."

Matt waited. He'd really like to have a short go with Ryan himself.

"He refused to back off, so I hit him." She glanced over her shoulder, smiling. "I broke his nose."

Matt's grinned back. He'd noticed the bump on Ryan's classic profile. It pleased him to know Tara had put it there.

Tara turned the faucet on and rinsed the brush. "He ran straight down to the sheriff's office before the bleeding stopped to press charges and file for a restraining order. He said that he'd tried to break up with me weeks ago and that I wouldn't take no for an answer and now I was getting violent." She squeezed the excess water out of the bristles and reshaped them.

"What happened?"

"Nothing. I denied it and added a few claims of my own, like assault. And trespassing. There were no witnesses to anything. It was his word against mine, according to the judge. That really irritated

Ryan. He couldn't believe that my word held as much weight as his." She laid the brush on the drain rack, then wiped her hands.

"Go figure."

"Now, this might surprise you," Tara said with a straight face, "but Ryan can be petulant and vindictive."

"No."

"Yes. He can. He needed revenge—I had disfigured and humiliated him, after all, and he couldn't really tell anyone how it happened, so he decided to use his clout to get me fired from the college. But Jack found out what was going on—Ben is the registrar's assistant at the college. And it just so happened that Ryan's accounting firm did the books for the Owl Club Casino...."

"I like where this is heading," Matt murmured.

"Long story short, Ryan's firm ultimately kept the accounts, but lost Ryan."

"He got fired?"

Tara nodded. "He'd been maneuvering to become a partner. Talk about a major blot on his employment record as well as a blow to his gigantic ego. Plus, Jack's boss must have put the word out. Ryan couldn't get a job anywhere to his liking. Martin finally had to bankroll him so that he could buy a small business here in Night Sky—

not anywhere near the status of his old firm. In fact, it's pretty darned Podunk. So now Ryan hates me and his dad hates me."

"But why doesn't Ryan hold a grudge against Jack?"

"He doesn't know Jack was involved. *I* wouldn't know if Nicky hadn't been friends with one of the junior associates at the accounting firm. Very 'hush, hush,' but Nicky can get anyone to blab. Jack's not a guy who looks for gratitude. It embarrasses him. He never said a word to me, before, during or after, so I've never said a word back. He just quietly saved my butt. He doesn't know Ryan holds me responsible." Her smile was humorless. "The thing that slays me is that Ryan's ego is so big he honestly thinks he's the victim in this."

She tilted her head then, her long braid sliding over her shoulder, reminding Matt of the day he'd run his fingers through her hair as he struggled to contain it in an elastic band. One of these days, he'd really like to undo that braid. Fill his hands with dark hair while he slowly showed Tara that not all men were self-centered, two-faced jerks.

It wouldn't happen. He wasn't at a point in his life to let it happen. And then his gaze met hers. And he realized that she was thinking something along the same lines as him.

For one long and very uncertain moment, they stared at each other, the atmosphere between them growing increasingly charged, until Tara swallowed and looked down.

Matt studied her profile.

*Say something.* "And that's why Martin Somers keeps throwing roadblocks at you?"

The question sounded forced, inane, but Tara didn't seem to care.

"That's why," she agreed in a slightly uneven voice. She started for the fridge. "Dinner might be a little late."

"We can go out to dinner," Matt suggested. The air in the kitchen still seemed charged with possibility.

"I don't think so, Matt. I have stuff to do."

She pulled the fridge door open, apparently thinking the conversation was over. She was wrong.

He pushed it shut. Tara's eyes widened. "Matt…"

He ignored her warning tone and settled his hands on her shoulders. "Tara, give yourself a break," he said quietly. "Take a night off."

"Matt—" She abruptly broke off. Biting her lip, she frowned.

"I don't know what to do here," she whispered, more to herself than to him, and Matt knew she wasn't talking about dinner. She brought her hands up to rest on his upper arms and let out a breath as her head slumped forward to rest against his chest. He felt her inhale, then exhale again. He waited, his thumbs unconsciously smoothing over her delicate clavicles, his nerves humming.

When she finally raised her head, she slid her hands from his arms up to his face. "Why don't you kiss me?" she asked quietly.

It was an invitation, not an inquiry. Matt's blood pressure jolted up, but he forced himself to stay still.

"Are you sure?"

She smiled. "Of course not. I'm too cautious to be sure."

That was when Matt knew he'd lost the battle. He gently put his arms around her and pulled her close.

Their lips met. Cautiously at first. Their tongues touched lightly and then Tara sighed as their mouths melded together. It was the kiss Matt had wanted to give Tara since their first encounter in the parlor, the kiss she'd apparently been waiting for. Mutual, deep and hungry in every sense of the word.

At first Matt did his best to hold himself in check, satisfying himself with running his fingers over her hair and down her back, lightly following the curve of her waist and skimming over the sides of her hips, telling himself he'd stop after just one more kiss.

*But there's so much time to make up for....*

Tara made another small sound in her throat as Matt's hands traveled slowly up her midsection to cup her breasts through the soft chambray of her shirt, his thumbs finding and lazily teasing her nipples through too many layers of fabric. It was a good sound, an encouraging sound, which Matt translated as an invitation to undo buttons.

"Tara?" he asked as his lips left hers. He needed to get a grip here.

"Shhh," she murmured, reaching up to pull his mouth back down, opening her lips, drawing him in, putting all thoughts of getting a grip firmly out of his mind.

He gave up on the buttons and pushed his hand up under her shirt, his fingers skimming over her incredibly smooth skin. He felt her shudder and then she buried her fingers in his hair, pressing her lower body against his.

Definitely a woman he could get lost in. And the stunning thing was that he wanted to get lost in her. They were teetering on a brink, about to go over...

He couldn't do it.

With a Herculean effort, Matt forced himself to pull back, to disengage his lustful body, engage his more logical brain. Logical brain seemed to be on hiatus, possibly due to lack of blood, but he sucked in a breath and gave it another try.

He looked down into Tara's beautiful face, his breathing still ridiculously uneven, and watched shifting emotions play over her features as she cautiously held his gaze. Confusion. Annoyance. Vulnerability rapidly masked by indifference.

She read him well, made no move to pull him back down to her. When she finally spoke, her voice was low, slightly husky, and self-protectively sardonic. "You need to be going?"

Matt grabbed the lifeline. "Yeah."

"Any particular reason?"

But before he could answer, she asked, "You aren't leaving for my own good or anything, are you?"

"I think maybe I'm leaving for my own good."

Tara gave him a suspicious look.

"You don't want to get involved with me." *Just ask my ex-girlfriend.*

"Not even for one night?"

A long beat of silence followed. "Is that all you're looking for?" The thought irritated him. Maybe he was getting more attached to this woman than he'd realized.

"Nothing more." She seemed to think that would reassure him.

Matt shook his head. He wouldn't do a one-nighter with Tara, for myriad reasons, none of which he cared to single out and analyze at the moment. But if he had to, protectiveness would be number one. He wouldn't start something that had the potential to do emotional damage to either of them, no matter what Tara wanted.

"You don't do casual?" She spoke with a forced indifference that told Matt exactly how hard it was for her to say the words.

"There are times," he admitted, "but frankly, in the long run, it isn't very fulfilling."

"Voice of experience?"

He nodded.

"Then I guess you're right," she said coolly. "You should be going."

"Tara, maybe we should talk about this."

She shook her head, her expression stony, and he knew then how much his rejection had stung. A strong desire to make things better, to ease the hurt, slammed into him.

"Please go." The words fell like chips of ice. "We can talk tomorrow."

Matt headed for the door.

The phone rang before he got there. He paused with his hand on the door handle as Tara picked up the receiver. She said hello, her eyes still on

Matt, her expression still carefully impassive, and then her demeanor abruptly changed.

At first he thought it was trouble, but after a few seconds, he realized it was Bidart, getting back to her about the cancelled reservation. She turned her back to him and Matt took that as a sign of dismissal. He pulled the door open and stepped out into the warm night air.

A decent guy probably would have stayed to find out what happened with Bidart, but Matt was afraid of what else might happen if he stayed. His willpower was shaky enough as it was.

He'd barely made it to the door.

TARA FORCED HERSELF to concentrate on what Nate Bidart was saying—none of which seemed to be positive—and ignore the taillights turning out of her driveway, as well as the disappointment and shame burning deep inside of her. What did he find so lacking in her? She wanted to think it was the one-night stand proposal, but he'd withdrawn well before that.

"Nothing personal, here, Miss Sullivan—" she forced herself to focus on Bidart's voice "—but tell me straight. Is your establishment ready for business?"

"It will be."

"That wasn't the question."

*No, it wasn't.* "Are you in Night Sky, by any chance?"

"I'll be leaving early tomorrow morning."

Tara went for broke. "Why don't you stop by for a few minutes on your way out of town. At least then you can judge for yourself."

"I'm leaving at close to four a.m." He paused and then said, "I can come by right now."

Tara glanced at her surroundings and then gave a fatalistic shrug. "I would appreciate it."

"All right. I'll be there in twenty minutes."

He hung up without a goodbye. Matt had left without a goodbye. *Kind of a theme here.* Tara sank into a chair, pushing the loose hair back from her face. If she closed her eyes, she could still feel Matt's mouth on hers. She opened her eyes. Plenty of time for that later. Right now she had to concentrate on Nate Bidart.

Tara resisted the urge to tidy up. She got up and tossed the two beer bottles in the trash and then paced from room to room as she waited for Bidart. If nothing else, he'd get an honest look at the place, and at her.

It was almost twenty minutes to the second when the car pulled into the drive and Tara wished for a wild moment that it was Matt coming back, that they hadn't argued. She was still trying to figure out what they had argued about.

When Bidart got out of his car, Tara's first thought was that she'd expected someone taller, but as soon as she came face-to-face with him, she knew that this was not a man to be messed with— or easily cajoled, either. He resembled a bird of prey with his closely cropped gray hair and intense black eyes. And he looked tired. A hawk exhausted after a hunt. It must have been a rough few days negotiating business in Night Sky, Tara thought as she stepped back to let the man into her three-story work in progress. Well, the past few days hadn't been that great for her, either.

"Good evening," she said. "I'm Tara Sullivan. Thanks for taking the time to drive over here."

"It was the least I could do under the circumstances." He moved past her into the foyer with the air of a man who was doing his duty and wanted to get it over with as quickly as possible.

Tara closed the door and watched as Bidart studied the room, taking in the stripped staircase, the gallons of paint sitting in the hallway, the sheet dropped over the hall valet, the hanging capped wires where a light fixture on back order was supposed to be.

"Pardon my dust," she said in an attempt to

lighten the mood and was rewarded with a cool, unsmiling stare.

*Okay...we'll keep things professional.*

"Well," she said, "let's start on the ground floor. I'll show you what I have and what I plan to have done."

Tara conducted the tour briskly. She talked and Bidart listened as she took him through the house, laying the project out before him. He remained silent, giving no indication of what he was thinking as Tara showed him everything, ending the tour on the disastrously incomplete, stiflingly hot third floor.

Bidart did a slow circuit of the large open room, taking in every detail, from the scarred floor and crumbling plaster walls to the cracked windowpane mended with tape.

When he was done, he turned back to her and Tara had to force herself not to shift uncomfortably under his hard gaze. "Nothing personal here, Miss Sullivan, but this place is a disaster."

"You should have seen it a week ago."

"I can imagine." His tone was not complimentary.

"This floor is a work in progress. I thought you should see the entire house so you could understand what had been accomplished on the lower floors."

"I understand, but you're still working under the gun on those lower floors, aren't you?"

"A bit." There was no use denying the fact.

Bidart pushed at a piece of broken wall plaster with the toe of his shoe. It left a trail in the dust.

"If it was just me, I wouldn't be too concerned. But this reservation isn't for me. I made it for my mother and her two sisters."

"I see," Tara said in a low voice.

"My mother has always loved this house. Once she tried to buy it from your aunt." His gaze traveled over the deeply disguised carved oak molding that framed the door. It had been painted at least a dozen times, but Tara knew what was underneath. She wondered if Nate knew, too, from the way he was studying it. "Your aunt wanted to keep it in the family."

"So do I," Tara murmured. "Will you be attending the reunion?"

"I have reservations at Somers Inn. I tried to get Mom to stay there, too, but she'd wanted to stay here. I have to tell you, I was under the impression the house was ready for business."

He gave the room one last critical inspection and then shook his head. "This isn't going to work."

He started walking toward the stairs.

"It could work."

Bidart stopped, surprised at Tara's blunt statement.

"The rooms will be ready, and, if you keep the reservation for your mother and aunts, you can stay here at no additional charge."

The offer was met by a very long silence and Tara felt her blood start to pound. Like saving a few bucks would be all that important to this man. Then, to her surprise, he came close to smiling. "Where?" he asked simply.

"We'll find room," she said, unable to suppress a hint of dryness. "We are starting this floor tomorrow."

"We?"

"My carpenter." *Who had better come back. If not, I am very, very sunk.* "And a few friends."

"I was under the impression you had difficulty keeping help."

Tara's eyebrows went up with mock surprise. *Yeah, I'll bet you've been given that impression.*

She swallowed the words and smiled. "My carpenter is very reliable."

Nate Bidart gave her a considering look. "I'll tell you what. We'll hold the cocktail party here regardless. Martin had me convinced the entire house was a shambles, but I see he was mistaken. I'd already made some alternate arrangements with him for the party, but seeing as that was all a misunderstanding, we'll change those."

*Misunderstanding, her butt.* Tara decided to go for broke.

"Look. You've been honest with me. I want to be honest with you."

Bidart nodded.

"My aunt took out a loan with the bank prior to her death to renovate this place. It has a hefty balloon attached to it. There are some other circumstances involved, but the bottom line is that I need to make this house start paying for itself. I can fill the rooms before the reunion. I've had calls, which is why I'm working on the third floor." She paused, met Bidart's steady gaze. "But having someone like you or your mother stay here…well, I was hoping that perhaps in the future, you'd keep my place in mind when you hold a retreat or meeting in the area. Or maybe you might recommend my place. I think if you keep your reservation, you'll be impressed." She glanced around. "And surprised."

For a moment she was afraid she'd been too candid, had looked too much like a money-grubber. She didn't want to grub money. She wanted to put Nicky through school, keep her house and survive during the process.

"How old was your aunt when she took out this loan?"

Tara was taken aback by the unexpected question. "Seventy-four, I think."

Bidart nodded. "Which lending institution?"

"U.S. Trust."

"Surprising."

Tara frowned and was about to ask why, but Bidart just shook his head.

"Never mind," he said.

He started down the flight of stairs without another word and Tara automatically followed, wishing she hadn't been quite so candid. It had been a calculated risk. She'd lost.

When they reached the ground floor, Bidart headed for the door, but he wasn't walking as quickly as before and Tara realized he was still assessing the lines and architectural details of her house. He stopped in the foyer and took a moment to study the carved oak molding that framed the archway, running his fingertips lightly over the newly finished surface.

"This house must have been something in its day," Bidart said, dropping his hand to his side. "I can see why Mom is so taken with it. But, frankly, you have a very long way to go."

"And I have several days to get there," she replied shortly.

His gaze settled on her. "You think you can pull this off?"

"I know I can."

Bidart's mouth worked for a moment. "I'll want to see the place before they arrive."

It was all Tara could do to keep a foolish grin from spreading across her face as the meaning of his words sunk in. "You'll keep the reservation?" she asked, wanting reassurance that she had not misunderstood.

"My mother wasn't too happy about the cancellation anyway," he admitted. "But—" his expression became matter-of-fact "—as far as business arrangements go, retreats and such, I've been using Somers Inn for a number of years. Martin is a friend. We have a mutually satisfactory arrangement and I have every reason to believe it will continue that way."

"I understand."

Nate reached for the door, then paused. "You do know that if I end up sharing a room at Somers Inn with my mother and two aunts...well, let's just say I'm not going to be happy with you or your establishment."

"That won't happen."

"It had better not. Or you won't get any referrals from me. Good night, Miss Sullivan."

She smiled. "Good night."

Tara gently closed the door behind him and turned to lean against it, blowing out a breath that lifted the tendrils of hair off her forehead.

She didn't have a promise of Bidart's return business, but she did have her reservations back, and the possibility of referrals, which she desperately wanted. She'd won. Kind of. On the professional front anyway.

As for the personal front…she wasn't even going to think about that. It was simply too humiliating and confusing.

"HEY, BABE." Jack's deep voice rumbled over the line early the next morning. "I hate to ask this of you. I know you're damned busy, but my mom's sick. Ben just took her to the hospital in Elko. They're running tests. I gotta get over there."

"When do you need me to work?" Tara immediately asked.

"Six to ten tonight."

"No problem." Matt's truck turned into the drive and Tara's heart jumped. Okay. He'd come back. They would work from there.

"Tonight and tomorrow…" Jack was saying.

"I'll plan to work every night until I hear from you." Matt shot a look her way as he came in the door. He crossed to the counter and filled his cup from the coffee carafe. He looked tired.

"Thanks, Tara. It'll only be those two nights. I have the rest of the shifts covered. And I promise I'll lend a hand fixing up your old barn in return."

"Thanks, Jack." Tara knew he'd have no time, but the offer was sincere. She hung up the phone and looked at Matt leaning against the counter, his expression distant, just as it had been when they'd first met. She'd managed to take them back to square one. She didn't particularly like it there, but she was going to live with it.

"Jack's mom," she explained, even though he hadn't asked. "She's in the hospital."

"Something serious?"

"They're running tests."

At the sound of a car coming up the drive, she went to the window and saw Hailey's station wagon pull to a stop next to Matt's truck.

"Hailey's here to set up her pottery stuff. I hadn't expected her quite this early, but she's excited to get started."

"Tara...about last night..."

Her heart rate increased in spite of herself, but her expression was purposefully cool.

"I didn't mean to insult you."

"I wasn't insulted," she said in a flat voice. "Confused is a better word." As were *hurt* and *abandoned*. She walked to the door and stepped out onto the porch before he could say anything else to tie her stomach in knots. She didn't move fast enough.

"It wasn't easy to leave last night," he muttered as he caught up with her.

"Oh, that makes rejection so much easier."

"It should."

She stopped on the top step, her hands on her hips. She wanted to put an end to this…rehash. Once and for all.

"Look. I got your messages loud and clear. You don't want to hurt me and I shouldn't get involved with you, even for *one night*. Fine. I understand and I am not insulted. I just want to move on without losing my carpenter. There? Does that cover all of the bases? Have we talked enough?"

"Just about." Matt grated out the words, his eyes narrowing. "What happened with Bidart last night?"

"I got the reservation. Thank you for asking." Tara's tone matched Matt's exactly.

Hailey had the tailgate open and was busy dragging a heavy bucket of clay out of the back as Tara and Matt approached.

"Let me get that," Matt said as he moved to the rear of the car. He easily hefted the remaining five-gallon plastic bucket and reached for the one Hailey had let thud to the ground.

"The shop?"

"The shop," Hailey said with a smile. "Thanks."

Both women watched Matt as he walked away, a bucket in each hand, flexing the muscles in his arms and back

"I've been meaning to ask you about him."

*No,* Tara thought with an edge of foreboding. *Don't ask me about him.* "I would think that working in the salon, you'd know everything there is to know."

"Well—" Hailey gave her a roguish grin "—it seems the ladies don't know much."

"Were you sent to find out more?" Tara asked darkly.

"It was suggested," Hailey confirmed. Tara gritted her teeth.

"Some of the ladies think he's sweet on you, and the rest think he's hanging around trying to get lucky. The general consensus there is 'good luck.'"

Tara felt her jaw tighten, but she liked Hailey and she kept her voice carefully even when she asked, "No chance that he could just be working here as a carpenter?"

"Nope," Hailey replied easily. "There has to be an ulterior motive."

"How do you stand that place?"

Hailey laughed. "There are only a few *really* nasty gossips, but for some reason, they always seem to be there at the same time."

Matt came back out of the shop and headed for the house. Tara watched him go, and then turned back to Hailey, who was looking at her now. Tara could see speculation in the blonde's eyes, but all her friend said was, "So you're working on the third floor?"

"I got another reservation," Tara answered, relieved, "and Matt said he could make it livable."

"Not much time," Hailey pointed out.

"Tell me about it," Tara replied, pushing her braid over her shoulder. "I need to get Matt's breakfast so we can go to work. Do you want something to eat?"

Hailey shook her head. "No. I've eaten. I'll just go and tidy up my work area. Grandpa is coming later with a couple of friends to move the kiln and table in."

"All right then…." Tara started for the house. Matt was in the kitchen, drinking his now-cold coffee.

"Luke should be here soon to help with the wallboard."

Matt nodded, his expression impersonal. Probably his cop face, Tara decided.

"I'll make you some pancakes and then maybe you and I could get some of the wallboard upstairs before he arrives.... You know, to kind of save his shoulder?"

"Good idea." Matt drained the cup and stood. "I'm not really hungry, so maybe we can get started."

Tara didn't argue.

Luke showed up twenty minutes later, just as Hailey came out of the shop. She greeted him like an old friend, and despite his protests, got on the other end of a piece of wallboard and helped him cart it up two flights of stairs.

Between the four of them, the wallboard was soon unloaded and transported to the third floor, where it waited for Matt to turn the framed-in bathroom into an actual room and replace what was once lath and plaster walls. Matt carried Luke's big circular saw up the stairs and set it on the floor next to the sawhorses. He straightened and wiped the sweat from his forehead with the back of his hand.

"It's going to be hot up here today," Tara said as she started opening windows and propping the fans in them to let a cross breeze through the already overheated room. "I'll turn the cooler on if you want."

"Don't," Matt answered automatically. "Too expensive. I'll survive." He turned his attention to the framed-in areas, mentally calculating. Fine, Tara thought, melt up here.

"Hey, Tara." Hailey came from the far end of the large room. "You know what you could do to this floor?"

"Cover it with about thirty rugs?"

Hailey shook her head. "Stencil it. Around the edges, like a border. If you hate it, you can strip it off, but it would be pretty without tons of work. We could put matching stencils around the walls and in the bathrooms."

"I don't know if I'll have time," Tara said dubiously.

"I'll help. I've done this before. In fact," she said with a smile, "I'm pretty good at it."

Tara hesitated, indecisive. She wasn't used to having people offer to help her. It felt strange. "All right."

"I'll bring my book by tonight and we can make some plans."

"I'm bartending tonight," Tara told her. "Six to ten."

"I'll bring it by the bar. How busy can it be?"

"There's a band tonight," Luke informed her. "You know what that means."

"There'll be really bad music at the Owl?"

Luke gave her a look that spoke volumes.

Hailey grinned. "I'll bring the book by anyway. Maybe we can look at it if you have a minute."

"Sounds good to me," Tara said, but her attention was already back on Matt, who was measuring the first wall. She headed for the stairs. She had work to do.

The rumble of a truck engine sounded through the open window and Hailey went to look.

"Grandpa," she said happily. "Come on, Luke. You want to do some lifting, we have a monster kiln for you down there."

LUKE POKED HIS HEAD into the kitchen to say goodbye late that afternoon. Matt hadn't come down to the first floor all day long, having skipped lunch as well as breakfast, so Tara finally went upstairs to see him before she left for the Owl. She just wanted to check on his progress. *Right*.

He was standing in the doorway of the new bathroom, a bottle of water in one hand, surveying his work.

"You've done a lot today." Tara pulled her eyes away from him and looked around at the newly covered walls. "Which I appreciate, since I contacted the lady on my waiting list, and I now have these—" she glanced around dubiously "—rooms booked."

"They'll be done." Matt leaned a shoulder against the doorframe, sipping at the water as he spoke. It was almost unbearably hot, even with the windows open and the fans pushing a breeze through the room. Matt's T-shirt was soaked with sweat and it clung to his chest. The white powder from the gypsum board streaked his face and dotted his glasses. He looked hot and male and sexy…and guarded. Whatever self-protective mechanism she'd triggered was a strong one.

"Luke's going to help tomorrow if his shoulder is still all right," he said.

"Don't—"

Matt raised a hand, cutting off her words. "I won't let him hurt himself." They both knew that Luke wanted to work. "You're tending bar until ten tonight?"

"I am. How much longer will you be here?"

"Another hour maybe. Do me a favor, okay?"

Tara tilted her head.

"Try," he said with a straight face, "really try, not to pick a fight with anyone."

"Right," Tara muttered, finding no humor in his

comment. She turned and trotted down the stairs, wondering why she put up with this guy who was turning her inside out and ticking her off to boot.

*Because he's the only carpenter you got...and, in spite of everything, he still makes your hormones sweat.*

## CHAPTER TEN

THE BAR WAS remarkably busy for a Thursday and it was entirely due to the band. BrushPopper was one of the area favorites, a garage band that had never moved out of the garage. The four men who'd formed the band in their teens were now in their forties and not yet close to quitting their day jobs.

Hailey arrived soon after the band, carrying a thick stencil pattern book, which she set on the end of the bar with a loud thump.

The band was beginning to set up their equipment and Tara knew the bar would soon be filled with the squeaks and squeals of numerous sound checks, followed by songs played through amps too large for the small room. She reached under the bar into the cache of disposable earplugs, automatically handing Hailey a pair before she pulled the stencil book closer, flipping the pages.

"Can you do this stuff here?" she asked, pointing to a picture of a multishaded trail of flowers and ivy. "All those colors blending together like that?"

"No problem. And look here," Hailey said, flipping to another page. "We can make the bathtub match the walls if you want."

"That would be kind of neat."

Tara was only able to look at the book for a few minutes before she had to start pouring drinks full-time.

"I thought Matt and Luke would be here," Hailey said as she resignedly flipped the book shut and shifted on her stool to look out across the barroom. The people kept coming in, happy to have something to do on a Thursday night. The band was playing for three days, and Tara was willing to bet that most of the people in the bar tonight would be back for the other two days.

"They'll be here later."

Hailey perched on the stool and leaned back against the bar, watching the crowd. Her eyes narrowed as they swept over the pool-table area. Tara followed her gaze and saw Rafe, wearing jeans and a white shirt that accentuated his olive complexion and dark hair. Tara glanced back at Hailey, whose soft lips had tightened ominously.

Becky arrived with an order from the restaurant and Tara lined up glasses and mixed drinks.

"Matt's here," Hailey said as Tara floated brandy on top of a pair of Picon Punches. Tara glanced up, her heart beating faster. She saw Matt ambling over to a pool table.

She glanced purposely back down at the drinks, rubbing the lemon twists around the rims of the glasses before dropping the curls into the drinks.

"Order up," she said to Becky, who was flirting with the guy two stools down from Hailey.

"You know," Hailey said, pushing off from the barstool with an air of determination, "I think I'll go and play some pool."

"Good idea," Tara said, and realized that she didn't mean a word of it as she watched her friend head toward her carpenter with a bright smile on her pretty face.

*I don't want Hailey hanging around Matt.* She swore under her breath. That was so not like her. She gave her head a shake. It didn't seem to help.

The last hour and a half of her shift passed rapidly, thanks to the band and the seemingly insatiable thirst of the crowd she was serving. But, even though she was very busy, her eyes strayed to Matt, Rafe and Hailey over and over again. Another woman that Tara had never seen before had joined the trio and was making a heavy play for Rafe, leaving Matt and Hailey free to do a lot of talking. Matt even laughed at one point, and Tara gritted her teeth. Sure, he laughs with Hailey, but not with her.

*Jealous.* She'd never been jealous in her life and she was jealous.

She hated it, but that didn't stop her from going straight to the pool table as soon as Becky took over the bar.

"Hey, about time," Hailey said with such obvious sincerity that Tara felt bad. "Now we can play guys against gals."

"I don't play," the woman cozying up to Rafe purred in explanation. Tara disliked her immediately and it had nothing to do with the expensively streaked hair, perfect makeup and manicured nails—or even the low-cut leopard print shirt. It had everything to do with the deadly this-is-my-prey-keep-your-distance look in her eye.

"Your loss," Tara said, taking a cue off the wall and sighting down it to make sure it wasn't the infamous U-cue that had warped when someone left it in the parking lot during a rainstorm. It wasn't. She chalked her hands, then turned to see that the woman had linked one arm through Rafe's. Tara looked Rafe straight in the eye, wondering whether he was a willing participant in this woman's game and, to her surprise, for once in her life, she couldn't read him like a book. She looked over at Hailey. "Would you like to break?"

"Yes," she said through her teeth. "I would."

As her partner prepared to shoot, Tara chanced a glance at Matt. He was staring across the room. Tara bit her lip and pulled her eyes away to watch Hailey make an excellent break.

"Stripes," Hailey muttered and proceeded to clean the table. "Eight in the side." The black ball slid into the appropriate pocket.

"What did you need me for?" Tara asked with an appreciative smile.

Rafe's new female friend looked unimpressed, but he was obviously of a different mind. He cast Hailey an odd look before retrieving the triangle and racking the balls. The tension between Rafe and Hailey was obvious and not to the liking of... "Excuse me," Tara said to Ms. Leopard Print, who was still watching Rafe with a predatory look in her eye. "I'm Tara. And you are..."

"Cat."

*Cat. Of course.* Tara fought to keep from smiling as she bent over the table to make the break.

They played another two games, and by that time the crowd on the dance floor had grown to the point that it was impossible to pull a stick back without making contact. After Hailey got bumped on an eight-ball shot and scratched, she put her stick back in the rack with a decisive thump. Then she turned to Matt, who had played all three games in relative silence, and held out a hand. When he frowned at her, she simply tipped her head to the dance floor, and with a shrug he put his hand in hers and followed.

Tara, feeling mean and more than a little annoyed at Cat's possessive attitude, turned to Rafe and held out her hand, mimicking Hailey. And to her surprise and Cat's obvious annoyance, Rafe didn't hesitate to take up the invitation.

"Not interested in Cat?" Tara asked over the music, watching the woman shoot daggers at her. Hailey and Matt were dancing several yards away, also in her line of sight. Hailey was smiling up at Matt and he was looking down at her with a tolerant half smile.

"Not much."

"How are you going to shake her?" Tara asked curiously.

"I think I'm going to get an emergency call pretty soon."

"Who is she?"

"Someone's cousin, in town for a visit," he answered absently and Tara noticed that he was also watching Matt and Hailey. Tara had a hunch it wasn't for the same reason she was watching them.

"Maybe you shouldn't have given her the ticket," Tara said, referring to Hailey.

"Didn't have much choice."

"How's that?"

Rafe looked down at her. "She ticked me off."

"*Really.*"

"Really. And it's not the first time."

"You know each other?"

"Oh yeah." In answer to Tara's perplexed expression, Rafe spun her in a quick circle. "Hailey moved here after we graduated and you'd left town. She was thirteen, I think. Anyway, by the time she was sixteen, I was a rookie deputy and she was flat-out trouble."

Tara smiled, incredulous. "You *really* know each other."

"Yeah."

"She doesn't seem like trouble now."

Rafe gave her a look that said he thought otherwise, but his words belied it. "She's changed. Grown up. The hard way, of course. I don't think she's ever done anything any other way."

"You gave her a *big* ticket."

"Yeah. Kind of let my temper get the best of

me. If she goes before the judge, she'll get it knocked down."

The music ended and Tara was surprised to find Matt and Hailey next to them.

"Going back to the Sheena, queen of the jungle?" Hailey asked Rafe in a sweet voice. His face hardened and Tara was intrigued by how quickly the girl could push his buttons. "Because if you're not," Hailey added, "I think we should dance."

And then she took his hand and led him away, leaving Tara and Matt staring after them.

They turned toward each other just as the music started and, after the briefest hesitation, Matt opened his arms. There wasn't much else he could do, short of walking off the dance floor and leaving her there. She knew Matt didn't do things like that.

Tara stepped into his light embrace, planning on a polite duty dance with a lot of air between the two of them, planning on showing him just how unaffected she could be, and was almost immediately bashed by a large man with a larger wife. Matt turned, putting himself in harm's way and pulling her more closely as he did. Tara surrendered without a fight.

Duty dance or not, his body felt good. More than good. It felt wonderful, dangerous. And he smelled good, too. Warm and masculine. She slid her hands up around the back of his neck and felt an immediate response in the part of his body that was pressed against her lower abdomen. Interesting. Definitely not insulting. Whatever problem he had with her, it wasn't lack of attraction.

"Dangerous place, this dance floor," he murmured.

"Mmm." She was feeling danger all right.

"I thought maybe we should stay close in case Rafe needs to be rescued. Hailey appeared to have murder in her eye."

"You know the look?" Tara asked. That was *not* why they were dancing.

"I've seen it a time or two," he replied in a low voice, his breath feathering the wisps of hair near her temple. Tara's pulse quivered and she caught her lip between her teeth, glad he couldn't see her face.

"How often?"

"Often enough to recognize it. Rafe has trouble on his hands."

*As do I.*

"Matt…"

Another human projectile bashed into them, nearly knocking Tara out of Matt's embrace.

"You okay?"

"Yeah."

"Come on." Matt eased them off the dance floor,

dropping his hold on her hand as soon as he led her around the pool tables to a relatively clear area near Edgar the Owl. "Rafe is going to have to take care of himself."

"He's capable."

"Let's hope." Matt smiled. "I'm heading home. Want me to walk you to your car?"

Tara considered and then nodded. An olive branch. She'd accept it. The rest she would work out later.

SOMEONE WAS CREEPING around in his yard. Matt had just watched Tara drive away and started down the alley when he saw the dark form moving stealthily past his opened windows and on around the corner of his house. He quietly moved closer, keeping to the shadows until he was at a vantage point.

He paused, waiting for his eyes to adjust, and listened. Then he heard it. A soft, "Kitty, kitty, kitty."

Matt let out the breath he'd been holding. Someone had lost a cat. He stayed in the shadows, though, wanting to make certain. "Can I help you?"

He heard a distressed squeal in response to his call and then a tentative, "Hello, Officer Connors."

His neighbor. The lady who took such joy watching him come and go, occasionally waving at him through her windows, unaware or uncaring that some people might find her behavior disconcerting. They certainly would in Reno.

Matt let himself in the back gate.

"I can't find Steve."

"Steve's a cat?" Matt deduced.

"Why, yes. He lives under your porch."

Oh, that Steve. The Steve he'd been hoping would go away. Apparently now he had.

"Is he your cat Ms....?"

"Mason. Iris Mason." She gave Matt a patient smile. "Cats don't have owners."

"Of course," Matt replied with equal patience, but he found himself smiling back.

"I had tuna casserole tonight and I wanted to bring him the leftovers, but he seems to have gone missing."

Steve's weight problem now made sense.

"Well, you know, it is early summer...."

The lady frowned and, after a few seconds, her face cleared and she smiled. "Oh," she murmured knowingly, "tomcatting around."

"That would be my guess." Although, Matt had a feeling old Steve wasn't going to lumber too far away to do his romancing. Must be some good-looking kitty nearby. He looked down at the neat plastic container in the woman's hands, brimming with tuna and noodles. "I could keep it for him and feed him when he shows back up."

"Oh, that would be lovely."

Matt took the container, but the lady stayed planted in front of him, studying him. "Will you be with us much longer, Officer Connors?"

Matt shook his head. "Just a few more days."

"Too bad. This has got to be so much nicer than living in Reno. And the criminal element...although we do have our share of trouble."

"Do we?"

"Oh, yes. Those meth labs you know. Springing up in all the farming areas. I haven't heard of one right in our community, but it could happen."

"I hope not."

"Me, too. This is a nice community. It just grows on you...but, I'm certain you have already figured that out." She smiled again. "I really should be getting back. One of my favorite movies is on in a few minutes."

"And what might that be?"

"*Psycho.*"

Matt somehow kept his expression from changing. "Have a good evening, Ms. Mason," he called as the woman let herself through his rear gate. She gave him a wave and disappeared into her own yard.

The lady was right, Matt thought as he opened the door and set Steve's casserole on the table. Night Sky, Nevada, had grown on him.

At first he'd missed the constant activity of a bigger city, the noise, the energy, the mix of anonymity and individualism. And then, slowly, almost without notice, new experiences had begun to replaced what he missed. People nodding at him for no reason. The mandatory wave all rural drivers exchanged. People trusting one another. People saving perfectly good leftovers for stray cats.

Luke would be pleased to know Matt was starting to appreciate the place, but staying in this town was not an option, no matter how much he liked it. Even if a deputy job did open up and he did manage to land it, and even if it would please Luke to no end to have someone around to talk to and take care of. He had a job to do in Reno. He was not going to walk away under a cloud and leave yet another dark Connors legacy in the Reno PD.

He filled a glass of water from the tap and then leaned back against the counter as he drank it. He glanced at Steve's casserole.

Where was that stupid cat? Other cats may go places at night, but this one tended to stay at home waiting for him. He'd at least check the street, make certain the animal hadn't been injured.

Matt looked out his front door. No cat. He ambled outside and down the street. He wasn't going to call the cat. He turned around after two blocks, figuring fat boy wouldn't make it much farther and started back. That's when he saw it sitting under the window of a neighbor's house, and sure enough, there was a classy-looking Siamese staring back at him through the screened window.

"Good taste, buddy," Matt muttered. "If you'd lose some weight, you'd be able to jump up on that windowsill and do some real courting." The cat blinked at him and then turned back to the feline Juliet in the balcony above.

*Man, he was getting soft,* Matt thought as he walked back, enjoying the quiet night. *Worried about a cat.* He had a lot bigger issues to be worrying about than some stupid animal.

He went in and headed for bed, halfway wishing Tara could be in it with him. She had felt so damned good pressed up against him while they danced....

The woman did seem to be developing an awesome hold on him and he was still trying to figure out how it had happened. He'd had no intention of going to the bar that night after work. He'd planned on an early evening, but he had been drawn to Tara, had felt the need to make peace with her after his poor behavior. He hadn't intended to play pool or dance, but he had lingered because of Tara, because he wanted to be near her.

Stubborn Tara with her invisible scars and protective barriers. Tara, who claimed she'd be happy with a one-night stand. He had a strong feeling that he'd need more than that—if he ever did sleep with Tara—and since he realized and accepted that, he knew it would be best if he simply kept his distance and left on cue. Easier on everyone. No pain. No regrets. He wouldn't have to watch Tara eventually leave because his life was screwed up and he couldn't help focusing on the job instead of the relationship.

His brain had it all figured out. Too bad the rest of him wasn't listening.

IT WAS JUST AFTER midnight when Tara climbed to the third floor and flicked on the overhead light. The bathrooms had walls and Matt had replaced some of the old plaster with Sheetrock. It was a good start, but there was still a long way to go before she could paint and Hailey could stencil.

Tara debated for a moment and then went down to her room and changed into her work clothes. The sooner the seams were finished, the sooner she could paint. The clock was ticking and she wanted the upstairs to be as perfect as it could be for her first and possibly most important customers.

It wasn't long until Tara discovered there was a knack to taping seams and feathering joint putty. It was definitely not as easy as it looked in the *Time-Life Home Improvement* series.

It was nearly three o'clock when a frustrated and exhausted Tara finally went downstairs, flicking lights off as she went, and she wasn't all that happy with the results of her efforts. She would try again in the morning.

The doors were all locked, the shades drawn. She flopped down onto the sofa to take off her shoes and that was the last thing she remembered until a knock on the kitchen door brought her up out of a crushingly heavy slumber.

She frowned at the second knock and glanced around, disoriented by the light streaming in around the edges of the shades and the fact that she was still fully dressed. By the third knock she sat bolt upright, finally putting the pieces together. She had fallen asleep fully clothed on the sofa and now either Matt or Luke was there, ready to go to work. She pushed the shade aside and glanced outside. Matt. Of course.

"I don't have breakfast ready yet," she said as she pulled the kitchen door open a few seconds later. "But—" she stifled a yawn, avoiding looking at his face, hoping to keep him from looking too closely at her bedraggled appearance "—if you want to get started, I'll call you when the coffee's done."

"All right."

To her relief, Matt refrained from comment and headed through the kitchen to the stairs. Tara waited until he was out of sight and then leaned both hands on the counter, letting her head hang. She stayed in that position for several seconds and then drew in a deep, determined breath and pushed herself upright. Three hours of sleep were plenty.

One, two, three…she began counting scoops into the coffeepot. She could hear Matt's progression up the old stairs, and then the noise stopped dead.

A few seconds later he was downstairs again, annoyance etched on his features.

"I was going to be polite. I wasn't going to mention the fact that you looked like you slept in your clothes, but—" his lips pressed together into a flat line before he went on "—this is stupid, Tara. Did you sleep at all last night?"

"Yes," Tara said in what was supposed to sound indignant, but came out more like a yawn.

"Look, it's not my business if you kill yourself, but this is crazy. And besides that, those seams are awful."

"Matt," she said wearily, "I would really appreciate it if you would just go back upstairs and go to work."

He cocked his head at an angle, looked at her from under hooded lids. "I will if you go to bed for a while."

"No."

He muttered an exasperated expletive.

"I have to get this house done plus I have another stupid committee meeting today. I lost time working for Jack. I was just trying to make up for it."

"Hire more help."

"I can't afford more help. You and Luke are it."

"Then don't pay me. Hell, don't pay Luke, either. Neither of us need it. Use the money to hire a couple more warm bodies—just for a few days."

"I don't work that way."

"No, it's a lot more sensible to work yourself into exhaustion and pay two guys who don't need the money."

Tara bit back a retort. "Can the three of us finish this place in time, even with my committee meetings?"

Matt hesitated and then said, "Probably." In Tara's mind that was a stubborn man's way of saying yes. "Barring any unforeseen delays," he added.

"Fine," she said. "Then if you wanted to get a start, I'll call you when the coffee is done."

He didn't move. She shook her head and turned back to the coffee machine, pouring in the water and flipping the switch. Her fingers had barely left the mechanism when she felt Matt move close behind her and every nerve in her body went on high alert. She clenched her teeth and turned in the small space. She met his eyes inquiringly, doing a pretty good job of faking disinterest. Pretty good. Not good enough.

"Tara," Matt murmured. His hands hovered for an indecisive moment near her face and then he gently brushed back the wisps of hair that had escaped from her braid while she slept. Her entire body seemed to respond to the feathery touch. "Sometimes you can let people do things for you. Sometimes people need to do things without recompense. Do *you* ever give without expecting to get something in return?"

Tara opened her mouth, and then closed it again. *Yeah. I offered myself the other night, no strings attached. You passed.* "Of course," she finally muttered.

"It works two ways. Everybody needs to give now and then. Sometimes you should let them."

"I'll keep that in mind," Tara said. "But in the meantime, I'm paying you and Luke."

"Just because someone gives you something, it doesn't mean you owe them," Matt snapped.

"I don't see you accepting a lot of help," she replied. "And I know you're dealing with something. Maybe I could help you."

Tara was saved from having to deal with his reply when the phone rang.

Nicky didn't even bother to say hello.

"Why didn't you tell me about this balloon payment on the house?" he demanded so loudly, Tara was certain Matt could clearly hear him. Her heart stuttered at her brother's uncharacteristically angry tone.

"Nicky—"

"The house is half mine, right? I have a right to know these things." Her brother was steamed.

"Yes, you do," Tara agreed, rapidly preparing a knee-jerk defense of her reasonable actions. He was her little brother. He hadn't even been legal when they inherited. Of course she had handled things. As for not telling him—

"Then why didn't you tell me?"

"I wanted you to concentrate on school, not

finances. You don't need to worry about this." Tara walked into the parlor as she spoke, not wanting Matt to hear her argue with her brother.

"That's not the impression I got," her brother barked.

"Who gave you this impression?"

"I applied for a bank loan to help with school and found out that I not only had half a house, I had half a huge debt. Do we have enough money to pay this?"

"I'll figure something out."

Nicky was silent for a moment and then said more calmly, "If we use Aunt Laura's life insurance money for school, then you won't be able to make this payment, will you? We might lose the house."

*We.* She wasn't the only one who would lose. Nicky would lose, too. But at least he would have his education.

"I'm working on refinancing." Not very successfully, but she was working on it.

There was another long silence before Nicky said in a tight un-Nickylike voice, "T, I'm not twelve years old anymore. You can stop trying to protect me from reality, you know. I don't need protecting and, frankly, you've got to stop. It's not healthy for either of us."

But she'd always been the boss, the protector. The one who kept Nicky safe.

"Look, we'll talk finances when I get back in a few days," he said. "I need to know what's going on. I need to be part of the decision-making process."

"All right," Tara agreed in a low voice.

"All right." There was a pause and then he added, "I love you, T. I'll see you in a few."

The line clicked dead and Tara stood for a moment holding the receiver before she returned to the kitchen and put it back in the cradle.

"Is everything all right?"

Tara turned to Matt. "Everything is fine."

A corner of his mouth tightened. "You don't need any help with anything?" he asked ironically.

Tara shook her head. "Nope."

"Good. Neither do I."

THE PROM-DRESS staging committee meeting was cancelled at the last minute because Dottie was under the weather, but Tara still had errands, so she drove into town and kept her luncheon date with Hailey in order to discuss the final stencil selection and supplies. She'd reluctantly made arrangements to pick Hailey up at the Hair Affaire after being assured it would be safe.

"None of the dragons will be there."

Hailey had been wrong. Well, not completely wrong. Tara had always thought of Sandra Hernandez as a witch, more of a dragon associate, but she bit the bullet and smiled at the woman, who gritted her teeth and smiled back.

"Very civilized," Hailey whispered in Tara's ear as she came up behind her. "Now, let's go get one of those jumbo burger things before I starve to death."

A jumbo burger was just what Tara needed, even if she only managed to plow through half of it in the time it took Hailey to clean up her entire plastic basket. Hailey grinned unapologetically as she dabbed at her mouth with a napkin. "Good metabolism," she said. "Grandma says it will catch up with me."

"Doesn't seem to have so far."

"I've gained weight," Hailey confided. "But that's a good thing. I lost a lot during the past few years." She shrugged. "Stress does bad things to your body."

"I know," Tara agreed after another bite.

"Yeah, I guess so. If you're interested, I think your stock is rising with the local ladies. The other day someone was trying to figure out what anyone had against you, other than your family." Hailey grinned. "That's when I found out that you used to be pretty handy with your fists."

"Not for a while," Tara retorted dryly as she dragged a fry through the ketchup. "These people have long memories."

"What about Ryan?"

Tara's eyes flashed up in spite of herself. "What about him?"

Hailey must've realized she had touched a nerve. She shrugged. "Rumor. Of course. Something about him filing a restraining order against you. Nobody knows the details."

"There's a good reason for that," Tara muttered. "I don't talk about it. Don't even like to think about it."

"I know what you mean."

And there was something in Hailey's quiet tone that made Tara believe she did.

"One bad experience shouldn't ruin a person for life, but you know what?" Hailey's mouth twisted ruefully. "No matter how many times I tell myself that, I'm still gun-shy. I like to date, but it will be a long, *long* time before I'm ready to commit again. Maybe never." She reached for one of Tara's fries. "I'll have to wait and see."

"So you just…date? With no intention of it ever developing any further?" *Hmm. That sounded mighty familiar.*

"I like company. I like fun. I'll be a friend. *But…*"

"But…?" Tara echoed. This was the closest she'd ever gotten to girl talk and it was good to get input from another female, especially when it was so close to her own way of thinking.

"But, my stomach churns when I think of letting it go any further, emotionally, you know. I don't think I will ever give anyone the power to hurt me again."

Tara leaned forward, resting her elbows on the table, concerned. "He must have done a number, that ex of yours."

Hailey nodded. "Yeah. He did." She reached for another fry and Tara pushed her basket closer, allowing Hailey easier access. "Maybe if I find someone rock solid…" Hailey's voice trailed and Tara wanted to tell her that Rafe was rock solid. "Even then," Hailey continued, "I don't know."

Tara thought for a moment, and then she did something she normally didn't do, since it gave a person the right to do the same to her. She asked a personal question. "What if you find yourself, you know, falling for some guy?"

"I'll enjoy him. He'll enjoy me. No commitment until I'm absolutely certain it will work. I'm not going to settle for anything less than absolute." She spoke adamantly. "And since there are no absolutes in this world—" she gave Tara a pert look and dipped a fry "—I will probably grow old alone, but at least I'll be in control of my own destiny." She gestured with the last fry. "Does that seem so wrong?'

Tara shook her head. *It seemed a little lonely, yes. But wrong? In her way of thinking it was the safest way to go.*

## CHAPTER ELEVEN

LYDIE HAD A BOX waiting for Tara when she dropped Hailey back at the salon.

"This needs to go to the convention center. Do you think you could drop it on your way home? I was supposed to have it there by noon, but Mrs. Reynolds stopped by and…"

"Sure," Tara said, taking the box off the counter.

"It's decorations for the luncheon," Lydie said as she patted the box. "Silk flowers and such. I do appreciate this."

"No problem."

And it wasn't a problem, until Tara got to the convention center and found it locked.

*What now?* She tried to peer through the darkened glass for a sign of life. Nothing. No lights, no movement. She'd have to take the box back to the salon. Tara had just loaded it into the passenger seat of her car when a familiar white Beemer drove into the lot.

Well, Tara thought as she pulled the box back out again, delivering it to Stacia was better than returning it to the shop.

"These decorations were supposed to be here by noon," Stacia said as she unlocked the door. She held it open with her toe, indicating that Tara should carry the box inside. Tara debated dropping the box on the sidewalk and walking away, and then decided she was past that. She'd be nice, if for no other reason than because Stacia expected her not to be.

"Something came up," Tara said evenly. She set the box on the reception table and turned to leave. Then she stopped and turned back. "You know, Stacia, since it's just you and me here, maybe it's time for us to clear the air."

"Excuse me?"

"We never had any problems before. Why are we having them now?"

"I guess it's the fact that you won't leave my fiancé alone."

Tara was genuinely taken aback. "I won't what?"

Stacia's expression hardened. "Oh, don't play innocent with me. Ryan told me."

Tara shook her head, trying to get rid of the twilight-zone feeling rapidly engulfing her. "Told you what?"

"Oh, for heaven's sake, Tara. He said you'd

deny it." Stacia took a few steps away, but Tara caught up with her.

"*What* did Ryan tell you?" She was angry now and she ground the words out.

"He told me that you've been harassing him and that I should let him handle it."

"When?"

"What do you mean, when?"

"I mean is he talking about after we dated a year ago, or is he talking about now?"

"Now," Stacia replied tightly. "Phone calls now."

Tara sucked in a breath. What was the bastard up to? "He's lying."

Stacia's chin went up. "He's my fiancé. He wouldn't lie to me. You, on the other hand, with your illustrious family history…"

Tara snorted. What was this about? What could he possibly get out of lying about her? Unless…an awful thought occurred to her. A thought she wasn't cruel enough to share—even with Stacia Logan. Not yet anyway. *Like father, like son?*

"*How* am I harassing him?"

"Like I said. Phone calls. Other things." For a brief moment, Tara thought the woman was going to start crying. But instead she drew herself up and said, "Tara, look. Just stop doing it and we'll all be better off. You're lucky he hasn't contacted the police."

*He isn't going to contact the police.* He wouldn't dare. But Stacia didn't know that. Tara pressed her lips together. Then she abruptly turned and left the building.

She got into her car and drove straight to Ryan's office, located in one of the refurbished brick-front buildings on Main Street. There was an old-fashioned sign just inside the door, identifying the various occupants of the building. Ryan's suite was on the ground floor. Tara didn't even give herself time to consider what she was doing. She strode purposefully into the office, past the woman at the front desk and into the opulent back office where Boy Wonder was busily tapping away at his computer. The woman shouted, "Hey," as she scrambled after Tara, but Ryan, after a quick, startled look, raised a hand.

"It's all right," he said. "You can close the door when you leave."

"Leave it open," Tara countered, suddenly realizing she didn't want to be trapped alone with him. The associate looked torn, then reached out and grasped the doorknob, pulling the heavy wooden door shut as she backed out of the room, effectively enclosing Tara in Ryan's lair.

Ryan picked up a heavy gold mechanical pencil and idly twisted the mechanism. "What brings you here today, Tara? Have you finally come to your senses and decided to unload that white elephant?"

"I do not appreciate being used."

Ryan's eyebrows went up, the pencil went down. "Used?" He looked genuinely perplexed.

"Used," Tara repeated. "By a man—that's you, although I use the term loosely—who's lying to his fiancée."

Ryan's lips curved, but she saw no humor in his eyes. "I have no idea what you're raving about," he said smoothly.

"All right. I'll spell it out," Tara replied, making an effort to keep her voice even as Ryan rose and came around the desk. She knew he was trying to intimidate her, but he couldn't hurt her with his associate so near, so she stood her ground until he leaned back against the front of his desk, prepared to listen with mockingly polite interest.

But he was interested. Tara could see that. He was wondering what she thought she knew. And belatedly she also knew, from the way he was looking at her, that she had made a mistake.

A monumental mistake.

He could now say, with the associate as a witness, that Tara Sullivan had burst into his office, had harassed him yet again, thus adding credence to the lie he'd told Stacia. And who knew what else he would do, now that she'd given him ammunition? All she needed was a restraining order during the reunion.

She had to get herself out of this. The best way to do that was to continue the full frontal assault.

"I know you think you're very clever, creeping around, trying to unnerve me, threatening my business in vague underhanded ways, but I am not going to put up with it. Stay away from me and *stop* using me as an excuse when your *paramours* call you at home!"

"You are unbalanced," Ryan replied matter-of-factly.

Tara narrowed her eyes. "Someday, Ryan, this will all catch up with you. You've bullied and assaulted me, you've lied to Stacia. In fact," she said as she yanked the door open, "I'll bet you cheat on your taxes, too. Your associate will probably be called in to testify." Tara nodded at the bewildered woman. "You'd better get your stories straight."

The last thing Tara heard was the associate asking Mr. Somers if he wanted her to contact the authorities. She was through the outer door before Ryan answered.

TARA FELT LIKE beating her head on the steering wheel.

*Why did her stupid moments always involve Ryan?*

She started the car and backed out of the parking lot, before the associate did call the authorities. She pulled the Camry out onto the street and headed home, occasionally checking her mirror for Rafe's rig. It would really tick him off if he had to arrest her for trespassing.

And as much as she was concerned about herself at the moment, she was also worried about Stacia. It was possible Ryan might not be happy about his fiancée's conversation with Tara and Tara knew from firsthand experience how charming Ryan could turn ugly when confronted or thwarted. There was a big difference between her and Stacia, though. Stacia had a lot of money. He wouldn't do anything to upset the golden goose. Anything direct, that is.

A girlfriend on the side…well, that did seem rather direct, but Ryan probably thought it was normal. It was, after all, a Somers tradition. Martin was infamous for his indiscretions and Ryan was just arrogant enough to believe he could do the same and not be caught. If he could have kept his girlfriend from calling his home.

Of course, as much as she liked the theory,

there were other explanations. The person calling his home could be an old girlfriend, someone who didn't want to let go. Or, more realistically from Tara's point of view, an ex with a grudge. Or maybe just some kind of a phone stalker.

Tara let out a sigh. She favored the first theory, but for Stacia's sake, she honestly hoped it was the second or third.

Tara made it home without the reds and blues showing up in her mirror, but she was dreading her shift at the bar that night. Soon the entire community would be aware that she had burst in on her former lover like some kind of a nut. Ryan would make certain they knew it, so that he could put his own spin on it. Tara Sullivan was harassing him again.

Matt was off picking up a final load of supplies to finish the bathrooms, and since Tara had a little time on her hands before she had to leave for her fun-packed evening, she sat at the computer and did what she always did when she had a few free moments. She opened a search engine, punched in the words "balloon payment refinance" and scrolled through the sites she'd already tried. She was on the third page, ready to click on the fourth, when an entry near the bottom caught her eye. *Balloon payment...predatory lending practices...elderly.*

Tara went to the site and began to read, her blood pressure rising steadily. The scenario perfectly fit what had happened to her aunt. Older people scammed into taking out low interest renovation loans with huge balloon payments they would be unable to make and then losing their homes. Aunt Laura had been taken in big-time.

The only way Laura's balloon could have been paid was through her life insurance, and Tara was pretty certain Aunt Laura had not intended to die to pay off her home. The bank manager had most probably assured her that the balloon would be refinanced, and up until refinancing time, she could take advantage of a very attractive interest rate. And then, according to the article, there would be no refinancing, the house would end up on the market and the predator could pick it up. Cheap.

Damn.

Tara printed out the document and bookmarked the page. She was still fuming as she dressed in her red satin cowboy shirt and jeans. She opened her jewelry box and pulled out the one piece of good jewelry her mother had left her, a gold nugget on a long chain, and fastened it around her neck, comforted by the heavy chunk of metal between her breasts. She'd have to do some research, but something could be done.

Becky happily relinquished the bar when Tara arrived, "Oh, did you hear about Ginny?"

"No," Tara replied absently, tying on an apron, her mind still working on the cheating bank manager.

"Martin Somers hired her at the Inn. She'd had an application in for almost a year and had given up hope, but he got hold of her yesterday...."

Tara caught her breath. Martin had hired away her day help. *That bastard.* It never stopped.

"Insurance benefits and everything. It's a lot better than what she was getting here."

"I'm sure it is," Tara said evenly. "Well, that's nice for her." Her lips tightened into a grim smile as she left the office to start manning the bar.

Ginny herself stopped by around eight o'clock, full of apologies. She had thought she'd be able to work around her schedule at the Inn and help Tara at the reunion as she had promised, but Martin wouldn't let her have the days off she needed. Tara was about as far from surprised as a person could be, but she didn't tell Ginny she was merely a pawn in a petty game. Instead Tara told her that she understood and that she was certain that she and Hailey could manage. *Somehow.*

Ginny left after a few more minutes of sincere

apologies, obviously still feeling guilty. She was a single mother. She needed a better paying job with benefits and now she had it. Tara wouldn't begrudge her that.

Then to top the evening off, Eddie Johnson came in just before the end of a long and busy shift. He pushed his way up to the bar, all but knocking a patron off his stool, and ordered a draft.

Tara slapped down a glass still dripping foam. "How're you doing, Eddie?" she asked, wondering if he'd gotten over the parking lot humiliation. She got her answer almost immediately.

"Fine," he announced. "That boyfriend of yours around?"

"I don't have a boyfriend."

Eddie sprayed a little beer as he made a disparaging snort. "Yeah. Well, when you see that guy who *ain't* your boyfriend, you tell him that old Ed hasn't forgotten."

*Tell him yourself because I'm not going to.* "Sure thing, Eddie."

"Cuz I haven't." He gave her what was supposed to be a dangerous look, grabbed the glass and tottered off the stool and into the restaurant. Tara watched him go with some relief. The last thing she needed on top of everything else was another incident with Eddie.

All the lights in Tara's house were off when she drove up later that evening. Even the porch light, which Matt always left burning, was dark. The observation had barely registered when her headlights flashed over the front porch and she saw that something was wrong. Very wrong.

No reflection. Her headlights usually reflected off the wavy old glass, but tonight they shined into complete blackness.

Someone had broken her two front windows. Tara immediately hit the automatic door locks and, thanking God for modern technology, reached for her cell phone. Rafe was on speed dial and he answered on the second ring.

"Don't leave your car. In fact, get out of there," he said in clipped tones after she explained. "I'll be there in ten minutes."

Tara didn't leave. She sat in her locked car with the engine running until Rafe's classic T-Bird and a sheriff's vehicle pulled into the drive and parked on either side of her car. She rolled the window down.

"I thought I told you..." Rafe stopped when he saw her face. "Stay put."

"I—"

"Stay put. Where's Connors?"

"Home, I guess. He doesn't spend *every* night here, Rafe."

Tara watched as the deputies went through the house. They made a thorough search, then came back to report that nothing seemed to be disturbed.

"You aren't going to stay here tonight, Tara." It was both a statement and a question, and for once Tara acquiesced without argument.

"I know." Even though whoever had done this was probably long gone—Rafe had looked in the shop and the barn as well as the house—Tara would never be able to sleep with gaping holes in her front windows.

"Stay with me," Rafe said. "I'm going on shift in the morning. I'll take the couch so you can get some sleep."

Tara nodded. "Thanks."

TARA'S CAR was gone when Matt pulled into her drive early the next morning. He frowned, wondering if she had gotten home all right, then his heart stopped when he saw the front windows.

Matt was not conscious of stopping his truck or getting out. He approached the house cautiously, then became aware of a vehicle on the gravel road behind him and turned. Rafe's official SUV.

"She's fine," Rafe said, getting out of the vehicle. "I stopped by your house to warn you this morning, but you'd left."

He'd gone to breakfast early, sitting and drinking bad coffee, but for once it wasn't a nightmare keeping him awake—it was thoughts of going back to the job, facing the FFD exam. And Tara. The woman made him restless. A case of wanting and knowing he couldn't pursue. A matter of integrity.

"Where is she?"

"My place."

Matt was immediately aware of a surging swell of emotions that swamped his initial anxiety. Relief, jealousy, anger. Relief.

Jealousy.

Matt swallowed. "Is she all right?"

"She's fine. She came home and found the windows broken and called me."

Matt didn't want to ask, but he had to. "Were you on duty?"

The deputy shook his head.

Matt shoved his thumbs in his back pockets and turned to face the old house. It didn't matter if Tara had spent the night at Rafe's place. It didn't even matter if they had slept together there. It was none of his business. So why did it feel like his business?

"Any ideas?" he asked Rafe.

"Could be random vandalism. Doesn't look like anyone went inside."

Matt nodded.

"I guess she had an ugly encounter with Stacia Logan yesterday."

"What about?"

"Stacia accused her of harassing Ryan."

"That's crazy."

"I know."

Matt shook his head and started for the porch. Tara may not have called him last night, but at least he could repair her windows.

"Luke's coming out to replace the glass," Rafe said, and when Matt turned to meet his gaze, he read something there that looked a lot like sympathy. Well, he didn't need it.

"Is Tara staying at your place again tonight?"

"She refuses," Rafe said mildly. "Not much I can do about it other than arrange a few drive-bys tonight. Jack is back, so she won't have to work."

Matt didn't know if that was good or bad. Rafe pursed his lips as his radio sounded and he took a few steps toward his rig. "I need to get going. Tara should be here soon."

When she arrived, Matt met her at her car door. "You could have called me."

"I called a deputy."

"Who didn't happen to be on duty."

"Does that matter to you?"

Matt pulled in a breath and then shook his head. *Nope. Didn't matter to him. Not one bit.*

TARA LEFT HAILEY putting primer on the third-floor walls while she went to the rescheduled prom-dress staging meeting. There was to be not one but two meetings that day—a dress fitting in the morning and a rehearsal walk in the evening. Definitely a full and rich day for Dottie.

Tara arrived ten minutes late, walking into the convention center to find the place buzzing with teenaged girls, mothers and community members all trying to decide which girl fit best into which formal. There were dresses spread over every available surface. Tara took an instinctive step backward at the sight of all the fluff and glitter, but Dottie saw her and waved her in.

Two girls were arguing over who would get to wear Tara's dress and no one, she noticed, was gravitating toward the unusual flamenco-styled dress she guessed was from the 1930s. Stacia was there, acting as referee to another pair of girls who were fighting over who *had* to wear a peasant dress from the '70s.

"You're wearing the dress, Ashley," Stacia said with a note of authority and was immediately rewarded with classic teenage rebellion.

"I don't want to. I want to wear my mother's dress."

"You don't fit your mother's dress," Stacia said bluntly and she had a point. Ashley was rather curvaceous and the peasant dress would look the best on her.

"Then I'm not—"

"Yes, you are, young lady." Ashley's mother cut into the argument at the same moment Stacia noticed Tara and reddened. Tara went to sort out the argument over her dress.

By the time the fitting was over, two other girls and Dottie were in tears and, Tara had to admit, Stacia handled the upset well. She'd explained that anyone who was unhappy with the dress she was modeling could easily be replaced, and she told Dottie that yes, the girl modeling her dress would remove her eyebrow and nose rings.

The girls left after making hair appointments with Lydie, who would give each model a hairdo to match the period of dress they were wearing. Surprisingly, after all of the ruckus, most of the girls were happy to be participating and more or less resigned to what they would be wearing. They all agreed to meet again at eight o'clock that evening to practice walking with the slides and music.

"That's nice of you to do their hair without a

charge," Stacia said to Lydie as she started hanging dresses. She seemed oddly subdued and Tara had noticed that the woman had taken great pains not to look at her during the fittings and modeling practice.

"It's nothing," Lydie said with a wave of her hand. "Come on, Dot. Dry those tears and let's get the rest of these dresses hung so we can get a cup of coffee."

"You two go ahead," Tara said. "Stacia and I will finish this."

Stacia's startled gaze swung toward her, but Tara pretended not to notice, focusing instead on the dress she was arranging on a hanger.

"Thank you," Lydie said hesitantly. When Stacia made no protest, she said, "Come on, Dottie. It's past noon and I don't know about you, but I could use a piece of pie with my coffee."

The outer door swung shut behind them, and Tara carefully hung a 1950s confection of pale yellow satin and chiffon in the coatroom. When she came back, Stacia was arranging the hated peasant dress, pinning it so that the wide shoulders would stay on the hanger.

The two women worked in silence, quickly smoothing and hanging the dresses, and then Stacia locked the closet while Tara found her shoulder bag.

*Now or never.* "I was wondering if you'd do me a favor and listen to me for a few minutes. It's about Ryan."

"All right." Stacia replied in an I'll-humor-you-so-you'll-go-away voice. "I knew you had something on your mind." She reached under the table for her designer bag. "I have another appointment in a few minutes, so if you could be brief."

"I'm not making phone calls to Ryan."

"So you say."

"So I say." Tara wanted to stop there, but she knew her conscience would eat at her if she didn't do this. "I know you'll have a hard time believing it, but I'm not trying to cause trouble between you and Ryan by telling you this. I just think you should know before you marry this guy."

"Know what?" Stacia asked coolly.

"Ryan hurt me." Tara held the other woman's gaze. "And I don't mean emotionally."

"Hurt you?" Stacia said incredulously.

"Physically."

"What has he done to you that you haven't driven him to?"

Tara swallowed a retort because what she was about to say next was difficult and she wanted Stacia to take it seriously. "The first time was pretty much date rape."

Stacia simply stared at Tara for a long moment, but with the exception of her rising color, she was unreadable.

"What else?"

"Dammit, Stacia, does there have to be anything else? Okay, let's see. He stopped by my place to threaten me. He grabbed me at the convention center hard enough to leave bruises on my shoulder. And, yes, I can see you think I drove him to that, too. Well, guess again."

"Tara, I really don't—"

"Whether you believe me or not, Stacia, this is the bottom line. Ryan is a man who hurts women who cross him. You have the information. You can do what you want with it."

Tara started for the door. She paused with her hand on the handle. "You might want to think about who's making those phone calls, Stacia, because I promise you, it isn't me."

MATT HAD PUT IN a pretty good day's work on the top floor of the house and he was pleased with the results. He only had two more days before he left Night Sky for good, returning to Reno and his own world, and it looked as if he would indeed have Tara's house done just as promised. Tara had only seen part of what he'd accomplished that day since she'd taken off for yet another prom-dress committee meeting, grumbling under her breath as she trudged down the stairs. But his Scout's Honor promise the house would absolutely, positively be done by Sunday had lightened her mood. A lot.

Matt smiled. She said she hated going, it took time away from the house, but she went anyway because it was her duty. He was beginning to suspect she secretly liked it.

He parked his truck in front of the Anderson house and was halfway to his gate when a Hulk-sized figure suddenly lurched out from behind the thick trunk of an elm tree, blocking the sidewalk.

Matt stopped in his tracks, cursing. His mind on Tara, he had blithely walked into...Eddie?

Matt rolled his eyes heavenward. Yes, it was Eddie, with his cap twisted around backward in fighting mode and his beady bloodshot eyes trying to focus on Matt's.

"Eddie, I'm not in the mood—"

Eddie tilted his head back belligerently and Matt changed his mind. Enough was enough. He wasn't back on the job yet. He still had a little leeway here. "All right, Eddie," he challenged, taking a stand. "You want a piece of me?"

To Matt's surprise, Eddie held his ground

"Are you a *cop?*" Eddie demanded in his nasally voice. "I heard you were a cop. That true?"

Matt dropped his hands a few inches. He thought everyone in town knew he was a cop. "Yes, I'm a cop."

Eddie screwed up his face and cursed. "Then I can't have a *piece of you*, can I?"

Matt shrugged, waiting to see where Eddie was going with this.

"And I'll bet you feel pretty *safe* cuz of that," the big man taunted.

Matt nodded. "You're right, Eddie. I do." As safe as a guy could feel with a drunk roughly the size of a rhinoceros looking to take him out. In spite of the size difference he could take Eddie; but, if he didn't have to waste the time or energy, he didn't want to.

"I can't assault no cop and you *know* it."

Matt nodded, suddenly feeling more positive about the outcome of the encounter. He may just get out of this, and with no superfluous blood on him.

"Well, shit." Eddie leaned hard to the right before he gave up the battle with gravity and sank to the curb. He picked up a pebble and tossed it across the street. "I did all that talking 'round town and now I can't do anything about it." He looked up at Matt with watery eyes. "And you knew it all along."

"How'd you find out I'm a cop?"

"Rafe warned me. Said I didn't want to mess with you, since I just got off probation. Said it wouldn't be advisable." Another pebble flew across the street.

"Nice of Rafe."

"Yeah."

Matt didn't trust Eddie enough to sit next to him, but he moved a few steps closer. "You break any windows lately, Eddie?"

Eddie's face twisted into a disgusted grimace. "Do I look like I'm eleven years old to you?"

"I'll take that as a no."

"Damn right it's a no." Eddie let out a snort. "I haven't broken any windows since the early nineties."

Matt smiled. "Hey, Ed..." Again the beady eyes turned his way. "You know, as long as you stay away from Tara, I've got no problems with you. How about a truce?"

"I haven't got a lot of choice here, do I?" Eddie asked grudgingly before muttering another curse. "I'll have to tell the guys we hashed things out." He sounded utterly disgusted at the prospect. "I'd 'preciate it if you backed me."

"You know, there was nothing personal that night," Matt pointed out. "You took the first swing."

"Did I? I don't remember."

"Do you remember waiting for Tara?"

"Hell. I was just having some fun."

"Yeah. No more of that. Understand?" Matt's tone was deadly serious and he could see that even in his stupor, the big man understood.

"You know Tara can take care of herself, don't ya?" Eddie said, his eyes squinting as he cocked his head. "I used to pick on her just because I liked watching her fight back. It wasn't ever serious, you know."

"I was new in town," Matt said dryly. "I didn't know. But all the same, I'd appreciate if you didn't do it anymore."

Eddie shrugged a big shoulder. "You don't need to worry. Being a cop and all."

"Good to hear it."

"Yeah. Hey. I hear you're leaving. When you coming back?"

"Soon," Matt said, thinking it would be best for Eddie to think he could appear at any moment. In the deep recesses of his mind, he rather wistfully wished it were true. He did like this town. The people.

"Well, you know what?" Eddie said as he heaved himself to his feet. "I think you'd better buy me a farewell drink. That way the guys will all see we're buds and I won't get crap from them."

Matt considered his options and then caved. "One drink," he said. "And not if you're going anywhere near a motor vehicle."

Eddie laughed. "Hell. I haven't been allowed near a motor vehicle in years."

## CHAPTER TWELVE

TARA THOUGHT IT WAS ODD, but not unprecedented, when the car following her down the highway also turned down her road. She didn't get a lot of traffic by her house since only a few people lived past her, but it was a county road and it was Saturday night—party time for kids.

The prom-dress rehearsal had gone without a hitch even though Stacia had been noticeably absent and Dottie had taken over. All in all, it was a decent evening.

She parked near the house and was already on her way up the porch steps when headlights swung across the front of the house, momentarily blinding her. She put a hand up to shade her eyes, then dropped it as she recognized the vehicle. A white BMW. Ryan. She walked to the door and calmly fit the key into the lock. She was not going to talk to him; she was not going to allow herself to be bullied by him. She went into the house, shut the door and turned the dead bolt. Then she stood for a moment wondering what to do. She decided to wait in the parlor with the lights off until he left. She heard his heavy footsteps on her porch, the faint rattle of glass as he knocked on the ornate front door.

She didn't move.

"Tara!"

He'd slurred the single word. He was drunk. Tara shook her head, feeling more secure. All she had to do was outwait him. He would tire and eventually—

The crash of glass shattered the thought.

Tara raced to the foyer in time to see Ryan's hand, dimly illuminated by the porch light, reach through what was left of the leaded glass front window and fumble with the lock. She grabbed the first thing at hand, an antique umbrella Aunt Laura had kept by the door for the infrequent Nevada rainstorms, and swung it at his arm. He howled with pain as she connected, then cursed and reached through the window with his other hand to flip open the lock.

Tara turned to run, making it all of three steps before she tripped over a rumpled drop cloth and went sprawling. She was scrambling to her feet when Ryan shoved the door open and switched on the light.

His arm was bleeding.

"Bitch!" His face contorted with anger. Tara held his eyes, her own wide and fearful in spite of herself, slowly working to get her feet under her so that she could bolt again. "You told Stacia lies!" he shouted.

Tara shook her head. She wasn't going to talk to him, knowing instinctively it would only amplify his rage if she argued. She'd never seen Ryan like this and she was scared. Very scared. She swallowed, holding his brutal gaze, slowly shifting her weight, gathering the strap of her small purse, in case she had to swing it as a weapon.

"Filthy bitch!"

He started toward her and she sprang up, praying she could make it through the kitchen and out the back door before he caught her. She heard him hit something that went clattering to the floor with a hollow metallic clang as she charged through the kitchen and slammed to a stop at the back door. She fumbled at the lock, finally sliding the bolt free. She jerked the door open, raced out onto the side porch and vaulted over the rail. He was behind her. Close. Too close. She darted to the side, heard him slip on the newly watered grass and go down. She raced across the dark lawn behind the gazebo and plunged into one of Luke's favorite hedges. Then she froze, huddled in the dark, itchy foliage.

She could hear Ryan's footsteps, stealthy now that he knew she was hiding. He was hunting her. Her purse had caught on something as she crawled into the hedge and she hoped desperately that he couldn't see it. And that he didn't have a flashlight in his car.

"Tara, baby, I know you're here somewhere… Tara," he singsonged her name, "come on out, sweetheart, we have something to discuss…. Get out here, you bitch!" Ryan didn't sound so drunk anymore. His voice was taking on an edge of hysteria.

"She thinks I'm cheating on her!" he screamed. "Because you told her I was!" He was getting closer. Tara held her breath as he kicked at a bush a few yards away. "She broke our engagement and it's all because of you. First my job and now this. I've had it with you, bitch!" He kicked another bush. "Where are you?"

Then, suddenly, he shut up and she heard him stride away.

He was trying to fake her out. He was walking off, hoping she'd make a break for it. Or he was—

She heard him climb the porch steps and enter her house. And then she heard the awful crash of things, her things, being broken and destroyed.

She crawled forward, wincing at the sound of a

particularly loud crash. Her purse...if she could find her purse, her phone was in it. Another crash. Tara poked her head out of the bush and saw the strap hooked on a branch.

It was suddenly silent in the house and she froze again. Then she heard him in her kitchen. She reached out to untangle the strap and then eased her way out the back of the bush. Now that she was shielded from view of the house, she crept toward the road. Ryan's car was parked haphazardly behind her own. She wanted more than anything to make a dash for her Camry, but the house had become quiet again. She had no idea where Ryan was.

She eased back into the willows and turned her phone on, shielding the keypad so Ryan wouldn't see the glow. The only numbers she had on speed dial were the Owl and Rafe. Rafe's voice mail came on. She silently cursed and pushed the other button, hoping for Jack. 911 would be her last resort, since it dialed into Elko and not Night Sky. A few minutes later a nasally voice answered.

"Eddie?" Tara whispered, her heart sinking. Why was Eddie answering the phone? "Put Jack on."

"Speak up, girl, I can't hear you."

"Jack," Tara growled.

"Not here."

"Eddie, this is Tara. Send the sheriff to my place, okay?"

"I can't hear you," Eddie complained so loudly that Tara was afraid Ryan might be able to hear the man's voice if he were outside. She was about to hang up when there was fumbling on the other end and then another voice came on—a very welcome voice.

"Rafe," she whispered, overwhelmed with relief. "Ryan's at my house. He's wrecking it."

And then her front door crashed open with a tinkling of glass and Tara hit the power button.

MATT'S HEART was hammering as he took the last corner to Tara's house too fast. Rafe was in front of him and already pulling into the drive. That bastard Somers…if he had hurt her in any way…

The lights were on in Tara's house and the BMW was parked behind Tara's Toyota. Matt swung his truck in behind the Beemer.

He heard a crash inside the house. The two men, both out of their vehicles, looked at each other. Rafe's hand went to his weapon. They moved silently up to the open front door taking a place on either side of it.

"Sheriff's department!" Rafe yelled. "Come on out, Somers."

There was a long silence. "It's about time." Ryan finally yelled. "I'm here trying to help Tara. Somebody tore her house apart."

"He's wasted," Rafe muttered, making eye contact with Matt. "Come out, Somers," he called again. "Don't make me come in and get you." He nodded when Matt indicated with a gesture of his head that he was going around back.

"You really should see what somebody did in here," Somers called. "It's a-appalling."

"I will come see it as soon as you come out."

The back door was wide open and Matt eased his way inside, listening as Rafe engaged Ryan. Every drawer in Tara's kitchen had been yanked out and its contents spilled, so Matt had to pick his way carefully across the floor.

*Where was Tara?* Hiding somewhere, he prayed. There was blood on the floor, but not enough to indicate a lethal injury. But still, if that bastard had hurt her in any way…

He carefully peered around the kitchen door and saw Ryan with his back to him, stealthily approaching the open front door with…an umbrella? Must have been the only weapon he could find, Matt reasoned as he came out into the hall and inched his way closer.

"Somers," Rafe called again. "Right now I only

have you for breaking and entering, but if you continue to—"

Matt brought Ryan down with a tackling lunge, grabbing the man's wrist and twisting it up behind his back just as Rafe came in the front door.

Ryan writhed and cursed and Matt pushed the wrist higher. "You're breaking my arm," Ryan protested in a high-pitched voice.

"Where's Tara?"

"You're brea—"

"I don't freaking care. Where is Tara?" Matt demanded, fully intent on snapping the man's bone if he had to.

"I'm here," she said from the front porch and then made her way into the foyer, stepping over a fallen coatrack "I thought I should stay out of the way."

Relief slammed into Matt. No blood, no torn clothing. She seemed fine, slightly dazed perhaps. Shock.

"You showed remarkable willpower, Tara," Rafe quipped as he snapped the cuff on one of Ryan's wrists and nodded to Matt that he could release his hold. "Too bad Big Alice wasn't that lucky when you took her on in gym class."

Matt got to his feet. He took a few steps toward her and she shifted her attention from Ryan to him. When he was close enough, he reached out to put an arm around her shoulders. She shivered as she leaned against him, but her voice was steady when she said, "How'd you get here so fast?"

"I was having a drink with Rafe and Eddie when Eddie answered the phone," Matt replied, lightly feathering his free hand down her face, convincing himself that she was indeed unharmed.

"You were having a drink with Eddie?"

"Long story. I'm just glad I was having a drink with Eddie."

Tara tore her eyes from his. "Look at this place." She swallowed. Hard. Rafe cleared his throat.

"I'm going to have to know what happened here, Tara, so I can make charges against this guy." The "as many as possible" was implied in his tone. "We'll talk outside," Rafe said as he hauled Golden Boy to his feet and marched him out to the waiting SUV. Tara eased herself out of Matt's embrace and followed. Matt noticed she didn't let her eyes linger in any one place too long. He didn't blame her. Ryan had gone berserk. Her house resembled a battlefield.

He and Tara waited by his truck while Rafe parked Ryan in the caged rear seat and shut the door, effectively drowning out the epithets and racial slurs that had been growing louder.

"Okay," Rafe said, moving away from his

vehicle. He took out a pad and placed it on the hood. "Take your time, Tara. We'll talk again tomorrow, in case you forget something, all right?"

"All right."

And then Tara described what had transpired in a steady, unemotional tone as Rafe wrote. Matt studied her as she spoke, impressed by her composure. He wondered whether she'd break later. Some people did, but it was often surprising who held together. Another shudder of relief went through him. *Damn, but he was grateful she hadn't been seriously hurt by that bastard.*

"He'll be out on bail in a heartbeat," Rafe said, flipping the book shut. "You need to understand that, Tara, but I'll see to it he's charged with as many things as I can think of and you might want to consider a restraining order. I'll be by in the morning to see what I can do to help."

She nodded.

Matt walked to the door of the SUV with Rafe, taking one last look at Ryan's sullen profile. Rafe cast a quick glance at Tara, then back at Matt. "You might see if you can get her out of here."

"Yeah." Matt gave Rafe a fat-chance look.

"I see your point," the deputy muttered and then he got into the vehicle and Ryan started voicing threats again. Lawyers. Life savings. Career-ending moves.

Rafe pulled the door shut and started the ignition. A few seconds later he was rolling down the driveway, taking Ryan off the Sullivan property, hopefully for good. Matt walked back to where Tara stood watching the SUV as it turned onto the road.

"Did he hurt you?" he asked, needing to hear her answer, even though he'd heard every word of her statement.

"He didn't have a chance." Tara started walking up the path. "But he ruined my house," she said icily. "I'll probably have to call Mr. Bidart in the morning." She raised her eyes toward the sky as though trying to hold back tears. Matt wanted to tell her she was entitled. "I don't want to call Mr. Bidart." For the first time since he arrived, her voice was shaky.

"Don't call. We'll fix it."

"We don't have time," Tara muttered as they topped the last porch step, but Matt could see she was already plotting her attack. He hoped she didn't start tonight, because he was probably going to have to stop her—for insurance reasons if nothing else.

"Let's close things up as best we can and get out of here."

"Where are we going?"

"My place."

Matt shut and locked the door, for all the good it would do with the broken stained-glass panes. He wouldn't have minded staying at the house to keep it secure, but he wanted to get Tara out of there, to a place where she could rest.

"I'm not leaving," she announced.

Matt regarded her for a moment, and then shook his head. He reached his hand back inside the broken window and unlatched the lock. "We'll stay."

He pulled the door open. Tara stood on the threshold for a moment.

"I'm not in shock, you know."

Matt didn't answer. He followed her as she walked into the house. She reached out and flipped on the light switch.

"Denial isn't healthy," she said more to herself than to him. "It's better to simply face things. Find out how bad they are so I can deal with them."

Matt followed a few steps behind her as Tara moved through the rooms facing the chaos head-on, taking silent inventory. She did all right until she reached the kitchen. There she stopped in front of her new refrigerator with its very damaged front panel. She bent to trace her fingers over the indentations. Tears started to roll down her face.

That was when Matt took action. It was time for a little denial, healthy or not. He knew Tara had to handle this in her own way—they all had to handle demons in their own way—but she could handle her demons later.

He took her arm, gently yet firmly propelling her down the hall to the bedrooms.

Ryan had trashed Tara's room. Matt closed the door and instead opened the door to Nicky's room, which was thankfully undefiled. They went inside and Matt closed the door, shutting out the reality they'd be facing again all too soon.

And then…they stood facing each other until Matt finally reached out and took Tara's hands in his own. They were like ice.

"Hell of a night, Sullivan," he said quietly.

"That's an understatement," she murmured back, clutching his hands. "I really am all right. The worst has happened and I've survived. Now I just need to figure out a way to fix it."

"Come on." Matt motioned to Nicky's double bed, which was pushed against the opposite wall. "Let's talk about it."

"All right."

Matt snapped off the overhead light and led her across the darkened room. He climbed onto the bed, pulling her with him as he turned to sit with his back against the wall, his legs stretched out in front of him. Tara settled beside him, her shoulder touching his. He slid his arm behind her, pulling her closer and her head came to rest on his shoulder.

"I don't know how I'm going to fix this."

Neither did Matt, but he was going to do whatever he could to make it right.

"Maybe now people will understand what Ryan is really like."

"I'd say that's a definite possibility."

"Or maybe they'll think I drove him to destroy my house."

"I don't think so."

Another silence. "How are we going to get this cleaned up before my guests arrive? I only have three days."

"We'll get it done." He felt her pull in a deep breath.

"I hate this," she muttered. "Feeling out of control. Lots of questions, no answers...no action."

"Control returns."

Spoken like a veteran of losing and regaining control. "So, what's your story, Connors?"

"My story?" He was more than a little surprised at the sudden change of topic.

"Yeah. You have a story, and you're about as good at sharing as I am." She lifted her head off his shoulder, peering at him through the darkness. "I'd go so far as to say that you're worse."

Matt raised his gaze toward the dark ceiling and compressed his lips for a moment as he dealt with possible ramifications of answering her question. It would take her mind off her house, but at what cost to him?

*Denial isn't healthy,* she'd said. He knew that from hard experience. And so what if he told her? What would it matter? He'd be heading back home the day after tomorrow anyway. He may as well talk. He could do this. For her.

"It was in the papers. On the news," he said in a low voice. "A standoff…an officer down."

"In Reno?"

"Yeah."

"I did hear about it."

Everyone had.

"You were the guy…"

"Who dragged the injured officer out of the line of fire. Yeah."

"You were a hero."

"No." There was no modesty in the word. It was a simple denial.

He felt her gaze shift toward his profile. "Why?"

Matt swallowed. "Because I was rash. I had something to prove."

"You're going to have to explain that one."

"The officer had been shot and went down, and then the shooter kept shooting at him while he was lying there. Fortunately the guy was a lousy shot, but he was shooting and no one could get to him. At that particular time in my life, I didn't feel like I had a lot to lose, and it seemed as if both the downed man and I had a lot to gain."

"Sounds like heroism to me."

"You weren't there," Matt said softly.

"Why did you have a lot to gain and not much to lose?"

"Because I was suspected, am still suspected, of being a crooked cop. I wanted to prove I'd put my life on the line—I was a good cop."

He felt her stiffen in surprise.

"You? A crooked cop?"

"Me."

"Why?" The disbelief in her voice almost made Matt smile. He swallowed hard and decided to explain about his dad. He finally understood that this was something he needed to do.

"Do you have a little time?"

"All night."

He told Tara everything.

He told her things he'd never told anyone...not even Luke. He told her because he knew she'd understand—because of what had happened to her with her dad. He told her because he knew she didn't want to have any kind of a lasting relationship with him...he could tell her and then walk away, knowing she wouldn't pass on what she heard.

When he was done, Tara shook her head. "You should have talked to me sooner, Connors. I never dreamed we had something like that in common."

"Felonious fathers?"

"Maybe we could start a club," she said without humor. "So, what do you do now?"

"I go back to work."

"With things to prove?"

He felt his back go up. "Just that I'm a decent cop who's not on the take."

"Considering your situation, you'd probably have to be the most honest cop on the force right now. Take it from one who knows, Matt. You can't change the past."

"Yes, but you still have to come up with ways to live with the aftermath."

"I can't argue with that." Tara lay her head back on his shoulder. "What's your plan?"

"I'm going back to work. I'm going to do a decent job. I'm going to change a few attitudes through time and persistence. I'm not going to disappear because the lieutenant is pissed that he wanted to pin stuff on me and couldn't. I'm going to ride this out, regardless, and—" his fingers tightened on her shoulder "—that's the reason you don't want to be involved with me."

"Because you need to prove you're not your father instead of living your own life?"

Matt felt a jolt of surprise that she understood so clearly what he was doing.

"Kind of a vendetta," Tara said so quietly he barely made out the words. She pressed her head closer to his shoulder.

Another long silence followed, so long that Matt thought that she might have fallen asleep.

"I know about vendettas. Ryan has one against me. I had one against this community…. They aren't good, Matt."

"It's more than a vendetta, Tara. I have a job in Reno. I have a career with ten years invested in it. I own a house. I am going to put things back on track, and yeah, I'm going to prove I am not my old man. I can do it if I just stick it out."

"Houses sell. Careers change. Vendettas and guilt…they suck the life out of you." He knew she was thinking about her ruined house. "Look what it got me."

His arm tightened around her. "Not quite the same."

"Close." She snuggled even closer, her head now comfortably situated on his chest. "You should rethink this, Matt. It's not healthy." She yawned and Matt knew exhaustion and the lingering effect of shock were taking over.

"Anything else?"

"Yeah. As long as we're being honest with each other. You know that other night…in my kitchen, when you thought you'd insulted me?"

*Oh yeah, he knew that night.*

"I wish you hadn't left."

"Why's that?" He regretted the words as soon as he said them, but her answer took him aback.

"I need to get over what Ryan did to me."

When Matt finally spoke, he forced himself to keep any trace of anger out of his voice. "Did he hurt you? Back then?"

"Yes," she replied simply. "And more than anything I want to move past it. I thought you could help me."

"Why me?"

"I trust you." Her voice was getting softer. "And you're leaving. I don't want a relationship, Matt. I don't think I'm cut out for one, but I want to know that I could have one, a physical one…sometime…maybe…" Her last words were barely audible. "With someone rock solid."

*Well, that put him out of the running.*

He felt her body start to relax against his.

He waited until he was certain she was asleep and then he shifted his position so that he was more comfortable, but still holding her.

So, he'd read the situation wrong. It hadn't exactly been a one-night stand she'd been asking for. She'd wanted him to make love to her to help her forget, to see if she could actually go through with it. No strings. Just two people who needed each other…for one night.

And she wanted it to be him.

Because he was leaving.

# CHAPTER THIRTEEN

WHEN TARA AWOKE, she was alone in Nicky's bed and she had a crick in her neck, as though she'd been sleeping in an odd position. She sat up, blinking into the bright sun and then an immediate, almost drowning wave of depression washed over her. Ryan had wrecked her house.

She got out of bed, wondering when Matt had left, and then another wave of horror hit her as she recalled what else had happened the night before.

*She'd told Matt she wanted him to make love to her...and she had told him why. Practically made an appointment.*

She felt an uncustomary flush of embarrassment. Maybe she'd been in shock the night before. *Please, Matt, make love to me—*

Matt who had made the priorities in his life pretty darned clear. Matt who was heading right back into Stressville, full steam ahead, and was taking no passengers with him.

She may not have actually said the words *make love to me,* but she'd implied them.

Tara glanced at her watch and was stunned to see how long she had slept. Must have been some protective instinct, a way for her mind to escape the reality of the situation…her house…Matt.

*And, oh, what a reality.*

Her first thought upon stepping into the hallway was that maybe the damage wasn't as bad as she had first thought; maybe it was mostly just clutter, things that could be picked up and either put back or thrown away. But as she walked into the kitchen, where Rafe was standing surveying the damage, she decided, yes, it was as bad as she had thought. Ryan had indeed kicked in her refrigerator and torn cabinet doors off their hinges. Two drawers had been shattered, probably stomped on. One of her antique chairs was broken. The purple penguin lay on the floor near the door.

"I called the insurance for you," Rafe said as Tara put the bird back in its place. "The adjuster will be here in half an hour."

Tara nodded her thanks, afraid that if she spoke, she might lose it. The reunion was days away. She was scheduled to have guests check in the day after tomorrow. Her house was a wreck. Damn. The Somerses may have actually won.

She straightened her back.

No. She wouldn't let them win.

"I know it looks bad, Tara, but the best revenge against that rat bastard is to get this place back into shape, pronto."

Tara smiled. "Thanks, Rafe. That's my plan." She was either going to win or die in the attempt. "Where's Matt?" She felt her cheeks warm at the hopefully innocent question.

"In the shop, doing what he can for the worst cabinet doors."

She nodded and went in the opposite direction from the shop, back into the parlor, stepping over debris as she went. The front door was propped open and Luke was busy forming a paper template to fit the broken pieces of leaded glass. Through the door she could see Ryan's car, still parked at an angle behind her own. She turned away. She couldn't really do anything until the insurance person came and assessed damages.

Maybe she should bolster her courage and go out to the shop and assess damages there. See how things looked in the light of day.

*Better to just face things.* At least she had two traumas to ping-pong back and forth between, she thought grimly as she headed toward the kitchen and the back door. When one became too overwhelming, she'd focus on the other. She wasn't sure what she was going to do when both became overwhelming.

"Oh…my…gosh." Hailey's voice came from the foyer. Tara had forgotten her friend was coming to help with curtains and finish the stenciling. Well, curtains and stenciling were certainly the last of her worries now. Tara reversed course.

Hailey stood in the mess and stared at Tara.

"Who did this?"

"Ryan Somers."

Hailey looked around the decimated room and, for a moment, it seemed as if she were on the edge of tears.

"You need help. I'm calling Grandma."

"No, don't," Tara automatically protested, but Hailey ignored her and walked to the phone, stepping over spilled plants and broken bric-a-brac. When she hung up a few minutes later she started picking things up, but Rafe stopped her. "We have to wait for the insurance adjuster."

"Well, maybe I'll go upstairs and do what I can on the stencils because later it looks like I'll be busy."

The insurance adjuster left an hour later. Two cars pulled into the drive as the adjuster's car pulled out. Ginny got out of the first one and Lydie and Dottie the other.

"I can't believe this, Tara," Ginny said once she'd had a moment to take in the disaster. "When I heard about it, I quit the Inn."

"You what?" Tara knew how much Ginny needed a steady income, being the sole support for her little girl.

"I didn't like it there. Now I know why he hired me, and he probably would have let me go as soon as the reunion was over anyway. I'm here to help in any way I can."

Lydie sailed into the house before Tara could reply, looking for all the world like a battleship steaming out of port. Dottie traveled at her side like a smaller escort ship. But apparently Hailey hadn't quite prepared them for what they would see. They stopped dead in their tracks.

"This is…oh, goodness." Lydie just stared, two circles of angry color forming on her cheeks, while Dottie bent down to pick up one of Aunt Laura's Hummel figurines, checking it for chips. Tara had the distinct impression that if it were marred in any way, Mrs. Gibson was going to take it out of Ryan's hide.

Dottie carefully set the figurine on the window-sill and pushed up the sleeves of her starched cotton blouse. "We have work ahead of us." She looked up at Tara. "You can't do this alone. We're staying."

Tara took a deep breath. "Yes, ma'am." No one followed her as she maneuvered through the debris to the kitchen, where she started randomly picking up scattered flatware.

She heard another car pull into the drive and frowned. This was getting weird. She dumped a couple handfuls of flatware into the sink with a clatter. She understood why Rafe and Matt were there, and even why Hailey was there, but Ginny? Lydie Manzo? Dottie Gibson, the woman Tara despised because of the embarrassment she'd caused her years ago?

"This is amazing," Tara said to Rafe a short while later, as more people began stopping by to pitch in, clearing debris, sorting items, assessing damage and possible solutions.

"You're part of the community," he pointed out as he helped her dump more flatware into a basin of soapy water.

Yeah, maybe she was. Finally.

"I didn't want to be the community charity," she pointed out grimly.

"Funny thing about charity—sometimes you're on the giving end, and sometimes the receiving end. It helps you appreciate both positions."

Tara didn't answer. She focused on washing the forks, knives and spoons until Hailey came to ask her advice on the parlor armoire that Ryan had pulled over, breaking a door. Rafe took over dishwashing.

Hailey and Tara made a list of what needed to be replaced immediately and what could wait for the insurance check. Tara still hadn't seen Matt. She wondered if he were hiding, hoping she wouldn't force him into lovemaking. If he didn't show soon, she'd have to go looking for him and let him off the hook.

"I just hope none of my guests come down to raid the fridge," Tara muttered as she opened and closed the dented door a couple of times.

"Can't make up your mind?"

Tara's breath caught. *Time to face the music*.

He was standing just behind her, holding a cabinet door in one hand. And he was looking at her...differently.

"Checking to see if it works," she said, suddenly having more trouble than usual pushing words up out of her throat.

"You've got a lot of help here."

"I'm the community cause."

"It looks like you might be ready for guests by Monday."

"Yes," she agreed, trying to read him. He held out his free hand. Tara automatically took the object he held there. It was her concho barrette, in one piece again.

"I thought you might want it fixed," he said. "Kind of a going-away present."

"How?"

"I soldered it."

She raised her eyebrows. "And you just happened to have silver solder?"

"I might have ordered it special."

Tara's lips trembled slightly and then she smiled. "Thank you, Matt." She gave in to impulse and hugged him. He hugged her back with his free hand, the cabinet door still suspended from the other. And then his arm tightened, holding her against him as she pressed her face in the crook of his shoulder, deeply inhaling his scent and feeling her body go liquid as his became hard.

Luke limped into the room, with one of the drawers he'd built to replace those that Ryan had stomped. "Oh." He started to backtrack, but Tara had already put some air between herself and Matt.

"Matt fixed my barrette," she said, holding it up.

Luke nodded and cast Matt a questioning look. Some sort of male signal fired back and then Luke came into the room and started fitting the drawer into the cabinet.

But even with Luke there, Tara felt the sparks of awareness between her and Matt. Finally, she had to leave the room and begin to work in another. It was the only way she could focus.

By late morning, Tara finally started to accept, as some people left and other people came to take their place, that she really was the community project. She, who had never accepted charity in her life, was accepting it in a big way today.

She had just finished helping Lydie place unbroken Victorian bric-a-brac in a cabinet in the foyer when an odd silence descended over her crew. She turned and found herself looking straight into the hawklike face of Nate Bidart. Her heart stopped.

Oh, no. So much for her reservations and referrals.

She moistened her dry lips. "Mr. Bidart—"

"Nate," he replied with a frown, his gaze traveling over the room which was about a zillion times better looking than it had been, but was still a shambles.

He shook his head. "And I thought it looked bad the last time I was here."

Lydie stiffened and Tara touched her arm.

Before either of them could say anything, Nate motioned with his head for Tara to follow him. She gave Lydie a "what now?" look and then followed him out.

They walked out the front door and Nate led the way to the old gazebo.

"I just got into town and stopped for lunch at the Owl," he said after gesturing for Tara to take a seat. "I heard the news and decided to come out and sort fact from fiction. I see that, for once, most of what I heard was fact." He sat on the bench opposite Tara.

"I've been doing some prying since I last saw you, and I have to tell you...I don't particularly like the things that have come to light." He glanced at the house, and then back down at her. "I'm beginning to think my friend Martin is a bit of a bully."

No argument there.

"This is not the time to go into it, of course, but I just wanted to tell you...well, you're not alone here. If you ever feel like you're being pushed around, if you ever feel like you might need the services of a decent attorney...well, give me a call. I'll see what I can do."

"I didn't know you still practiced," she said. She'd thought he'd given it up for his business ventures.

"I keep a finger in the pie."

She did have questions about what had happened to her aunt and about unethical lending practices aimed at the elderly. Nate might be just the man to help her.

"I appreciate the offer."

"Least I could do."

Nate stayed for almost three hours after his talk with Tara and she soon understood that he was not afraid to get his hands dirty. Before he left, he went over to pat Billie and Buddy, smiling as he did.

"I like stubborn folk."

Tara grinned. "Then you're going to love me."

"You'll have the rooms ready for my mother?"

"You know I will."

Nate drove away a few minutes later. "I need to feed these people," Tara told Rafe. He shook his head.

"Ben is on his way from Elko. He picked up fried chicken and salads at the grocery there."

Ben and the lunch arrived and people ate on the move. The work continued into the evening, at which point the pizzas arrived, and Tara wasn't all that surprised when she was asked where she had the upstairs furniture stored. She led the way to the barn and in a matter of an hour, the three second-floor bedrooms were furnished and ready for rugs and linens.

It was midnight when the last car pulled out of the drive.

Her house looked great. Well, not as great as it had before Ryan's rampage, but better than she had dreamed possible in so short a time—and she was utterly exhausted. Physically. Mentally. Emotionally.

Where was Matt? He'd been in and out all day, between the shop and the kitchen. They hadn't had any time alone after he'd delivered his going-away present, but Tara had been so aware of him, both his presence and his absence.

She glanced out the window, just in case. He hadn't left. His truck was still parked next to hers, moonlight reflecting off its hood.

"Looking for something?"

Tara slowly turned, leaning back against the counter as she held his gaze from across the room.

"Yeah," she said softly. "I'm looking for you."

"Any particular reason?" Matt asked, propping a shoulder against the doorframe. Behind his glasses, his eyes were hooded.

Tara could feel the undercurrent swirling around her, engulfing her. Seducing her.

A tingle traveled up her spine.

Matt, studying her, loose-limbed, handsome… watchful.

It was Matt who finally moved, pushing off from the doorframe and slowly crossing the room to Tara. He stopped in front of her and looked down at her for a heartbeat before settling his hands at her waist. Tara thought he'd pull her close, but instead he surprised her by boosting her up onto the counter and, once she was settled, nudging her knees open to move into the V of her thighs. His eyes never left hers.

*So that is how it's going to be.*

She reached up to remove his glasses and found the act oddly intimate. She set the glasses aside and looked into those gorgeous hazel eyes. And what she saw there made her shiver in anticipation.

With slow deliberation, she reached out to take his face between her hands, sliding her sensitive palms over the lightly stubbled planes of his cheeks. The corners of her mouth tilted up at the sensation and then she leaned forward until her lips just touched his in the lightest of kisses. A butterfly touch. Brief. Promising.

She pulled back and his mouth followed hers. When the back of her head touched the cabinet behind her, his lips settled.

His mouth was warm, wet and demanding. No teasing, no light caresses this time. Serious kisses, deep kisses, kisses meant to inflame.

Kisses that were doing exactly what he intended them to do.

She felt herself dampening and she pushed herself against the hardness in his jeans, growing wetter at the intimate contact. She hooked her legs around his hips pulling him even closer, savoring every nuance of the sensations traveling through her body.

She let out a sigh when Matt's hot mouth finally left hers and he leaned back.

"I've been thinking about what you said last night," he said.

"Yeah?"

"I have to leave tomorrow. I go to work on Monday."

"I know."

"So, I guess what I'm asking is—"

"I meant what I said last night."

Matt took a moment to consider her flat statement, and then asked, "What exactly did Somers do to you?"

Tara's gaze didn't waver. "He was rough."

He gave her a long, searching look and apparently understood that that was all the answer he was going to get. "And if we do this, what about tomorrow? When I have to leave?"

Tara still held his gaze. "You leave. I stay." It sounded so simple…she hoped it was. She cared for him, trusted him, but realistically there was nothing to hold them together. They'd both survived without each other for a long time. They would no doubt continue to.

"As long as we understand each other."

"We understand," Tara murmured. "Totally. And now—" she tilted her head "—I really, really think you should kiss me again."

Matt didn't have to be asked twice. He reached behind her to slide his hands under her seat and pull her even more tightly against him as his tongue pushed into her waiting mouth in a hot kiss so intense that Tara felt as if a fuse had been lit inside of her.

He brought one hand up to pop the silver concho barrette and it rattled to the counter, not breaking for once. He buried his hands in the thick hair as he continued to lean into her, kissing her.

"Are we going to do this…here?" Tara finally asked on a moan. Here would be okay. She was already working on the buttons of his shirt.

Matt let her finish the job, even though her fingers were clumsier than usual. When she was done, she pushed the blue chambray off his shoulders. It slid down his arms and landed in a heap behind him. She immediately leaned forward to do something she had wanted to do for weeks. She tasted him, trailing her tongue over the faintly salty surface of his shoulder muscles, teasing her lips with the smattering of dark hair on his chest. She circled a nipple, first tentatively, then more boldly as his hands bunched in her hair. She nipped him and he groaned. She traveled on, up his chest, up his throat, over the stubble on his chin to his lips. And then she buried her tongue in his mouth, pressing herself against him.

Matt never answered her question, but when he lifted her up off the counter and carried her down the short hall to her bedroom with her legs still hooked around his hips, she figured his answer was no. They wouldn't do it in the kitchen. At least, not yet.

It wasn't until he gently set her back on her feet in her bedroom that she felt the quick and brutal stab of anxiety.

What on earth was she doing? Had she not learned this lesson the hard way? That sex was not her friend? That it hurt? Badly?

And then she looked at Matt and the anxiety ebbed.

"I need you to...go slow."

He brought his head down to touch hers. "I will go very, very slow. And anytime you say stop, I'll stop."

Tara nodded against his forehead and he briefly tasted her lips before he took her by the hand and led her to the bed. He sat and pulled her, still standing, between his knees, looking up at her.

"Slowly," he reiterated and then he punctuated his words by peeling the T-shirt she wore up and over her head. Tara pulled her hair free and shook it down her back. Matt watched the movement with fascination. His hands came up to span her bare waist as the heavy strands dropped into place, and he kept his eyes on her face as he slowly pressed a kiss to her abdomen. Tara pulled in a sharp breath. He slid his mouth over her smooth skin, making circles, tickling her navel with his tongue. Tara's muscles seized and she unconsciously fisted her hands in his hair.

She made a little noise and bit her lip to keep from making more as Matt's slick mouth traveled up to the edge of her bra. He flicked his tongue under the lace and her nipples contracted, almost painfully.

She glanced down, color rising in her cheeks as she saw that he was watching her, keeping his eyes on her as he teased her, waiting, no doubt, for some sign that she wanted to stop. But she didn't want to stop. Not yet.

Matt raised his hand to her bra, continuing to

hold her gaze as he flicked a finger against the plastic clasp. It popped open. Tara's breasts fell free and only then did Matt pull his eyes away from hers. He touched her, lightly at first, caressing the silk of her skin with his rough-edged fingers, cupping her fullness, filling his palms. Tara pressed herself forward into his hands and he took her up on the unspoken invitation, flicking his tongue over one nipple, causing Tara to suck in a sharp breath.

And then he suckled.

Tara thought she was going to lose control right there. She had never, ever felt anything quite so exquisite as Matt's tongue, his lips, his teeth, on her sensitive nipples, first one, then the other and back again. By the time he was finished, her breath was shaky. Her entire body was shaky.

"Are you all right?" Matt asked quietly.

"Fine," Tara responded breathlessly. Her voice was shaky, too.

He continued to nuzzle her breast as his fingers trailed back down her abdomen, and the ends of his fingers hooked on the waistband of her jeans. She stilled as Matt worked on the snap closure, then froze as he started to drag the zipper down.

Matt stopped instantly.

Tara frowned, annoyed with herself and her

reaction. She didn't want to stop. She didn't want to be a victim of Ryan. She yanked her zipper down in one quick movement and quickly shucked out of both her panties and her jeans.

And then she just stood there. In front of him. Naked and uncertain.

Matt reached for her and pulled her to his chest, rolling her over him and tumbling her onto the bed, coming to rest partially on top of her. And then he kissed her, wiping all uncertainty out of her mind. His mouth was demanding, but his hands were gentle, caressing, creating a dichotomy of sensation.

The denim of his jeans was rough against her bare skin, creating another surprisingly erotic contrast, but it was his hands that Tara was most aware of, hands that were finally traveling down to where she wanted…something.

He touched her then, rubbing his thumb over the most sensitive part of her body and she gasped. He kept kissing her, but it was his fingers she concentrated on as they moved over the slick dampness between her legs. She gasped again as one finger penetrated her, felt herself close in on it, move against it. He kept rubbing with his thumb, dipping into her with his fingers.

Tara was losing control. She tried to stop. She

really did, but his fingers would not stop, they gave her no reprieve, showed her no mercy. She cried out, biting her lips as the sensation built to an unbearable level and then, suddenly, the world exploded around her. Blood pounded in her temples. Colors flashed. It went on, an eternity of throbbing sensation, until finally she dropped her head against Matt's chest and took a shaky breath. Only then did his fingers still.

She couldn't believe it. She raised her head to look at Matt in wonder. So this was sex? This was an orgasm? No wonder people were so enthusiastic.

He smiled.

Tara pushed her hair back and took another breath. She reached for Matt's jeans, deliberately popping open the buttons on the classic 501s one after the other. She was glad he wasn't wearing a zipper because she had a feeling she'd have had a difficult time getting it down. He raised his hips and she worked the jeans over his legs, while he kicked his shoes off, letting her fingers travel over the taut hair-covered muscles of his thighs and calves, loving the sensual contrast between his body and hers. She dumped the jeans on the floor and went back then to take his boxers on the same slow trail. But as soon as her hands touched the navy blue cotton she stopped.

"Something wrong?" Tara heard the concern in his voice and she forced herself to shake her head. He propped himself up and reached for her chin, tilting it so he could see her face.

"Scared?"

She hesitated, then nodded.

"We can stop," he said. Her eyes flashed up to his.

"I don't want to stop."

A gentle hand came up to stroke her hair then, pushing it away from her face so he could see her.

"Are you sure?" She gave him an ironic look and he smiled again. "I know...you're too cautious to be sure. But you have to be this time."

She smiled a little. "I'm sure." And then his expression sobered. He took her hand and guided it down, letting her run her palm over the hard length of him. His eyes went shut as her fingers closed around him through the cotton of his boxers, then he forced them open again.

He gently worked his boxers free of her grip and slipped out of them, then rolled over and reached for his pants. A second later he held a condom packet. He reached down and rolled the latex sheath into place before guiding her hand back down to encircle him. "Like an Eagle Scout..."

"I like the way you think," Tara murmured, trying to hide her nerves as he moved gently on top of her, nudging her thighs apart with his knee. She felt her body go rigid. This was when the pain had started before, when, despite his promise to go slow her first time, Ryan had lost all patience, and roughly shoved his way home. And that had only been the beginning.

"Shh," Matt soothed, bringing her back to the here and now. He kissed the corner of her mouth, stroked her hair, traced his tongue lightly over her lips. She was starting to go liquid again, starting to relax, but then he shifted and she felt the blunt pressure of him against her and once again she felt the panic. Her eyes flashed up to his, seeking reassurance. He smiled down at her. Patient. Gentle.

"Just say stop. Anytime."

The tender words were what she needed. She made a move against him and he in turn, pushed gently against her, causing one of the most incredible sensations she had ever felt. She reached down for him then, sliding her hand between their bodies, encircling him once again with her fingers, arching a little as he started to ease into her, slowly...oh, so slowly.

Tara's eyes drifted shut, focusing on the exquisite pressure she felt as he moved farther inside of her, filling her.

He held himself still for a moment as she arched against him, and then he eased back out. Tara bit her lip as he pushed back in again. All the way in. In one smooth stroke this time. Then out. *Oh. My. Goodness.*

She became aware that her breath was coming in pants as he moved in her. And then, at some hazy point, she noticed that his movements were no longer slow and sensually deliberate. He pushed into her harder and faster. Tara clutched at his back, then fisted her hands in his hair, drowning in sensation as he drove himself into her again and again.

It didn't seem possible. Couldn't be possible... could not...but it was.

Tara cried out as she exploded around him, arching against Matt's body just seconds before she felt the muscles in his back go rigid. He gave one last thrust as his body emptied into hers. And then he carefully lowered himself down to rest on top of her.

Matt lay still for a moment, his breathing rough and unsteady. Tara cradled his head to her breast, loving the feel of him sprawled possessively on top of her. Then he lifted himself up and reached out to tenderly brush the hair back from Tara's face.

"Did I hurt you?"

"If you did, I hope you do it again real soon,"

she murmured. He rolled over onto his back, bringing her with him, holding her against his chest, her hair spilling over them.

"Trust me. That can be arranged."

# CHAPTER FOURTEEN

WEAK SUNLIGHT FILTERED in through the lace curtains covering Tara's bedroom windows. It was probably close to four-thirty. She couldn't see the clock because of Matt's shoulder, and she was afraid to move, afraid of waking Matt, afraid of having to face the reality she had so blithely created without any thought of consequence. The night had been incredible...she'd never known passion before, had never felt so close to a person in her life—a person who'd be walking out of her life in just hours....

To say she was confused was a massive understatement.

She'd known for quite a while she trusted Matt, but last night she came to realize that the feelings she had for him went beyond trust. The depth of emotion he provoked in her both terrified and astonished her. She'd never felt anything like this before. She didn't have any idea how to deal with it. Didn't even know if it was real.

She needed time to think, without being swayed by Matt's nearness.

She'd been lying awake for over an hour when Matt finally shifted and then got out of bed, crossing to the hall leading to the bathroom without looking back. She swallowed as she watched his impersonal exit. Already she missed his warmth. A very bad sign, no doubt.

She forced herself out of bed, feeling numb as she started picking up her scattered clothing. It took some time. She found her missing sock under the dresser, her left shoe in the hallway.

Matt came out of the bathroom as she was buttoning her blouse, which seemed to be missing a button. She gave him what she hoped was an acceptable morning-after smile. He smiled back, but she could see that he, too, was dealing with the reality brought on by daylight. He looked as if he wanted to be anywhere except for where he was.

*Say something.*

She didn't know what to say. She could face down bullies in parking lots, she could tell people off in public meetings…but she had never, not even with Nicky, discussed her deepest fears and feelings.

How was she supposed to start now, when she didn't even know what she was dealing with?

TARA STOOD NEXT to the rumpled bed, her fingers working on the buttons of her blouse but not quite getting the job done. It was all Matt could do not to brush her fingers away and finish up himself, but he was afraid he might start working in the wrong direction. He'd been afraid to kiss her good-morning for the same reason. He wanted to make love to her one more time, but he'd felt her lying tensely next to him, wide-awake, for a good hour. He might have worked his way around that, but she made no move to touch him, kept as much distance between them as her undersized bed would allow. The one time he had eased his body against hers, she'd moved away. Obviously, she intended to abide by their verbal contract and Matt knew that, for her sake and his, he needed to do the same.

He had to face that he was heading back to his world today. Making love to Tara again would only prolong the inevitable.

Her words of the night before echoed in his head as he shrugged into his shirt. *You leave. I stay.*

It made sense and Tara appeared to be satisfied with the agreement. She even looked as if she wanted him to leave as soon as decorum allowed. He decided to give her a break and take off.

"I need to get going," he said, but he couldn't help making one last shot at reviving the togetherness they had shared the night before. "I do have time to make breakfast before I go." He tried a smile. "No oatmeal."

Tara shook her head. "No breakfast, but thanks."

Enough said.

TARA WATCHED MATT drive away after a stilted goodbye that had been uncomfortable to both of them, a brief embrace, an impersonal brush of lips. And that was it. He was out of her life. She took a shaky breath.

Think. She had to think about this.

She was the one who'd laid down the rules, but he had agreed to them, had given no indication this morning that he regretted them. He seemed to cling to them in the same way a drowning man clutched a life preserver.

He'd been clear about his no-relationship policy, as had she. It made sense. It was logical.

So why did it seem such a rotten idea right now? She had gotten her wish. He'd made love to her. He'd wiped Ryan right out of her brain, and now she regretted it. Not the lovemaking, but rather, the aftermath.

Tara had turned to go into the house when she heard another car and looked back. To her amazement, Martin Somers got out of the white Continental that had pulled to a stop next to her Camry.

She started down the steps, wondering what this was all about. It couldn't have happened at a better time. At the moment she didn't give two hoots about much of anything, except for the turmoil she had created for herself with Matt.

"Tara."

"Mr. Somers." Tara chose to go formal with the father of the man who had ruined her house.

"I'm here to discuss—" he paused very briefly "—the incident two nights ago."

*The incident. How wonderfully impersonal.* Tara waited.

"I want you to consider dropping charges against my son."

Tara slowly yet adamantly shook her head. "I don't think so."

"If you drop the charges, I will see to it that the damages are fully recompensed."

"I believe you'll be seeing to that anyway."

"You might find going to court expensive."

"I'm sure I'll get court costs."

"If you win."

"Why wouldn't I?"

"There is no evidence Ryan did what you claim he did. He saw the door hanging open from the road as he was driving. He stopped, found the place ruined. It's possible you did it yourself for the insurance money."

Tara shook her head again. "You need to think about your public image here, Martin. You see, I'm used to being a pariah. You are not." She tilted her head, regarding the man and for once she felt as if she were in the driver's seat. "I think you're going to find that public opinion in Night Sky has changed. A lot of people came to help me yesterday and they saw firsthand what your son had done. And now you're trying to get him off the hook and I don't think that's going to look so good. You can put all the spin on this you want but you and Ryan are not going to come out of this unscathed."

Martin turned toward his car. His hand was on the handle when he looked back. "You don't know what you're doing here."

Tara shrugged. "I'll take my chances. Win, lose or draw, dirty laundry will come out. Most of it yours, since mine is already out there."

"Do not threaten me, Miss Sullivan."

"It's not a threat. Just a warning. I may not have your resources, so I have to play hardball with whatever I have." She paused. "And you're wrong about no evidence, Martin. Rafe swabbed the blood on the door where Ryan broke my window. In fact, he took a lot of samples, because there was blood everywhere. Did Ryan run in to stop me and then proceed to bleed all over the house in the process?" Her forehead wrinkled in a frown. "That won't look good."

Martin showed no emotion. Tara hadn't expected him to. "I might consider working out a deal," she said.

"What kind of deal?"

"Let's talk punitive damages. If Ryan pled no contest to the charges and accepted his punishment, I wouldn't be able to pursue punitive damages in civil court, and *you* would look a heck of a lot better than if you spent tons of money trying to get your obviously guilty son off the hook." She raised a shoulder. "Just a suggestion."

"Anything else?" Martin asked with a sneer.

"Yes. You seem to carry some weight with the manager of U.S. Trust. Before I consider any kind of deal I want my loan refinanced."

"I can't—"

"Of course not," Tara agreed. "Just like you didn't influence the loan *not* being refinanced." She crossed her arms over her chest. "You might mention the term predatory loan practices aimed at the elderly to the bank manager if you see him."

She hadn't had much time to look into it, just a few minutes here and there, but what she had found made for interesting reading. She was certain Nate Bidart would think so, too.

Martin opened his car door.

"Oh. One more thing," she added conversationally. "I have quite a list of people who were suddenly *unable* to work for me but still worked for you. A lot of little coincidences." Her nose wrinkled a little. "Well documented, and when added to Ryan's destruction, wow, it looks like a conspiracy."

"You'll need a good lawyer to prove that."

"How does Nate Bidart sound?"

Martin turned without another word and got into his car, and that in itself told Tara that she might soon find herself on the trail to financial recovery. And if she didn't...well, she was pretty certain now she'd survive. She seemed to be getting a lot of practice at survival lately.

Lydie dropped Hailey off at 8:00 a.m. to help with the cooking for tomorrow's guests and then decided to pitch in herself until her first appointment at the salon.

"I heard Ryan is already out on bail," she announced as she tied on an apron, "but that Martin is so embarrassed that he has forbidden him from showing up at the reunion. Rumor has it Ryan is going *out of town* very soon." Lydie gave Tara a significant look as she said the last words. "Probably an all-expense paid vacation to somewhere warm and far away to keep him out of his father's hair."

*Martin is afraid of becoming a target of a lawsuit and wants his son in a place where he can do no more damage.*

"Let's see, what else?" Lydie said as she chopped onions. "I guess Stacia has figured out who Ryan was seeing on the side. It was an old girlfriend from Elko who Ryan just wasn't quite ready to part company with. Or rather, *she* wasn't ready to part company with *him* after a short post-engagement fling. A hot little number I hear." She gave Tara a meaningful sideways glance. "Martin's the same way, you know. That old coot had a girl on the side for most of his married life. I don't know how his wife stood for it."

Lydie continued passing on the gossip she had picked up in the shop for another forty-five minutes as she helped chop, slice and mix. "Well," she finally said as she untied her borrowed apron. "I have a perm and it's Mrs. Martini. I can't be late or I'll never hear the end of it."

Lydie bustled out the door. Tara looked at

Hailey and shook her head, a reluctant smile tugging at her lips. "You must know everything, working at that place."

"I can't wait to get out of there and not know everything," Hailey said on a sigh. "Exhausting."

Tara glanced at her watch. "Would you mind finishing piping these shells? I have to get to—"

"Your stupid committee meeting," Hailey finished for her. "You bet."

"The meetings don't seem as stupid as they used to."

Hailey raised her eyes, the piping bag hovering dangerously unattended over a shell.

"Someone usually ends up crying," Tara explained with a nonchalant wave of her hand, making an attempt to sound like her old self. "Lots of unexpected action and drama."

The meeting, of course, lasted forever, but this time there were no tears. Dottie still had a few tricks up her sleeve, though. It seemed that after the dress parade, she thought it was the best of ideas to have all of the queens present walk the length of the runway with an escort while slides of their original coronation were shown. She'd already found the slides, and had the escorts lined up.

Great. On top of everything else, now she'd get to relive her sucky prom in front of an audience.

It was obvious that Dottie had been planning this for some time, but had waited to spring it on the women until it was virtually fait accompli. She'd probably been afraid that someone—like, oh say, Tara—would nix it, and Tara was tempted, but she also knew how important it was for Dottie to relive her moment of glory.

She raised her hand though, knowing Dottie would expect at least a token resistance.

"I won't be escorted by Principal Gates, will I?" There was a short silence and then Dottie laughed.

"No," she promised, waving her hand at Tara in a dismissive gesture. Sandra Hernandez turned red.

"Great," Tara said as she collected her shoulder bag and got to her feet. "In that case, I'll find something nice to wear. Now, if you'll excuse me, I still have a few things I need to settle." She headed for the door, knowing that, regardless of the reunion preparations she still had to make, the main thing she needed to settle was in her own mind. Was she actually in love with Matt? And if so, what was she supposed to do about it?

Luke was industriously clipping a hedge when Tara drove in, but no greenery seemed to be coming off. He was faking it, waiting for her, obviously to put his two cents in. A few weeks ago, she would have been furious if someone had tried to push their nose into her private business, but at the moment she welcomed any insight she could get.

"Hey, Luke."

He gave her a searching look, and Tara realized that he knew more than she probably wanted him to. Nothing was ever private.

"Tara."

"Did you see Matt before he left?" she asked, taking the bull by the horns.

That appeared to be all the opening Luke needed. "I did. Did you know about the FFD exam?"

"The FFD? What's that?"

"Fitness for Duty."

Tara felt as if she'd just been sucker punched. Matt had to take a fitness for duty exam? When he poured his guts out a few nights ago, he hadn't seen reason to share that bit of information. Trust issues or privacy issues? Pride perhaps.

"Neither did I. Not until he returned his key."

"What does it involve?"

"Basically a visit to the shrink. He has to pass the exam before he can go back on patrol. Until then he'll be parked behind a desk or not working at all. Just another way for the lieutenant to try to get to him." Luke added in a low voice, "And that woman helped him."

*What woman?* Tara felt her insides go hot and

then cold. She hated the thought of some other woman doing anything to Matt, good or bad. "He never said a word."

"He's an idiot." He took a step back and studied the hedge. "That may go for both of you."

"Now, wait a minute—"

"No. I won't wait a minute," he said, waving the clippers. "Matt has always been too fixated on right and wrong for his own good. He's been wronged and he wants to make it right. Regardless of everything else. He's just like you. Handling everything alone, his own way. Tunnel-visioned. Bullheaded—"

"Wait a minute—"

"You're the first crack I've seen in his facade."

Tara frowned. *Crack in his facade?* "What woman?" she finally demanded.

"What would it matter to you?"

Tara opened her mouth and then closed it again. She took a deep breath and then said, "I don't know, but I plan to find out."

And with that she turned and marched toward the house.

Nicky pulled into the drive a few minutes later and burst into the kitchen with his usual enthusiasm. Tara had called him the day before to explain what had happened to their house. That was when Nicky had informed her that he'd landed a part-time job with the school in California, starting in September. It would take time away from his studies, but he thought he could handle it. Tara reined in her protectiveness and told him to go for it. It wouldn't solve their financial problems, but it wouldn't hurt, either.

"The house looks good, T. A lot better than I thought it was going to." His eyes traveled around the room. "Except for maybe the fridge." He went to smooth a hand over the dents, then checked the seal.

"I had a lot of help," Tara replied, her mind still on Matt and his FFD and the mystery woman. What should she do about this? Back off? Cool off? Let Matt live his own life?

Okay. There were things he hadn't told her, things he didn't want her to know. Private things. What right did she have to butt in after her famous no-commitments speech?

The right given to her by the fact that she had some feelings for the guy. She wasn't sure what they were, but how sure could a person be? At what point did the heart, the hormones and the brain all synchronize?

And at what point was a risk no longer a risk? She'd thought she had it all worked out, how to feel close to a person with no risks. The single requirement was that no one fall in love.

Well, she was beginning to feel she'd blown that one.

But maybe Matt had, too. Maybe that was why he'd backed off so fast. Something deep within her suspected no man made love that tenderly without caring about the person he was with.

She needed to know the truth and, impatient person that she was, she wanted to know it now. She hated living with shades of gray. Four long days until the reunion was over. Four long days to brood. It might be good for her. Yeah.

She glanced at her watch, thoughts of doing the impossible edging into her mind.

"I saw Luke. Where's Matt?" Nicky asked.

"Gone." Tara pulled the fridge open before she had to explain. Ginny was chopping mushrooms in preparation for a hot appetizer for the Bidart party and she smiled shyly over her shoulder at Nicky.

"Hi, Ginny," Nicky said with his easy grin, accepting the glass of lemonade his sister pushed into his hand. He downed it in a couple of swallows and then Tara gestured toward the hall with her head and Nicky, always one to take a hint, followed her.

"What's up?" he asked as Tara closed her

bedroom door. "Whoa," he added as he glanced around. Her room had only been touched upon during the cleanup.

"This is nothing," Tara said. She'd cleared the floor, dumped her personal items and books into a couple of boxes, put the empty shelves back in place, and thanked heaven that her laptop had been under the bed. Ryan had ruined the main computer. "You should have seen the house before."

Nicky sank down onto the bed.

"I talked to Martin this morning."

"On purpose?" he asked.

Tara gave a tolerant smile and then described her discussion with the man, the deal she'd suggested.

"Why no contest?"

"To tell you the truth, Nicky, I'm halfway afraid he might hire a megalawyer and get Ryan off the hook somehow. Weirder things have happened and he has a lot of money and a lot of connections. And then we'd still have to go through a civil suit to try to collect damages. This way Ryan gets his lumps—" and it was important to her that Ryan get those lumps "—we get the damages paid for. I think Martin is tempted. This will be easier and quieter than a trial." She focused on the worn leather of the recliner. "I need you to do me a favor."

"Name it."

"I want to talk to Matt."

"Who is…"

"In Reno."

Nicky unclipped the phone from his belt and held it out. Tara shook her head.

"This isn't a phone matter."

"That serious?"

"I don't know," she said. "I need to find out. I figure if I leave now…head back very early tomorrow morning at the latest…I won't quite make it here in time for the earlier guests. But I'll be close."

Nicky smoothed back his hair with exaggerated style. "I think that maybe I can welcome a few guests and get them settled without help."

Tara smiled. "I know. But I didn't want you to think I'm shirking my duty."

He stood. "Shirk away, T. Nicky's here." He put a hand on her shoulder. "But you might want to arrange to have someone else do the cooking."

MATT DID NOT HAVE a sense of homecoming as he drove into Sparks and snarled his way down 395 in the mid-afternoon traffic, heading for his house in the south of Reno. If anything, he was surprised at how congested the roadways were.

Night Sky's lazy pace had definitely gotten under his skin. But he wasn't in Night Sky anymore.

He already had a tension headache.

Thirty minutes later, which was twenty minutes longer than it should have taken, he was home. He hadn't realized before he'd left just how unhomey it was.

Stark. The functional mode of décor was understandable in Luke's rental, but this was his home, the place where he'd been living for six years. He barely even had any pictures on the walls. This was more of a crash pad than a home.

Tara would hate it.

Ah, Tara. He rubbed a hand over the back of his neck, trying to ease the tight muscles.

Had she given any sign, any indication that her feelings had changed...but now that he was away from her, thinking with his brain, he knew that it was a good thing she hadn't. A damned good thing.

Luke had not agreed when Matt stopped by to give him the key. *So, what happens now with Tara?* had been the old man's exact words.

*Nothing,* Matt had said. Luke had not been impressed, even when Matt laid out a few solid truths: the effect of his job on relationships, the upcoming FFD, and the fact that Luke had managed to survive without hooking up.

"I wouldn't wish this life on anyone." And that,

too, had eaten at Matt as he had driven home. Luke was lonely and Matt was bailing on him.

Well, at least Tara hadn't been all that sorry to see him go. She'd practically packed his bags.

He went to the grocery store late that afternoon when his stomach started to growl and loaded up on the easy-to-fix food he ate while on shift. Frozen everything. He actually liked to cook, but after Lisa had left him…cooking for one was a pain in the ass.

Shopping done and food put away, he opened the windows to let a breeze through his stuffy house…the place still didn't seem like home.

Matt popped the top of a beer and opened a bag of chips. He sat out on his back patio and looked at his overgrown grass. A kid was supposed to come by and cut it while he was gone, but there must have been a miscommunication. He'd get the job done after shift tomorrow. No, after the scheduled FFD.

Hearing a knock on his door, Matt halfway considered ignoring it. But it might be the lawn-mowing kid, there to explain himself. He set the beer down and went to open the front door. His heart did a slow slide into his throat.

"Can I come in for a minute?" Tara asked after a few seconds of staring.

"Sure." He stepped back, still working on the

fact that she was here…right here, looking tired, yet determined. She glanced around at the spotty décor, then back at him.

*Welcome to the world of Matt.*

"Who's running the business?" he asked.

"Nicky."

Another uncomfortable beat of silence.

"It must be pretty obvious why I'm here."

Matt had a general idea, but there were some areas that needed firming up.

She took a few paces into the room, glanced around. "You really should fire your decorator."

"I'll make a note."

"I didn't like the way we parted company this morning."

"And you drove four and a half hours to tell me that?"

She had that no-nonsense, get-it-done expression in her eyes. "Yes. I don't like having things up in the air. You know that."

He nodded. If she were any more beautiful it would be unbearable.

"Did you consider phoning?"

"I wanted to talk in person."

Yeah. And that worried him.

"I realized after we'd made love…I had made a mistake."

The words jabbed at Matt. She had regrets, but they would work through them. Move on, go their separate ways.

"I thought I could compartmentalize everything. I thought I could put the physical here and the emotional over there and never let the two overlap and that way avoid getting blitzed again." She glanced down at the coffee table, which was covered with a film of dust he hadn't noticed until now. "I was wrong. I didn't have a lot of control over the emotional."

Matt sucked in a breath as the implication of her words sank in. "Tara, before you go any further—"

"What? Are you going to say 'it's been fun, but…'?" She shook her head. "I don't buy it. You have feelings for me, too."

Okay, she had him there.

"I can't deny that, but there's a lot more to the situation. I'm not really the guy you got to know in Night Sky. Once I go back to the job…things will change. I probably won't be able to help that." He pressed his lips together. "I know what my life is going to be like. I know what *I'm* going to be like."

"You do," she said flatly.

"Yes."

He did. Vividly. He remembered how it had been with Lisa, the deterioration of the relationship as the insomnia, fatigue, lack of appetite and shortness of temper all took their toll. She had tried to be patient, had tried to understand, but eventually it had just been too much for her.

And the situation that had caused the symptoms hadn't changed.

"Did she walk out on you because you were too focused on the job?"

"Lisa?" He didn't need to wonder how she knew about Lisa. Luke. And if Tara knew about Lisa, then she must also know about the exam. "No. She's a lawyer and as much of a workaholic as I am." Their relationship, he saw now, had been more like parallel play than a commitment between two people.

"But you broke up?"

"She left me just before my so-called heroic deed. She had her reasons."

"What does she have to do with this exam?"

Matt sent Tara another sharp look. "I think my superiors might have sought her out and she might have thought she was doing me some good by talking."

Matt didn't want to go into it, but he would if it made Tara understand the situation.

"Things worked with Lisa and me, while they worked, because we were both committed to our jobs. We understood that about each other." He was surprised at how cold that sounded now.

"Why did they quit working?"

"The stress," Matt said simply. "After the truth came out about my dad, it raised issues in the department. I wasn't too pleasant to be around while I dealt with them...I don't see things being any better in the near future. Even with you."

He saw the pain in her eyes, but, rather than giving in to it, she pulled herself together. "Have you ever considered quitting?"

*Exactly the words he'd known were coming.*

"I haven't done anything wrong, so I shouldn't have to quit," Matt snapped. "If I leave now, I'm as good as guilty."

"Looking guilty and being guilty are not the same thing."

"Easy to say when you're not the one in question. I don't need platitudes and helpful advice." He knew he sounded arrogant, but he was going to get this point across. Tara was threatening the one thing he had to do if he was going to live with himself.

"Okay, so you stay and you prove you're not your father. You prove you're not guilty of anything. Somehow. How many times do you prove it? Once? Twice? A dozen times? Will you ever be able to prove it enough to satisfy yourself?"

He was silent.

"Is the purpose of your life to pay penance for something you didn't do?" Tara shook her head. "That would be a sad thing, Matt. What will they put on your gravestone? 'I showed them'?"

*Twist the knife again, Tara.* He did not need to hear this.

"So what do you suggest?" he asked coldly.

"Try letting go, a little at a time. You don't have to quit your job…just let this thing go."

*She didn't get it.* "Just say 'no'? It won't work."

"Because you don't want it to." She could think what she'd like as long as she didn't waste her time trying to rescue him.

"And you ragged at *me* about not accepting help?" she asked incredulously. "Look at you. Now I know why you understand me so well. You're just the same, except you don't seem to be able to heed your own advice."

"I know what I'll be dealing with. You don't."

"I can learn," she said after a beat.

Those three sincere words were as good as a declaration and they rocked Matt to his core.

"Matt?" she whispered and his gut twisted.

He hauled out the only gun he had left. The big, cold, hurtful one. With as much indifference as he could muster, he said, "We had a deal, Tara. We slept together with no strings, no commitments. It was your idea. You wanted it to be me because I was leaving." He held her gaze. "Maybe I felt the same."

Tara's beautiful eyes narrowed. But, when she spoke, it wasn't what he'd expected to hear.

"Damn, you're stubborn. Well, go ahead. Protect me all you want while you slowly kill yourself. If you ever come to your senses—which seems highly unlikely—and if you ever want to see me again, you're going to have to work for it."

And then she turned on her heel, wrenched the door open and left without looking back.

Matt hesitated for only a second before he started after her. He wasn't going to let her drive off like this. Shit. If she had an accident or something because he'd upset her…

She was already at her car by the time he made the porch. He headed across the lawn and vaulted the fence as she peeled away from the curb, leaving him standing like the fool that he was at the curb.

He walked back in, scooped up the phone.

Nicky answered on the second ring. "Where's Tara staying?" Matt asked without saying hello.

"I don't know."

*Great.* "Could I have her cell number?" Nicky didn't answer immediately. "I'm worried about her, Nick. She just left here. I want to talk to her."

"I'll talk to her."

"Nick...please."

"Sorry. I'll call you if there's anything you need to know."

The kid hung up, leaving Matt staring at the receiver.

*What now? What freaking now?*

## CHAPTER FIFTEEN

THIRTY-SIX VERY long hours later, Matt pulled up to Tara's house to find the gravel parking area surprisingly empty of vehicles. Even Tara's truck was gone. She had gotten back to Night Sky safely according to a decidedly cool Luke. However, he hadn't been able to get away from Reno himself until after the FFD exam.

Where was everyone? He glanced at the dash-board clock.

The luncheon. That dress thing. Matt turned his truck around and headed for town. The convention center was packed. He edged in the back door and watched as a teenaged girl strutted down the catwalk in an odd yellow flouncy dress. It looked like something his great-grand-mother would have worn. It was followed by a missile-fronted frock straight out of a 1960s James Bond movie.

Matt searched the crowd until he found Tara.

She was seated close to the stage, her hair tumbling down her back like an ebony waterfall.

Matt kept his eyes on her as though she would vanish if he looked away. She did anyway. She got to her feet along with several other women and disappeared behind the curtains as the last teenage girl paraded down the runway. A few seconds later the emcee explained why. The queens were coming. There was a swell of dramatic music. An elderly woman stepped out onto the stage, accepted a beribboned rose and then tottered the length of the catwalk while a grainy black-and-white photo of her wearing a tiara and gown, probably fifty years ago, was projected behind her. The crowd applauded. The woman beamed. A young man met her at the steps, offered his arm and helped her down the stairs before escorting her to her seat.

The slide changed, another woman appeared, a little younger than the first. Matt started edging through the crowd.

WHEN TARA'S TURN CAME, she couldn't help herself. She craned her neck to see if Principal Gates was waiting at the end of the catwalk. Nope…just some really skinny kid in a suit jacket and boutonniere. Dottie caught her eye and gave her a thumbs-up. Tara smiled back, even though she didn't feel like it. She felt like crawling into her bedroom and spending about a week licking her wounds. But she was made of tougher stuff than that. She hoped.

She'd taken a huge risk, faced her worst fear. She hurt. A lot. It was going to take some time to recover, but she knew that given the opportunity, she'd take the risk again. She would have regretted it forever if she hadn't at least tried to get that stubborn man back.

Back. What was she thinking? She'd never really had him. The part of him that cared for her wasn't as strong as the part that was focused on proving himself. And there was nothing she could do about it. Just thinking about it filled her with frustration. And pain.

The theme from her prom came up and Tara forced her mouth into a smile so as not to ruin Dottie's big finale. She only hoped she didn't look like she was grimacing. The mini floodlights shining up from the edge of the plywood platform made it difficult to see the crowd as she walked, but she could hear the applause grow. She wondered what photo was being projected behind her and then decided it didn't matter. Mug shots, handcuffs—all part of the Sullivan legacy. But it didn't have to be her legacy. She had figured that out long ago. Too bad Matt couldn't do the same.

She made it to the end of the runway and reached out for the extended hand, startled when a large, warm, masculine hand closed firmly around hers instead of the clammy teenaged one she'd been expecting.

Her lips parted as, bewildered, she stepped past the glare of the floodlights and saw it was Matt's. And then she clamped her mouth shut. *What?* and *How?* were two reasonable thoughts that popped into her head, followed by *It's not going to be that easy, buster.*

Matt gave her fingers a gentle tug, and she allowed herself to be led down the short aisle so as not to cause a scene. There was a murmur in the crowd. She expected no less in Night Sky. Something new to talk about.

She wasn't surprised when, instead of turning toward the seats, Matt pushed the door open and escorted her outside. She wondered if he was surprised that she went quietly. Somewhere along the way she'd lost the rose he'd handed her.

When the door shut, closing them off from the view of the gawking crowd, Tara pulled her hand out of his and took a step backward, putting herself out of reach.

And then she just looked at him—every delicious inch.

He was back. He'd knocked her for a loop two days ago, had all but broken her heart and now he was back…and she was ridiculously glad to see him. It ticked her off royally. She gave him a cool look.

"Well, I guess I should thank you for rescuing me from my second prom experience."

"Was it any better than the first?"

"Marginally." She glanced down at the shiny blue sheath she wore. "The dress isn't as spectacular, but the ambiance is much improved."

"I owe you an apology."

Her chin angled up. "And you drove four and a half hours to deliver it?"

His reply was much better than hers had been.

"I'd have driven a hundred. More if I had to."

Tara's heart stuttered, but she caught herself. "Well said, Matt."

"You're a difficult woman, Tara."

Her lips curved ironically. "And look what it's gotten me." She spread her hands, indicating a whole lot of nothing. "Besides, you're not much easier to deal with yourself."

"That is what I am here to talk about," he said in a low voice. Tara heard the door creak open behind her and Matt verified her suspicion that they were being spied on by gesturing toward the street with his head. "Shall we walk, or do you want to go back to your prom?"

"I'd rather walk."

They fell in step, walking slowly because of Tara's heels, which clicked a gentle rhythm on the asphalt. She told herself she was going to keep her distance, at least until she'd heard him out, but her nerves were humming. He was here. That had to be good.

Didn't it?

She still wanted him. That had to be good.

Regardless of what he thought, she wasn't difficult. She was too damned easy.

"You know, Tara," he said, "I thought I was a brave man until you came to see me Sunday night."

She cast him a sidelong glance, but he focused straight ahead.

"I have some problems in my life, but I'm facing them. Bravely, I thought...and shoving everything else of importance off to the side in the process." He shook his head, but still did not look at her. "I began to wonder how brave that was. It didn't take all that long to figure it out. He pushed aside a long weeping willow branch as they passed under the tree.

"I realized after you'd left—okay, one sleepless night after you left—that perhaps the bravest thing I could do would be to follow your advice and let go of the need to rewrite my father's legacy." He fell silent as they continued to walk. Tara allowed herself to move a little closer. "To accept that I will be living with suspicion and I can't do anything about it…. To accept that life is a gift and I shouldn't waste mine on a personal crusade that has no end." He looked over at her. "Especially when there are other things in life more fulfilling."

She kept walking. She didn't even stumble.

"I was a good cop before all of this happened with my dad. I can be a good cop again. I went to the lieutenant and I laid everything out for him. I actually talked to him, instead of being angry and defensive. I was honest. I think I might have gotten his attention."

"What'd he say?"

"Nothing, really. But I think he listened."

"What happened with the FFD?"

"That's confidential, but between you and me, I passed. Nothing official yet, but the shrink gave me the nod. I think he thought I was amazingly normal."

"You faked it?"

He smiled. "Like a champ."

He turned and settled his hands lightly on her

shoulders, and she was having a difficult time with her resolution to keep her distance.

"I tried to find you after you left my house. I wanted to make things better."

"Nicky told me."

"But I'm glad I didn't know where you were. It forced me to figure out what I wanted, and what I was willing to give up. It became pretty obvious that the thing I was not willing to give up was you. I want a life with you and I'm willing to adjust the other aspects of my life to do that. And so now—" he swallowed "—it's just a matter of seeing how you feel. Especially after the way we parted last time."

He waited and then, a few seconds later, said gruffly, "I wouldn't mind it if you said something here."

She smiled.

"You're not going to make this easy, are you?"

Tara took a step closer, so that her body was almost, but not quite, touching his. "If things are easy, Matt, you don't appreciate them, and, trust me, because of that, I appreciate everything in my life…including you. Especially you."

Tara slid her hands around his waist and leaned into him, her head in the crook of his shoulder. She so loved this man. Alone, they were decent fighters. Together…they could handle anything.

"No more protecting me for my own good," she murmured against his chest.

"No more," he agreed. "And you'll be patient with me while I deal with this thing with my dad. I don't know if I'm going to be able to let go... cold turkey, you know. It'll take some time. I might backslide."

"I'll be right by your side, beating you up until you stop."

He held her for a moment and then he tipped her chin up to kiss her. First sweetly. Then hungrily.

On the third kiss, they almost drowned.

Fortunately, the obese cat came lumbering across the street to throw himself against Matt's legs, bringing them both back to the surface before either of them lost consciousness.

Tara glanced around. Nothing like losing control in public, and it was indeed public. People were now spilling out of the convention center and heading for their cars, walking across the street, most of them craning their necks to see what was going on with Tara and her carpenter cop. Eddie Johnson was propped against the side of the convention center. He raised his longneck beer in their direction in a silent toast.

"I...uh...will need to get back to my place now. My guests."

"I know." Matt leaned down to scratch the cat's ears. The animal threw himself against Matt again.

"And you?" she asked.

"I have to go back to work." She tried not to show her disappointment. "I leave tomorrow."

"Tomorrow."

"Yeah. And there don't seem to be any rooms available in this town."

"That could be a problem...unless of course, you're willing to share a bed."

Matt smiled. "Bed sharing happens to be one of the things I will not be giving up."

"Then I think I might have something that will suit you."

*Ten months later*

"BEIGE MAY NOT BE your best color, but I like this uniform better than your last one."

Matt smiled as Tara reached out and adjusted his collar, and then he captured her hand. She raised her eyebrows and pulled it back.

"No. You are not going to be late on your first day."

"I can be quick."

"I like it better when you're not."

"Okay. Pencil me in for tonight. Slow."

"Noted. Now get out of here." Matt started for the door. Tara followed even though it was a windy day. She usually did, regardless of the weather, waiting on the porch that he rebuilt almost a year ago until he'd driven out of sight. But today he wasn't heading back to Reno. He began his first day of duty as a sworn deputy of Night Sky County, Nevada. She gave a wave as he turned the truck around and then she disappeared back into the house. The slightly thinner fat cat waddled out from under the porch to take her place.

Matt's first weeks back on the job in Reno had not been easy, but they'd been better than expected because he'd finally gotten his priorities straight. He knew the danger signs of stress and when they started to sneak up on him, he took the time to reassess. A couple of times he'd even talked to Luke.

He'd made a tenuous peace with the lieutenant, had begun to reestablish relationships with his colleagues and peers, and he simply learned to live with the suspicion some of his fellow officers had that he would eventually be retiring to a beach in the Caribbean. Little did they know that his heart was actually set on a piece of desert property that had finally been refinanced. He was hoping to help Tara pay it off soon.

He was eventually able to set the issues with his

father aside for the most part. If Tara could do it, so could he. He had other things to focus on.

The future looked bright in Night Sky. Luke was making noises about becoming a great-uncle one of these days, but Matt and Tara planned to hold off on children for a while. They'd only been married for a month and wanted time together.

Matt smiled as he made the final turn into Night Sky and slowed to let a couple of quail run across the street.

*Maybe, just maybe, there was something to this small-town cure....*

* * * * *

*Experience entertaining women's fiction
about rediscovery and reconnection—
warm, compelling stories that are relevant
for every woman who has wondered
"What's next?" in their lives.
After all, there's the life you planned.
And there's what comes next.*

*Turn the page for a sneak preview
of a new book from Harlequin NEXT.*

## CONFESSIONS OF A NOT-SO-DEAD LIBIDO
*by Peggy Webb*

*On sale November 2006,
wherever books are sold.*

My husband could see beauty in a mud puddle. Literally. "Look at that, Louise," he'd say after a heavy spring rain. "Have you ever seen so many amazing colors in mud?"

I'd look and see nothing except brown, but he'd pick up a stick and swirl the mud till the colors of the earth emerged, and all of a sudden I'd see the world through his eyes—extraordinary instead of mundane.

Roy was my mirror to life. Four years ago when he died, it cracked wide open, and I've been living a smashed-up, sleepwalking life ever since.

If he were here on this balmy August night I'd be sailing with him instead of baking cheese straws in preparation for Tuesday-night quilting club with Patsy. I'd be striving for sex appeal in

Bermuda shorts and bare-toed sandals instead of opting for comfort in walking shoes and a twill skirt with enough elastic around the waist to make allowances for two helpings of lemon-cream pie.

Not that I mind Patsy. Just the opposite. I love her. She's the only person besides Roy who creates wonder wherever she goes. (She creates mayhem, too, but we won't get into that.) She's my mirror now, as well as my compass.

Of course, I have my daughter, Diana, but I refuse to be the kind of mother who defines herself through her children. Besides, she has her own life now, a husband and a baby on the way.

I slide the last cheese straws into the oven and then go into my office and open e-mail.

From: "Miss Sass" <patsyleslie@hotmail.com>
To: "The Lady" <louisejernigan@yahoo.com>
Sent: Tuesday, August 15, 6:00 PM
Subject: Dangerous Tonight
Hey Lady,
I'm feeling dangerous tonight. Hot to trot, if you know what I mean. Or can you even re-member? ☺ Look out, bridge club, here I come. I'm liable to end up dancing on the tables

instead of bidding three spades. Whose turn is it to drive, anyhow? Mine or thine?
XOXOX
Patsy
P.S. Lord, how did we end up in a club with no men?

This e-mail is typical "Patsy." She's the only person I know who makes me laugh all the time. I guess that's why I e-mail her about ten times a day. She lives right next door, but e-mail satisfies my urge to be instantly and constantly in touch with her without having to interrupt the flow of my life. Sometimes we even save the good stuff for e-mail.

From: "The Lady" <louisejernigan@yahoo.com>
To: "Miss Sass" <patsyleslie@hotmail.com>
Sent: Tuesday, August 15, 6:10 PM
Subject: Re: Dangerous Tonight
So, what else is new, Miss Sass? You're always dangerous. If you had a weapon, you'd be lethal. ☺
Hugs,
Louise
P.S. What's this about men? I thought you said your libido was dead?

I press Send then wait. Her reply is almost instantaneous.

From: "Miss Sass" <patsyleslie@hotmail.com>
To: "The Lady" <louisejernigan@yahoo.com>
Sent: Tuesday, August 15, 6:12 PM
Subject: Re: Dangerous Tonight
Ha! If I had a *brain* I'd be lethal.
And I said my libido was in hibernation, not DEAD!
Jeez, Louise!!!!!
P

Patsy loves to have the last word, so I shut off my computer.

\* \* \* \* \*

*Want to find out what happens to their friendship when Patsy and Louise both find the perfect man?*

***Don't miss
CONFESSIONS OF A NOT-SO-DEAD LIBIDO
by Peggy Webb,
coming to Harlequin NEXT
in November 2006.***

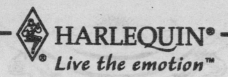

## Harlequin® Historical
### Historical Romantic Adventure!

*Imagine a time of chivalrous
knights and unconventional ladies,
roguish rakes and impetuous
heiresses, rugged cowboys
and spirited frontierswomen—
these rich and vivid tales will
capture your imagination!*

*Harlequin Historical...
they're too good to miss!*

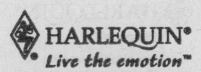

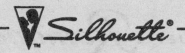